Daydream Retriever

Susan C. Daffron

An Alpine Grove Romantic Comedy

Book 10

Published by Magic Fur Press
An imprint of Logical Expressions, Inc.
P.O. Box 383
Ponderay, ID 83852

Daydream Retriever

ISBN: 978-1-61038-046-1 (paperback)
        978-1-61038-047-8 (EPUB)

Like all of my books, *Daydream Retriever* is dedicated to
my husband James Byrd,
my best friend and biggest supporter.
Thanks for everything!

Books by Susan C. Daffron
The Alpine Grove Romantic Comedies
Chez Stinky

Fuzzy Logic

The Art of Wag

Snow Furries

Bark to the Future

Howl at the Loon

The Good, the Bad, and the Pugly

The Treasure of the Hairy Cadre

The Luck of the Paw

Daydream Retriever

The Hound of Music

The Jennings & O'Shea Mysteries
Sensing Trouble

Sensing Secrets

Sensing Truth

Chapter 1

A Family Matter

It was a sad commentary on the current state of her life that getting a phone with caller ID was arguably the best thing to happen to Lisa Lowell in 1997. She'd finally purchased a new telephone with a display, so she was empowered. Now, like the rest of the world, she could identify and evade telemarketers and other annoying callers.

Because of this newly acquired knowledge, Lisa had been able to successfully dodge calls from her brother Larry for the past week. Of her three siblings, Lisa found her brother Larry the most irritating. Maybe it was because he was the youngest. Everyone had always doted on Larry, and because of the wide gap in their ages, Lisa and Larry had been blessed with vastly different experiences growing up.

Larry was a lawyer and ever since he'd graduated from law school, he'd taken on a pompous air and manner of speech that drove Lisa nuts. And since her divorce, Lisa was perfectly happy to never talk to another lawyer, ever again.

Of course, even considering their age difference, Lisa and Larry *had* experienced life with the same parents, which was why he was calling her. He wanted her help with a "family matter," and when Larry wanted something, he could be extremely persistent. Like most lawyers, he loved to pontificate, and nothing made him happier than a good debate, even when it was with Lisa's answering machine.

Lisa had avoided returning Larry's calls because she hadn't been feeling well and couldn't face talking to him. But it wasn't like she could avoid him forever. With a sigh, Lisa dialed the number for Larry's law office in the small town of Alpine Grove. A woman with a businesslike voice answered, proclaiming her name was Brigid. Momentarily startled that Larry wasn't answering his own phone anymore, Lisa said, "Hello, I'd like to speak to Larry. It's his sister Lisa and I'm returning his call...or calls."

After a protracted delay, Larry came on the line. "Hello, Lisa. I've been attempting to reach you for quite some time. How is your health? Are you feeling well?"

"I'm a little snuffly and my throat hurts, but I think it's just a cold. I'm sorry I didn't call you back sooner." Lisa didn't want to get into the details of her recent doctor visit and was glad Larry couldn't see her rolling her eyes. He was in hard-core stuffy lawyer mode again. Ugh.

Larry continued, "We have a situation here and I would like to request your assistance."

"What kind of situation? Are Mom and Dad okay?" Lisa's parents owned the hardware store in Alpine Grove and all of their children had worked there at one time or another. Stocking shelves and doing inventory at Lowell's Hardware had been a big part of Lisa's life when she was growing up. She had counted more nuts and bolts than anyone she'd ever met, aside from her siblings. If anyone asked her what a Lenker rod or mortar hawk was, she could tell them. But so far no one ever had, and her knowledge of obscure hardware wasn't something she wanted to include on her resume.

Larry cleared his throat emphatically as if he were about to launch into a closing argument. "Our parents are fine, but Mom is insisting on a vacation. However, Dad won't go anywhere until the house sells."

"The house *still* hasn't sold? I just assumed it had and no one bothered to mention it to me. What's taking so long? I know the interior is dated, but the place is huge." More than a year earlier, their parents had moved out of the house Lisa had grown up in and purchased a small cottage in town that was closer to the hardware store.

"The real estate agent is requesting that we do some work on it. Or, in her words, 'it will sit up there on that hill like a petrified dead squirrel forever.' Sitting empty also isn't helping matters. I'm afraid it will fall into disrepair, especially if we have another bad winter like last year."

Lisa was pretty sure she knew where this was going. "You don't expect *me* to do something about this, do you? I don't live in Alpine Grove."

"Bev told me that you are on winter break from your classes, and you aren't doing anything right now. You're the only one who has the time to deal with this issue."

Lisa's best friend Bev still lived in Alpine Grove and always said she never talked to Larry, a claim that obviously wasn't true. "Why don't you ask Leo to help? He lives there."

"You know he's at the hardware store every day. Mom and Dad wouldn't know what to do without their heir to the family enterprise."

Lisa put her palm over her eyes. Larry wasn't wrong about that. Their brother Leo had lived and breathed hardware almost from the moment he could walk. Her sister Lynn wasn't an option because she lived on the East Coast. Lisa knew what Larry was going to say next, but she asked anyway. "What exactly do you want *me* to do?"

"Clean out the house, sell the old furniture, and remodel the place. I'm told magenta is no longer in style and the decor should be modernized."

"What does Mom think about this? We've been telling her to get rid of that ugly furniture and carpet for decades and she wouldn't budge. She loves her 'color palette,' as she calls it."

"Dad asserts that he's more interested in the money from selling the house than he is in sixties decor."

"That doesn't answer my question. How many times have I heard Mom go on and on about the 'professional decorator' she hired? Someone would have to use a blowtorch to get that wallpaper off. And how are you supposed to cover kelly green paint? Even after thirty years, it's still practically fluorescent. Then there's the magenta room, which we all know hasn't improved with age. I was embarrassed to bring friends over when I was twelve. Now it's beyond saving."

Larry didn't say anything for a long moment. "There's another complication."

"Beyond the fact that you expect me to go behind my mother's back and remodel her house? That's fantastic. What is this *complication*?"

"You know that Aunt Betty has been residing at the nursing home here in town, right?"

"Yes, I visited her last summer after she moved there."

"She's quite a bit better. Or I thought she was. But I think, well, I'm not sure, she may be having a few other issues. She has embarked on a peaceful protest."

"What is she protesting?"

"She's convinced that if someone cleans out the house, precious items of hers that she has stored there will be lost forever. She wants to make sure nothing is sold that she wants to keep." Larry cleared his throat. "Betty requested that I make up a legal document giving her first right of refusal."

"What precious items? And why would anything precious be left in Mom and Dad's place after they moved?"

"I'm not entirely sure."

"Assuming these precious items actually exist, what is Betty going to do with them? She's in a nursing home and doesn't have any place to put much of anything anymore."

"Those questions did come up, but she was adamant. You know how she can be. She is worried about what she terms 'her stuff' to a rather extraordinary degree."

Lisa sighed. "Betty was always a little off. That's not news. I'm told she prefers the term *eccentric* though. She thinks it sounds classy."

"Yes, I'm aware of that. However, she went on a hunger strike until I acquiesced."

"*Acquiesced?*" Lisa wanted to reach through the phone and strangle her brother. "In other words, you caved. Larry! How *could* you?"

"Please don't talk to me like one of your children. You weren't there. Betty can be extremely persuasive."

"If you're going to act like a child, I'll treat you like one. And let's face it, Betty knows you're a wimp."

"I'm going to choose to ignore that comment."

"I don't understand. What stuff is Betty worried about? It's not even her house. This makes no sense at all."

"I'm sure you can determine what she wants after you get here. The bottom line is that your family needs your help, Lisa. I am unable to assist because I have a tremendous amount of work to do right now. In fact, I would also be willing to hire you part-time temporarily to help me file documents with the courthouse and do other errands. I need someone with a flexible schedule whom I can trust."

"Why would I want to do that?"

"Bev says you have nothing else to do."

"Bev has a big mouth. I have no interest in visiting Alpine Grove in the winter and I don't have a car right now. It finally died." Lisa tried not to dwell on the recent demise of her faithful 1973 Volvo 144. It had racked up two hundred and seventy-three thousand miles before it went toes up. The car was one of the last mementos of Lisa's many years of motherhood and relegating the old boxy beast to the junkyard had been almost physically painful.

"You can rent a car to get here and then I'd be happy to loan you my truck during your visit."

"You mean the ratty old hardware truck that you painted that disgusting pink color? I can't believe you still have that thing." The truck had been her father's before it was passed down to Larry. Originally, it had been brown with the words *Lowell's Hardware* painted on the side doors. Larry had painted the truck to cover up the text, although Lisa thought the color was far worse than the words ever were.

"For the record, the truck isn't pink. The Dodge is salmon colored and has four-wheel drive. It also runs, which is more than you can say about your car." Larry cleared his throat again. "Lisa, you have to help me. There's no one else I can ask."

Lisa couldn't think of anyone else Larry could call either. No one other than a family member would be able to go through the thirty years of memory-laden artifacts lurking in their childhood home. She was going to kill Bev for this. What a blabbermouth.

Unfortunately, to kill Bev Lisa would have to return to Alpine Grove, and after she hung up with Larry, she was going to have a long conversation with her friend. Being best friends entailed certain responsibilities.

Lisa put her palm over her eyes, wishing she had any other alternative, but she finally relented. He was right. It was her family and she should help. "All right Larry, fine. I'll do this and help you, but if you and Dad are keeping this from Mom, I want no part of your lies." Even though it went against her better judgment, after all these years she was finally going to visit her home town of Alpine Grove in the wintertime, which was something she'd vowed never to do.

～

Beverly Kinnear had been Lisa's best friend practically since the day they met in third grade. No one was better at talking Lisa down off the ledge than Bev.

Lisa dialed the phone and smiled at the sound of Bev's voice. "Hi, it's me. Are you busy?"

"I'm always busy; hold on a sec."

Lisa could hear the sound of the phone thumping onto the table and Bev shouting at her kids.

"Okay, I'm back. What's up?"

"I went to the doctor," Lisa said. "And because of you, now I have to go to Alpine Grove."

"The doctor? What happened? I thought you had a cold. Are you coming here for some type of treatment, honey? What's going on?"

"No, well, yes, I'm going there, but not for treatment. I do have a cold, but it could have been something worse." Lisa touched her neck with her fingertips, prodding at it gingerly. "I was worried my glands might be swollen. It could have been the cancer coming back. The doctor called me back for another test, and I almost had a nervous breakdown."

"What test?"

"They wanted to test for strep."

"But nothing to do with cancer, right?"

"Nothing at all."

"Do you have anything other than a cold?"

"No. The strep test was negative. But you remember what happened the last time the doctor called me back. He felt a lump, and then you know what happened after that too." Lisa touched the scar at the base of her neck. The next few weeks had been a whirlwind of tests that confirmed her doctor's suspicions. She'd had to undergo surgery to remove her thyroid gland. Afterward, she'd spent several days in the hospital, in isolation, while she received treatment with radioactive iodine to eliminate any remaining cancer cells.

Bev said, "Of course I remember. But right now, everything is fine, right? So what's the problem? You're all panicky. I can hear it in your voice." Bev paused and Lisa could tell she was covering the mouthpiece with her hand, but Lisa could still hear the faint sound of Bev's voice yelling at one of her kids. "Don't you even think of doing that, Kenny. I'm watching you."

Lisa ignored the interruption and continued, "Well, I don't feel well. I just...I don't know. I feel unsettled, like something's not right. I don't feel good."

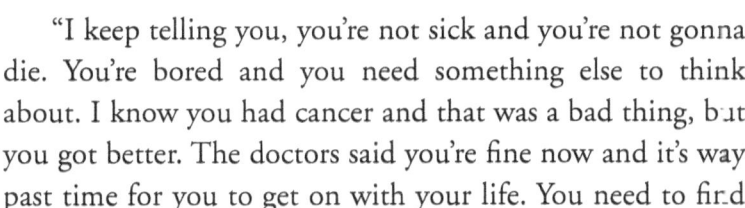

"I keep telling you, you're not sick and you're not gonna die. You're bored and you need something else to think about. I know you had cancer and that was a bad thing, but you got better. The doctors said you're fine now and it's way past time for you to get on with your life. You need to find something to do."

"I am doing something. I'm going to school!"

"And we all know that's been working out mighty fine for you." When Bev was frustrated, her Texas accent reasserted itself. Even though she hadn't lived there since she was nine years old, traces of the slow drawl still lurked in the background. "You hated your classes and said it was a waste of time. And the term just ended, so now what? Did you ever decide what you're gonna sign up for next?"

"I was thinking about maybe making some decisions, but then the car died and Larry called."

"The ancient green machine finally bit the dust?"

"Yes, I'm afraid it's terminal this time. I need a new car."

Bev cleared her throat. "Honey, I hate to say this, but since your kids left all you do is think about being sick. It's a good thing you don't have a cat or you'd spend all day mumbling at the critter about your aches and pains."

"I had cancer! What if it comes back?"

"You told me all the tests are clear. They gave you a completely clean bill of health. Heck, you're probably in better shape than I am."

"That's not true. I don't feel good."

"You never feel good. When was the last time you actually felt good?"

Lisa gazed up at the ceiling. "Well, before the divorce and the girls left for college, I guess. It was before I got sick."

"When you were diagnosed with thyroid cancer, you had no symptoms. Now you have symptoms and no cancer."

"I know. But I don't feel good."

"You told me you got your drugs figured out."

"I know. It's not the thyroid medication. That's fine, and I don't feel tired or cold like I did before. I suppose maybe I am okay, except for the sniffles and sore throat. But I feel all antsy and anxious."

"I think that's because you have no friends there anymore. All the kids left, the whole mommy circle broke up, and now you're bored."

"Gosh, that makes me feel a ton better. Thank you. At least I always have you to cheer me up."

"You do, but I'm in Alpine Grove. If you're so convinced you're going to die any minute, you should be closer to the people who care about you, just in case."

"Gleasonville isn't far away. I can visit whenever I want."

"But you never do."

"I know. It's complicated."

"No, it's not. We've had this conversation. You're the one making it complicated."

Lisa tried not to sigh audibly because it would undoubtedly annoy her friend. Bev had known Lisa forever and had no patience for Lisa's "complications."

Opting to change the subject, Lisa continued, "Larry called about four hundred times and I put off calling him back because every time I talk to him, it seems like I'm giving him bad news."

Bev said, "You're fine, so you can call him back."

"Well, I finally did."

"Good. It's about time! You should talk to your baby brother. I heard through the grapevine that he's really busy. He even got a new assistant at the law office. That's a good thing because supposedly he's working on some big case. I met his assistant and she seems nice enough. Very organized too. I think she's helping him get his act together."

"For someone who never talks to Larry, you seem pretty well informed. What big new case? Larry always says he only does family and corporate stuff. Divorces, real estate, that kind of thing. I don't think he's ever seen the inside of a courtroom."

"Well, it's not like he's become a high-powered prosecuting attorney while you weren't paying attention. I mean, come on. This is Larry we're talking about. He's got a one-person practice in a teeny-tiny town. But the ski resort is changing ownership, so there's a ton of legal paperwork. For Larry, it's a pretty high-profile job. He even got quoted in the newspaper."

"You're kidding. Snow Grove has been sold?"

"Yes, remember that place where we used to ski all the time. High school? Ski team? Remember all that?"

Lisa snorted. "Don't be snotty. Of course I remember. But you know I hate thinking about that place. I'm surprised they sold it. The Greenfield family has owned the resort forever."

"Times change, honey. After all these years, they're probably ready to do something else."

"Well, now I know why Larry said he was so busy. I guess I'll find out more when I get there."

"Wait, you're coming here during the winter? You never do that."

"I know, and that's why I called. It's all your fault because you blabbed to Larry that I have nothing to do. So I told him I'd work on fixing up Mom and Dad's house for sale."

"That's an intriguing project, but..." Bev snarled in exasperation. "Dammit, I really want to talk to you more about this, but right now, I gotta go. Robby is up in that big tree out back and I think he's about to do something really, really dumb. But I do want to say that this is a perfect time to visit! The holidays are over and the girls are back in college. You don't have any excuse not to, and I miss you tons—it's been way too long since I've seen your face."

"I know. I miss you too."

They said their goodbyes and Lisa hung up the phone. Part of her couldn't quite believe she'd actually agreed to go to Alpine Grove in January. She'd avoided visiting in the winter for years, which had entailed lots of awkward conversations with her kids trying to explain why they never spent Christmas at grandma and grandpa's house.

Her daughters never understood why Lisa was so firm in her decision, but seeing the snow and the mountains brought back a lot of memories that Lisa preferred to forget.

∼

Lisa spent the rest of the afternoon getting organized for her visit to Alpine Grove and doing exciting things like paying her electric bill. She also went to bid a final farewell to the old green Volvo and clean her stuff out of it. The ancient green machine was going to be towed to its final resting place in a massive junkyard south of Gleasonville.

After she had pulled the old maps from the glove compartment, she turned to peer at the backseat of the car.

Memories swirled through her mind, first of two battered car seats and then of twin blonde girls strapped safely into their seat belts, bickering with one another. The Volvo's worn beige interior had seen a lot of hard road time. There were stains on the seats and floor, undoubtedly from long-ago soda spills.

When she didn't have the car to remind her, what if she started to feel as if all those trips to dance classes and soccer games had never happened? Would she simply forget? She'd already lost so much; she didn't want to lose those memories of being a mom too.

The only good thing about going to Alpine Grove was that she could avoid buying another car for a while. She dreaded the idea of having to negotiate with her ex-husband about money again. Although they'd had an unusually amicable divorce, discussions about money with Mike still were never anything even close to enjoyable.

The next morning, she rented a car for the journey north to Alpine Grove. Heading to the mountains in January sometimes wasn't a great idea, but the weather forecast was for sunny skies. After so many years of driving the Volvo, it felt odd to drive a different car. For one thing, it was an automatic, not a manual.

Years of yanking on the Volvo's stiff gearshift and smashing her foot onto the clutch made driving the rental seem downright dull. It was strange having so little to do. The rental car was a boring white Ford sedan with no character at all. On the other hand, it was clean. The prospect of driving the former hardware store pickup was not appealing, since it was unlikely it had gotten any less filthy since she'd last seen it. Maybe she'd search for a new car after she got to Alpine Grove.

When she slowed at the outskirts of her hometown, Lisa was flooded with memories. Larry's office was in an old building near the single traffic light. The red brick building had housed a dry cleaner when she was a little kid. Later, it had been a gift store, then it was converted to office space, and a few years ago Larry had set up his law practice there.

After she returned the rental car, Lisa walked along the main street of town toward the office. The sidewalks had been cleared of snow and the brilliant blue sky reminded Lisa of the crisp cold days that were perfect for skiing when she was growing up. Shaking off memories of alpine sporting events, Lisa opened the door to the Law Offices of Lawrence Lowell. She found a petite woman with disheveled flaming red hair sitting at the desk out front. The woman was surrounded by piles of paper and as she looked up at Lisa, her eyes widened in surprise. Clearly, Larry didn't get a whole lot of visitors.

The redhead smiled politely. "May I help you?"

"Yes, I'm Lisa Lowell, Larry's sister. Is he around?"

"Oh yes, I forgot you were stopping by." The woman stood up and held out her hand. "I think I spoke to you the other day. It's nice to meet you. I'm Brigid Fitzpatrick." She inclined her head toward the back of the room. "Larry is in his office."

Lisa thanked Brigid, walked around the desk, and went back to the larger office beyond. She tapped on the door, which was ajar.

Larry looked up from a pile of papers that was even larger than the stacks on the desk out front. He tilted his head. "What did you do to your hair?"

Lisa put her hand to her head. "I had blonde highlights added."

"Oh, it's…different. It makes you look kind of like Mom."

"Gee, thanks." Although her eyes might be the same amber-brown shade as her mother's, Lisa didn't think she looked much like her mother at all. Mom was petite and compact, whereas Lisa had inherited her father's long, leggy build. Like her siblings, Lisa's hair had been a warm chestnut color. She certainly wasn't going to volunteer to Larry that the absurdly expensive salon streaking and frosting helped cover the increasing amount of gray in her shoulder-length hair.

After her divorce, Lisa had wanted a change and she liked the new tawny look of her hair. She gestured toward the towering pile of papers. "What happened here? You used to be so neat and tidy about everything."

"I told you I have a tremendous amount of work to do. I'm absolutely drowning in it." He stood up and walked around the desk. A few papers fluttered to the floor and he bent to pick them up. "I confess that at this point, I'm regretting taking on this project. They should have gone with a larger law firm."

Her brother looked so distressed that Lisa walked around the desk and gave him a hug. "It will be okay. For the next few weeks, I can help you out."

"Here are the keys to my truck. It's parked in the alley out back. Do you still have a key to the house?"

"It's on my key chain."

"Good. After a year, I'm afraid things may be a bit dusty in there."

They both turned at the sound of a dog barking out front. Larry frowned. "Oh dear. It sounds like Harley has returned."

"You have a dog named Harley?"

"No, he's one of Brigid's dogs." Larry walked toward his office door and Lisa followed. She looked around his shoulder to the outer office where Brigid was attempting to corral a large, boisterous yellow Labrador retriever.

Larry said, "Brigid, why is he here again?"

Brigid pushed the dog's rump to the floor, "Harley, sit!" The dog looked momentarily confused, sat, opened his mouth to pant happily, and stood up again.

Brigid mumbled, "Good boy," and looked up at Larry and Lisa. "I'm sorry. Clay dropped him off for a few minutes while he goes to pick up some photos down the street. He'll be right back. I promise."

"After that beagle ate the Lombardi contract, I think I made it clear that we can't have dogs in the office." Larry put his fists on his hips. "The last time Harley was here he knocked over that banker's box full of Snow Grove deeds and easement information. It took me hours to get everything back in order."

Brigid pushed Harley's rear end down again. "I know, I know! I'm trying to find a placement for him. He's not adapting to the ranch at all. Clay has to take Harley everywhere. If he leaves Harley at home, this dog manages to find some way to get out and then he chases after the truck. At least he hasn't made it to the highway yet, but I'm tearing my hair out. All my regular foster families have dogs they're caring for already. I need to find a temporary foster home, and I'm hoping a place will free up soon."

Larry scowled. "Perhaps in the short term, you could take him outside."

Brigid gathered up the leash and glanced at Lisa. "Larry said you're here for a couple of weeks. I don't suppose you could foster Harley, could you?"

Larry added, "Brigid runs the local dog-rescue group and Harley is staying at the V Bar H ranch north of town. Remember the Hadleys? It's their old place. Clay owns it now."

"I remember his sister TJ from high school, although I didn't know her very well," Lisa said.

Brigid rubbed the dog's ears. "Harley would be much happier in a foster home where he gets more attention, even if it's only for a little while."

Lisa shook her head. "I have a cold and I'm not feeling well. I have a lot to do while I'm here."

Larry said, "You're going to be in that huge house all by yourself. You used to love dogs, and he'd keep you company."

Brigid's expression brightened. "Yes! Harley is a wonderful dog. He just wants to be with you. He's like a shadow, and I know if Larry says you like dogs, you'd be great with him. If I didn't have to work here, he'd be the perfect dog. He might need a little training though."

Lisa looked down at the dog, who appeared to be using his leash to hog-tie Brigid's legs. A little training? More like a *lot* of training. She turned to Brigid. "I really don't want to take on the responsibility of a dog. I'm sick."

"You said you have a cold." Larry frowned. "You're not seriously ill, are you? There's not some kind of recurrence is there?"

At his concerned expression, Lisa waved both hands in front of her. "No, it's nothing to do with that. I promise."

"Remember Buster? He was a great dog. Harley kind of reminds me of him in a way," Larry said.

Brigid pushed Harley's butt back to the floor again and said, "There's a boarding kennel north of town, and if you foster Harley, you get two free days of boarding. Normally they only offer free days for dogs that have been adopted, but the owner, Kat Stevens, said she'd add an incentive for anyone who would be willing to foster Harley. Please?"

Larry turned to Lisa. "Harley has become a frequent visitor here, and it will improve my work life if you take him. I'll also feel better knowing you aren't out at the house all by yourself."

Lisa gazed down at the dog, who was wagging his tail eagerly. Harley was kind of cute in a goofy, happy, Lab type of way. It was hard not to smile at his enthusiasm and Larry wasn't wrong about the potential of her being lonely at the house all by herself, surrounded by nothing but memories. At least with a dog, the place wouldn't be so quiet. She shrugged. "All right, I guess I can take him, as long as it's only temporary."

Brigid clapped her hands together, and Harley jumped up with a mighty *woof.* Brigid put her hands on his back and attempted to settle him down. "I'll get his things. He'll be great. You'll love having him around—I promise!"

Lisa wasn't so sure about that, but she took the leash from Brigid and smiled at Harley. "So you wanna see where I grew up?"

Harley started for the front door, which Lisa took as a "yes."

Chapter 2

Welcome Home

The second Lisa opened the office door, Harley leaped forward, causing her to stumble out the door to the snowy sidewalk. Lisa yelped, "Harley, no!"

Undeterred, Harley continued dragging as Lisa hauled back on the leash, struggling to control him. The journey around the block to get to the truck was like a mini Iditarod, with Lisa acting as the sled. She was five feet eight and could probably stand to lose a few pounds, so it wasn't like she was a tiny waif of a woman. How did Brigid control this animal?

"Come on Harley, this way." She pulled on the leash and pointed Harley toward the alley where the trucked was parked. Larry's salmon-colored pickup was just as hideous as she remembered. The old Dodge was as ugly as it had ever been when it was used to haul hardware and building supplies.

Seeing the old vehicle brought back embarrassing memories of high school. Who goes to their homecoming formal in a hardware-store truck? At least she didn't have to feel bad about putting a dog into it. A little dog hair would add a new furry layer to the years of debris that had collected in the interior.

The door creaked as Lisa opened it. Harley leaped into the cab and faced forward, looking ready to drive off. She patted his head. "Good boy. I guess if you've been hanging out at a ranch, you've done the whole riding-in-trucks thing before."

Lisa slammed the passenger door and got in on the driver's side. Even though it had been years since she'd driven the truck, when she started the engine she recognized the familiar rumble and the peculiar putrid scent of decades of sweaty men mixed with decomposing vinyl. Harley thumped his tail enthusiastically on the bench seat, seemingly oblivious to the odd odor and ready for his next adventure.

Lisa's parents' house was located about three miles out of town. The rambling two-story ranch sat up on a knoll on a large grassy lot that Leo used to complain bitterly about mowing. With four bedrooms, three baths, an office, and a family room, Larry wasn't exaggerating about her rattling around in such a large house by herself. The swing on the covered front porch overlooked Mom's big fenced garden, and Lisa recalled the peaceful summer afternoons she'd spent reading stories to her girls. The twins liked to curl up with her on the swing after they'd tired themselves out playing or splashing around in the kiddie pool Mom used to set up for them in the yard.

Lisa turned the last corner and drove up the street to the house. The exterior looked more or less the same as it always had, but the place had that empty, abandoned look that houses get when they've been for sale for months and received little interest. Sure, it was sappy and sentimental to be sad about a house, but nonetheless Lisa found she was a little choked up as she parked in the driveway. The poor old house looked lonely. It was going to feel strange to be there alone after she'd spent so many years fighting with her three siblings and then later visiting with her own kids.

She opened the truck door and Harley leaped out with enthusiasm. After stomping around the snow in the front yard for a few minutes while Harley took care of his business, Lisa waded through the snow to the front porch and up the four steps. She opened the door and Harley charged into the house first. He stopped short and sneezed loudly.

Lisa followed the dog inside and turned on the light. All of the furniture was covered with white sheets, undoubtedly to keep the dust from settling onto the upholstery. She could see the outline of the symmetric semi-circle couches that surrounded the oversized glass coffee table in the living room.

Under the sheets, she knew she'd find the same horrifying kelly-green-and-white print covering the sofas. Like the rest of the decor, the fabric was a throwback to the late sixties. The kelly green in the upholstery pattern was a perfect match for the carpet, which stretched out like a sea of brilliant Astroturf, seemingly indestructible and immune to the passage of time.

Lisa let out a long breath. Rehabbing this house wasn't going to be easy, and it wasn't a huge shock that the house hadn't sold. Although it was a large home, a buyer would need to have amazing vision to see beyond the dated decor. No one had been able to convince Mom to part with the old furniture and it had been far too large for their new cottage, so it had stayed in place, exactly where it had sat for decades.

Mom always argued that the house had been "done by a decorator" and she refused to change anything. What an avant garde few might have considered stylish and ornate in the late sixties and early seventies now was outdated and just plain ugly to virtually everyone.

Although Lisa could no longer remember the name of the person who had committed the awful acts of interior design, whoever he was must have had some type of color-matching fetish, because each room had a color theme. The living room and dining room sported the kelly green, the master bedroom was magenta, Leo's room was dark blue, Larry's was harvest gold, and the bedroom Lisa had shared with her sister Lynn was orange. After growing up feeling like she was living inside a gigantic piece of fruit, Lynn claimed she couldn't even bear the thought of drinking orange juice.

Lisa followed Harley into the kitchen and put the bag of canine supplies on the counter. The walls had striped wallpaper with roses that matched the bubble-gum pink curtains exactly. At least the counters and appliances were white. The prospect of removing all the wallpaper throughout the house was too exhausting to contemplate, not to mention unloading the furniture. The whole place was like a grotesque Lowell family museum and updating it was now her problem. How on earth had she let herself get roped into this?

Harley was obviously enjoying sniffing around the house. He wagged happily as he pressed his nose to the floor, snuffling along and undoubtedly learning all kinds of great things about the happenings of the last twenty-five years or so. Lisa smiled. Weren't dogs color blind? If so, that would certainly help him deal with living in this house. "What do you think, Harley?"

The dog looked up expectantly. Brigid had given Lisa a bag of dog food and bought Lisa a sandwich, so Lisa fed Harley and sat down at the kitchen table to have her lunch. After she finished eating, she called Bev to let her friend know she had arrived.

Bev answered on the first ring and greeted Lisa enthusiastically. "You're here!"

"Yes, I stopped by Larry's office to pick up the old hardware-store truck and now Harley and I are hanging out at the house."

"Who is Harley? Do you have a date? Well hallelujah to that! It's about time."

"Calm down, Bev. Harley is a dog. He's sitting here drooling on my foot. I fed him, so now he loves me."

"Since when do you have a dog? How did I miss that?"

"You haven't missed anything. I got talked into it. Larry's new assistant or whatever she is…that Brigid woman…talked me into fostering a dog. I don't know what is wrong with me. First I get roped into trying to fix up this house so it will sell, and then I end up responsible for a dog."

"Aww don't feel bad, honey. I met Brigid, and as my momma would say, she speaks ten words a second, with gusts to fifty. You probably just nodded your head and she ran with it. You've always loved animals, so I'm sure it will be fine. He'll keep you company."

"I suppose. He's cute and it *is* a little odd being here alone."

"It's time to fix that. I have a leftover bottle of champagne from New Year's Eve because my oh-so-sexy husband fell asleep too early for us to drink it. So I'm gonna grab it and come over right now. We need to celebrate your return to Alpine Grove!"

"Is it okay to drop everything and leave your family alone?"

"Are you kidding? I'm getting my coat. See ya."

Lisa giggled and said, "Drive carefully," but the line was already dead. Some things never changed. Once Bev was on the move, she was unstoppable.

~

By the time Bev knocked on the door, Lisa had removed most of the sheets from the downstairs rooms, so the house no longer looked like the setting of a Scooby-Doo cartoon. Harley barked madly and ran around in circles. He had the bark of a much larger dog and sounded quite ferocious. At least Lisa wouldn't have to worry about break-ins while he was around. "Quiet, Harley!"

She grabbed his collar with one hand and opened the door with the other. Bev was holding a tote bag and bent to pet Harley as she walked by. "Dang, I thought you had Cujo in here."

Lisa closed the door and took the tote bag. "No, just a goofball Labrador retriever. Meet Harley."

Bev gave Harley a final pat. "Definitely not Cujo."

"Well, he can dream."

"Hey, I love your hair! The sun-bleached look works." Bev opened her arms for a big hug. "How are you doing, sweetie? I missed you!"

Lisa embraced her friend and leaned her head on her shoulder. "It's so good to see you."

Bev released her, grabbed her tote bag back from Lisa, and started for the kitchen. "Let's celebrate the farewell to the horrible magenta and green. This is a major event. A turning point in the Lowell family history! Can you imagine what this house might be like once this seventies horror show is over?"

"I know. I'm trying to envision it, but it's difficult, since I lived with these colors for so long."

Bev busied herself opening the champagne and then got some glasses from a cabinet near the sink. "Once you start down the remodeling road, you'll probably get into it. Getting rid of the carpet is your first step."

"I agree, but I hope my mother doesn't have a heart attack. Every time I've mentioned replacing it, she says, 'But it's in great shape, dear. Why would you want to do that?'"

"It frightens me when you imitate your mom, because you sound exactly like her." Bev handed Lisa a glass of the champagne. "Here's to finding a pretty house under here somewhere."

"Cheers." Lisa took a sip and tipped the glass toward Bev. "I do *not* sound like my mother."

Bev rolled her eyes melodramatically. "So how did your family convince your mom to let you do all this remodeling?"

"Larry was a little vague on that. I'm guessing he and my father didn't mention it."

"How did they explain why you're here?"

Lisa shrugged. "Larry didn't say. He said I should send all the bills to him, but I told him I'm not going to lie to Mom if she asks me about all this. It sounds like he and Dad have some type of agreement or bank account for it that Mom doesn't know about. I figure if Larry signs the checks, it's not my problem."

"Your mom is going to freak out."

"Not if you don't tell her." Lisa waved her glass. "But that's not even the worst part! Larry said that he drew up a legal document that gives my Aunt Betty first right of refusal on anything we decide to unload."

"Did he forget that she's completely off her rocker?"

"I don't know. This is a massive family disaster waiting to happen. How did I get myself into the middle of this mess?"

Bev tipped her glass toward Lisa. "See what happens when you don't stand up for yourself? How many times do I have to tell you—if you don't make decisions, someone else will make them for you. You let Mike make all the decisions for years."

"Until he divorced me. Thank you for that special reminder."

"Well, I think coming here and helping out is a good thing. You're one of those people who needs to be needed. Right now, your family needs you."

"And since you blabbed about how I wasn't sure about school, they figured I'm a pushover."

"Well yes, that too. You've been trying to figure out what to do with yourself since you got divorced."

"Again with the special reminder of my failed marriage? So tell me again why we're friends?"

Bev grinned. "Because we've known each other since third grade. And you know you love me and that I'll always look out for you. At least you took your maiden name back. That's a step in the right direction. And I have another one for you."

Lisa frowned. "Why do I have a feeling I'm not going to like this?"

"I fixed you up."

"No."

"Yes! He's really nice. I met him last week and told him all about you. And now you're in Alpine Grove, so it's even better."

"No. I mean it, Bev. Absolutely not. You just finished telling me I'm a pushover and now you go and do this?"

"You have to get out there and meet new people sometime. It's been two years. How long are you going to pine after a marriage that stank like a clogged septic tank?"

Lisa gulped down the last of the champagne in her glass. "I'm not pining and my marriage was fine for years."

"Cut the BS. It's me you're talking to, sweetie."

"All right, it wasn't fine for a while. Maybe a long while, and the end did stink. But I'm done with men and relationships. I need to figure things out first."

Bev raised her eyebrows "What things?"

"I'm still working on that. But it doesn't include men. I've decided they're like television."

"What are you talking about? Does this relate to something you saw on *Oprah*?"

"I don't watch that show. I mean television, the thing. Remember when you were really, really little and getting a TV was a big deal? No one wanted to be the only family on the block without a TV."

"Yeah, so what?"

"Everyone was so excited to get a tiny TV with grainy black-and-white pictures and three channels. It was a momentous event."

"Okay, what does this have to do with men?"

Lisa shook her head as she poured more champagne into her glass. "Then everyone was excited about color television. When your family got a color TV before mine did, I was so jealous. The pretty peacock was in living color and it was amazing."

Bev took a sip and put down her glass. "Okay, so it was cool at the time. I'll give you that. What's your point?"

"Now, everyone has cable with 350 channels and you can't find anything worthwhile to watch. So you give up and go read a book." Lisa gestured toward the windows with her glass, spilling some champagne on the counter. "The whole thing with men is like that. First you have the gee-whiz factor. 'Wow, a date!' Then you graduate to sex. 'Yippee, now I know what everyone is talking about.' Then you get married and you can have sex whenever you want. But you don't, because it's boring like all the junk you don't want to watch on cable. So you say 'forget it.' That's where I am now. I'd rather read a book than deal with a man again."

Bev grinned. "You've put some thought into this, haven't you?"

"Maybe a little. But I'm serious. After Mike and the whole divorce mess, I've had it. I'm done with men."

"I promise this guy isn't like cable and it's not like you have to marry him. When we chatted, he was interesting and told me about how he used to work in an advertising department. He did lots of creative stuff."

"The last guy you fixed me up with in high school was about as fascinating as a lint-covered Dorito."

"Aww come on! Harold wasn't that bad."

"I don't want you to fix me up with anyone, Bev. I'm serious. I hate blind dates now just as much as I did then." Lisa reached down to pet Harley. "And I have a dog now. I can't just leave him alone. This poor guy is an orphan."

"He seems pretty well adjusted to me. I doubt he'd mind if you got someone to take care of him for one evening." Bev pointed at Lisa. "Hey, I thought of something—there's a new boarding kennel in Alpine Grove. You can take him there."

"I heard about that place. The owner is named Kat, which I thought was a little ironic for someone who deals with dogs. Brigid said I have two free days of boarding coming to me because I'm fostering Harley." Lisa squeezed her eyes shut. "Never mind. You didn't hear that."

"Oh, but I surely did." Bev put her arm around Lisa's shoulder. "You're fresh out of excuses then, sweetie. I'll tell Jonah you can't wait to meet him."

"If by 'can't wait,' you mean, 'would rather have a root canal,' then, yes, I can't wait."

Bev hugged Lisa. "I refuse to let you turn into a hermit."

"Just like old times, huh?"

"You betcha. Welcome home."

～

After spending the remainder of the evening laughing and drinking champagne with Bev, Lisa had almost forgiven her friend for fixing her up with the allegedly captivating Jonah. Bev also offered a list of suggestions of people in the construction trade who might be available to help begin shredding the interior of the Lowell family homestead.

Harley was the perfect dog all evening. According to Brigid, he was great except when he was left alone, and that assessment seemed to be true. The dog seemed to enjoy the conversation and reminiscing as much as Lisa had. After Bev left, Lisa was too tired to make up a bed and besides, all the sheets were dirty, since they'd been draped over furniture collecting dust for months. She laid out a couple of blankets on her childhood bed and curled up, exhausted from the long day. Harley daintily hopped up on the end of the bed, turned around a few times, curled up in a ball, and began snoring.

The next day, Lisa got up and made quite possibly the worst cup of coffee in her forty-two years of life. She filled the teakettle, placed it on the stove, then scooped some instant coffee and nasty powdered creamer into a cup. Gazing down at the mound of chemicals, she pondered their age. How long had those jars been sitting in that cabinet? She poured in the hot water and stirred. It was as if she were conducting a chemistry experiment made of ingredients dating from the Mesozoic era. And yet, she was going to drink it. Even awful, possibly poisonous coffee was better than no coffee. The noxious brew also made it clear that she needed to go to the grocery store as soon as possible.

As she sipped the vile concoction, Lisa made a grocery list, went through Bev's list of contractors, and began making a few phone calls to line up meetings. Quite a bit of destruction was going to have to precede the redecorating process. While flooring people and laborers were tearing up the house, Lisa could go through the various rooms, boxing up stuff and cataloging the furniture.

Although most of the furniture wasn't old enough or nice enough to qualify as antique, some of the mid-century modern vintage oddities might appeal to somebody. If someone had a taste for white French provincial dressers and tables with gold trim, they'd be in luck. Most of the furniture was incredibly ornate and heavy, and Lisa loathed it. The orange bedroom she'd shared with Lynn was notable for the hideous brown, orange, and gold plaid bedspreads that still graced the pair of twin beds.

Along with the many house-related calls, Lisa also called the boarding kennel. She needed to make arrangements to board Harley because much to Lisa's dismay when she'd talked to Bev that morning, her friend confessed that she'd set up the date with Jonah. *Already*!

Bev had apparently been confident that she could convince Lisa to go on the date if she pressed the issue. Bev then confirmed the date with the guy for that evening. Way to set that ball in motion. Since everything was already set up, it was easier for Lisa not to argue about it. She loved Bev like a sister and even though she could be bossy, her friend had always been there when she needed her.

One good thing about getting thyroid cancer—okay, the *only* good thing—was that having a major illness showed you who your real friends were. Bev, Lisa's siblings, parents, and her daughters had been by her side and supportive throughout the entire ordeal.

Mike, on the other hand, who was supposed to be her partner in life, had treated her like she was another patient at the hospital. Yes, he was a doctor, but his response to her illness had taken professional detachment to a new level. She'd been his wife, for heaven's sake, not a lab rat or an amoeba in a petri dish.

Although Lisa no longer harbored any ill will toward him, going through her diagnosis, surgery, and treatment had revealed fundamental problems in their marriage. Their mutual dissatisfaction had happened slowly, over time, like tiny cracks in a piece of china. Getting cancer was the hammer that had finally shattered their marriage into tiny shards.

She shook her head, forcing herself to let go of the depressing train of thought. How many times had she told herself that it was time to leave the past behind? Lisa vowed yet again that she was done rehashing her divorce in her mind. She had moved on and was healthy now. Although right at this particular moment, she did feel tired and listless. Maybe it was the champagne. She pressed her fingertips to her neck. Were her glands swollen? What if it was something with her lymph nodes?

Maybe she shouldn't go out on this ridiculous blind date. But she'd already set everything up with Kat Stevens, the owner of the dog-boarding kennel, who'd said Harley was welcome. Backing out now after giving Kat so little notice in the first place would be incredibly rude.

When Lisa had talked to Kat, it sounded like she already knew about Harley. It wasn't really a surprise. Alpine Grove was so small that if you owned a kennel and lived in the area long enough, it was inevitable that eventually you'd know every dog in town.

After completing her arguments with herself, Lisa got ready to take Harley to the kennel, which was located out in the woods north of town. If Lisa was remembering correctly, it sounded like the place was somewhere near where Abigail Goodman used to live. Lisa's parents had been friends with Abigail for years. If she had time, maybe Lisa could stop by for a visit while she was in town.

Harley happily leaped into the truck again. At least the dog was good about riding around. He'd be a great dog for a family that liked to get out and hike. Or maybe he'd be a good farm dog. Lisa felt a little bad dumping him at the kennel after only one day. Harley had been so sweet sleeping at her feet all night. Any little kid would adore this dog. She could easily imagine how her girls, Carol and Cheryl, would have loved playing with him. They'd always wanted a dog.

Lisa drove out of Alpine Grove and up the highway past the Kmart and the Enchanted Moose Motel and RV Park. The Moose appeared to be under construction. That was a novelty. The owners had managed to get away with minimal maintenance for years, thanks to a serious lack of competition. Maybe people had finally noticed it was turning into a dump and made an effort to find somewhere less disgusting to stay.

Lisa turned onto a road that led back toward the deeply forested areas northeast of town, thankful it hadn't snowed lately. These back roads were awful in the winter. Although Larry had assured Lisa that the ugly truck had four-wheel drive, she would prefer to avoid having to count on it. The evergreen trees were bright green against the backdrop of snow and mountains. Although Lisa hated to admit it, Alpine Grove was stunningly beautiful in the winter, with everything all sparkly and white. She probably should have come up here more often when the girls were growing up. Oh well. It was too late now and the girls always had seemed to enjoy visiting Mike's parents over the holidays and spending time in Alpine Grove in the summer.

Finally Lisa found a driveway with a sign that said Wag On Inn. Not only was this near Abigail Goodman's house, it *was* Abigail's house. Did Kat buy it from her? What had happened to Abigail? A knot formed in Lisa's stomach. Like everyone else, Abigail must be getting older. Was she still alive?

The long gravel driveway was bracketed by mounds of snow and weaved through a section of forest filled with huge trees. Everything looked the same as Lisa remembered from her visits out here years ago.

Lisa stopped when she reached a gate across the driveway. That was new. In the past, she'd been able to go all the way up to Abigail's house. A sign indicated she should turn left toward the dog-boarding kennels. She parked the truck in front of the kennel buildings and told Harley to wait. She got out of the truck and took a deep breath. At least the forest smelled the same. The winter sun was warming the evergreens in the clearing and even though it was cold, the breeze was unusually redolent with the scent of pine.

A sign attached to the kennel building instructed visitors to ring the buzzer. Lisa followed the directions and dutifully pressed the button. She stood and looked up at the trees, waiting, clasping her gloved hands in front of her.

At the sound of a door slamming, Lisa turned. A petite woman walked down the steps of the log house at the end of the driveway. She must be the owner, Kat Stevens. From a distance, she looked like Abigail, with a long braid hanging down her back. It was like a flash back to days gone by, which would make more sense if Lisa had done lots of drugs in the sixties. But unlike almost everyone else, she'd been too busy training for ski competitions to engage in that type of recreational activity.

Harley was leaping around in the cab of the truck, obviously eager to escape. Lisa turned and managed to extricate him from the vehicle, unravel the leash from herself, and get him under control.

As the woman walked up, Lisa pushed a clump of hair away from her face. "I'm sorry. He's been so mellow. I don't know what happened to him."

"Harley is probably excited about getting to play with his friends again. I'm Kat Stevens. It's nice to meet you in person." Kat bent and reached out toward the dog. "Hey Harley. Welcome back. Why don't you settle down?"

Lisa rearranged the leash and shook Kat's hand. "Yes, you too. I think I've been here before. Did you buy this house from someone named Abigail Goodman?"

"Not exactly. I inherited it."

"Oh no, you mean Abigail is…she *died?* When? I'm so sorry. She was a wonderful person." Lisa stared down at Harley. "I didn't think she had kids."

"She died a year ago and I was her closest relative. I'm surprised Larry didn't mention it. He dealt with all the estate issues. He was really helpful."

Lisa made a face. "Well, I, ah, had some of my own things going on then and I didn't talk to my brother much about what was happening in Alpine Grove. I can't believe no one told me. Again, I'm so very sorry. You must miss her."

"I hadn't seen her in a long time, but yes, I wish I could talk to her now." Kat gestured toward the trees. "I have about a million questions."

"I can imagine."

"I should get Harley settled. Are you still planning to pick him up tomorrow?"

"Yes, I'll be by to get him during the morning pick-up hours."

"That sounds great. We'll see you then."

They said their goodbyes and Lisa clambered back into Larry's truck. Abigail was dead and Larry had never bothered to mention it to her. Didn't he think she'd want to know? Abigail had been a friend of the family for years. On the other hand, it probably wasn't entirely his fault. After she'd been sick, Lisa had retreated from family, feeling like she'd burdened everyone enough with her health problems.

As Lisa drove down the driveway, her regrets were replaced with apprehension about her upcoming date. Even though it had been a long time, her experiences with the men of Alpine Grove hadn't exactly been electrifying. If Jonah spoke in complete sentences and had all his teeth, it would be a welcome surprise.

Chapter 3

Little Piggy

After taking Harley on a walk through the forest, Kat led him into the kennel building, opened one of the chain-link doors, and went inside the enclosure with him. She ran her hand across the smooth golden fur on his head. "Remember this place? It's your extra-special, super-reinforced, escape-proof kennel."

Harley wagged his tail uncertainly and Kat smiled. "It's going to be fine. I have a peanut-butter filled Kong right over there with your name on it."

Kat exited the kennel and returned with a bowl of water and the Kong. Harley took the toy from her and curled up on the dog bed in the back of the kennel to begin working on his peanut-butter-extraction project. Kat left as quietly as she could, hoping that the thrill of PB would keep him from fixating on the fact that there was no human to keep him company.

She left the building and met her dog-walker, Mia, who was returning from a walk with four dogs on leashes.

Mia grinned at Kat as she rearranged the leashes in her hand. "We're back. Is Harley in there yet?"

"Yes, and he has a Kong, but please keep an eye on him while you're brushing out Ziggy. I'm going back to work on my horrible book now. Let me know if you need anything."

Mia nodded and disappeared inside with the dogs, which led to a burst of barking as the canines greeted their kennelmates.

Kat walked up the driveway toward the house, her mind whirring with all the things she was supposed to remember to add into the book chapter she was working on. It was the last section she had to write for a deadline on Friday. The FedEx guy would be by bright and early to collect the package filled with her peerless prose. By the end of the month, the whole dreadful project would finally be over and she'd be able to sleep again. What a novelty that would be.

The book deadlines over the holidays had been murder. The outline for the software book had been due right after Thanksgiving, four chapters were due after Christmas, and now four more were due Friday. The last chapters would be due at the end of January. Writer's block had become a luxury Kat couldn't afford. She smiled at the quaint notion she used to have of "not feeling like writing." Or that sometimes the "creative juices weren't flowing." Or maybe she wasn't "feeling inspired today." What a joke.

At this point in the book project, Kat had written thousands upon thousands of words when she was not in the mood. In the process, she taken the term "crabby" to a new and extremely disagreeable level. It was a miracle her fiancé Joel hadn't decided to move out. Although he was generally a quiet and even-tempered person, he had become increasingly silent and distant, which was worrisome, although understandable. To be fair, Kat didn't want to be around herself either. But once January was over and the manuscript was safely in the publisher's hands, she'd make it up to Joel. She'd known the book project would be a lot of work, but she hadn't expected her entire life to revolve around deadlines.

She opened the door to the house and was greeted by the sound of her five dogs barking from downstairs. Joel was in the kitchen leaning against the counter and eating an apple. He raised his pinky finger and wiggled it in greeting as he took a huge bite of the Red Delicious.

Kat walked over, stood in front of him, and looked up into his face.

He swallowed and raised an eyebrow at her. "Something wrong?"

She shook her head. "Not exactly. Other than I feel like I never see you anymore."

"I'm not far away. If you left your office more often, you'd see me more."

"I know. I hate this book and I hate how grumpy I've been. I'm sorry."

"You've apologized before, and I understand." He put his hand on her shoulder. "I'm going back outside to dig out more wood."

Kat reached up and put her hand on his to keep him from leaving. "You look tired."

"I *am* tired. My clothes got soaked, so I came in to change."

"I wish I could help."

He pulled his hand away. "It's fine. You have deadlines. See you later."

Kat watched as he went to the hallway, put his winter coat on, and left. He was definitely not happy. It didn't help that the lean-to where they'd been storing wood had collapsed under the weight of soggy snow. Pretty, light, fluffy snow had a habit of turning to mushy, heavy cement when it was rained on for an extended period of time. The poor old lean-to wasn't up to the task and the roof had caved in, burying the firewood under a mess of snow and broken boards.

Because the lean-to was no longer useful for keeping firewood dry, Joel had spent hours digging out the firewood and carting it over to the Tessa Hut. The old outbuilding had been used for dog boarding before the kennel construction was completed. They had nicknamed it the Tessa Hut because Kat's golden retriever Tessa was the first occupant.

Joel had removed the chain-link kennel from the Hut and rearranged the interior so it could house the wet firewood instead of a dog. Unfortunately, the outbuilding was not as close to the house as the old lean-to was, so getting wood for the woodstove in bad weather had become more of a chore.

Kat reluctantly went downstairs to her office to return to the tedious task of cranking out more words. The dogs gathered around and she smiled at them. "Thanks for the moral support, guys. Let's go finish up this chapter." Amid wagging tails, she settled back into her chair for another writing marathon.

Kat stayed glued to her chair writing, even though she desperately wanted to leave and do something else. Anything else. But she needed to finish this chapter so that the next day she could read everything over, print it out, and package it up for FedEx to pick up Friday morning.

Fortunately, Mia was well aware of Kat's work schedule and was handling the care, walking, and feeding of the boarding dogs. Kat paused for a small thank you to the universe for sending Mia to Alpine Grove. Hiring a dog walker to manage the day-to-day operations of the kennel had made it possible for Kat to write.

If this book ever saw the light of day, Kat was going to thank Mia in the acknowledgments and dedicate the tome to Joel for putting up with life with a book author. It was the least she could do.

~

After spending an outrageously long time selecting her clothes and doing her hair and makeup, Lisa left the house and drove to the Italian restaurant in town. Although the ownership had changed a few times over the years, the restaurant had been the de facto first-date restaurant in Alpine Grove for as long as Lisa could remember. It also was practically Larry's second home. She often wondered if her brother ate all of his meals there. The man never seemed to cook anything for himself.

Because it was Alpine Grove, quite a few people recognized Lisa and the pretty blonde hostess patiently attempted to get her customer to the designated table. The hostess waited with her hands in front of her clutching the menus while Lisa said hello to everyone from former teachers and classmates to customers from the hardware store she hadn't seen in decades.

At last, Lisa was seated at one of her favorite tables near the fireplace, gazing at the flickering flame of the votive candle. She'd sat right here across from Randy Houston before a spring formal they'd attended together. In some ways, that felt like it was a million years ago; in others it seemed like yesterday. Where had the time gone?

She was startled from her reverie when a tall, handsome man stopped in front of her table. He bent slightly and said quietly, "Are you Lisa?"

Lisa looked up into his face. Now she knew why Bev had fixed her up with Jonah. This guy was extremely easy on the eyes. Wow. With his jet black hair and smoldering dark eyes, he should be in a movie featuring a Scottish lord. A kilt would absolutely work for him. She gestured toward the seat across from her. "You must be Jonah. It's a pleasure to meet you. Please sit down."

After settling himself, he picked up the menu, held it in both hands, and leaned forward toward her. "I've never been here before? Have you?"

Lisa smiled politely. *Only about a thousand times.* "I have. Didn't Bev mention that we grew up here in Alpine Grove?"

"No, but it must have been a great place to be a kid, with skiing and the lake and all that. I like it here."

"Bev and I had a lot of fun." Lisa picked up her napkin and put it in her lap. Jonah seemed pleasant enough. Maybe this hadn't been such a bad idea, after all. Having someone to go places with while she was in town could be enjoyable. It was utterly pathetic, but one side effect of getting divorced that people often didn't think about was that you no longer had a date for events. When they'd been married, Mike might have ignored her half the time, but at least he was obligated to be her 'plus one.' She smiled at Jonah again. "Bev said you met last week?"

His only response was a gigantic sneeze that reverberated through the low hum of ambient conversation, startling the restaurant into silence. Reaching into his pocket, he yanked out a handkerchief and blew his nose like a trumpet. "Sorry. Allergies."

"You have allergies in the winter? Are you allergic to pet hair?"

"I have allergies all the time because I'm allergic to everything. Hair, dust, mold, grass, trees, leaves—you name it. If it's floating in the air, my sinuses don't like it and stage a revolt. I keep trying new drugs, but nothing seems to do much."

"I'm sorry to hear that." Lisa struggled to think of something to say that wasn't related to nasal passages. "Bev told me you're in advertising."

"Well, I was, but I retired. The medical-equipment company I worked for got bought out by a gigantic conglomerate and they wanted everyone to move to Cleveland, so I took early retirement."

"How nice that you were able to do that. Do you miss the work? Bev made it sound like it was very creative and interesting."

He shook his head. "Not really. There's only so much you can say about enemas and I think by the time I left, I'd said it all."

Lisa paused, mentally flailing for a response that wouldn't be completely inappropriate. *Enemas?* She was going to kill Bev. "So, ah, what's next for you?"

"Not sure. Just kinda floating around, doing a little traveling. I tried out skiing at Snow Grove. Turns out I'm really bad at it."

"I haven't been skiing in many years. It sounds like you're finding yourself. What a wonderful opportunity. Now you have time to explore new ideas and look for the answers to the big questions."

He tilted his head. "What questions? I don't have any questions."

"You know, all the big questions of the universe. Why am I here? What is my purpose in life?" Lisa smiled. "I can relate to that, since I'm at a bit of a crossroads myself."

"I guess I never thought about it. You're kinda intense aren't you?"

"Intense?" Lisa pursed her lips. She'd certainly never thought of herself that way. Or not in a long time anyway. "I don't think so. Maybe years ago I was, but after I got married, I was focused on raising my two girls."

"You're married?"

"Divorced. Now that I'm alone and the girls are off in college living their own lives, I'm not sure what's next for me."

"Are you scared of being alone? Is that it? The whole empty-nest deal?"

"Maybe. I suppose so."

"Yeah, I'm a little worried I'll be alone forever. Because of my allergies, people avoid me. But I'm not sick. I mean, it's not contagious or anything."

"That's good to hear."

"I guess I could spew out something gross when I sneeze, but I do cover my mouth, since that's what you have to do to be polite, you know. But sometimes I get this itching all over my skin too, particularly in hot spots like the genital area. Oh, and because I have a severe case of allergic rhinitis, as the specialists call it, that means I snore like a rusty old diesel freight train. And there's nothing anyone can do about it."

"Ah, that's interesting." Lisa took a sip of water. That was *vastly* more information than she needed to know.

"Yeah, it stinks." He sighed. "I really shouldn't be telling you all this personal stuff."

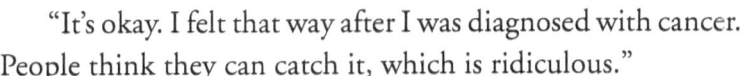

"It's okay. I felt that way after I was diagnosed with cancer. People think they can catch it, which is ridiculous."

Jonah raised his eyebrows. "You have cancer? But you look really healthy and alive."

"I had thyroid cancer, but it's in remission."

"But wow, cancer? You musta been really sick. Like dying and stuff."

"Ironically, none of the symptoms I had related to the cancer. I used to go to doctors a lot...I suppose some people might say I was a bit of a hypochondriac. In any case, I asked them to do all these tests because I didn't feel well. It turned out there was nothing wrong with me that had anything to do with my symptoms, but in the process they did find the cancer. So I still don't feel great, but the cancer is gone. With cancer, they generally don't say cured, so technically I'm in remission."

"But wait, remission means it could come back, right? Aren't you scared you're going to die?"

"Well, yes, I do think about that sometimes. I never want to go through that type of thing again, and to be honest, like I said, I still haven't been feeling great." Lisa touched her neck absently. "It could be a cold. But I don't feel good. I have this sort of clogged and foggy feeling, you know?"

"So you're going to *die*?" Jonah leaned back away from her in his chair. "Jeez. Cancer. The Big C. That's scary. Bev didn't say you were dying."

"Well, everyone is going to die someday, and it's not like I'm going to keel over and cork off right this second. I had surgery and radiation and received the all-clear." Lisa turned her palms up toward the ceiling. "I mean, you're going to die eventually too, you know."

Jonah looked toward the door. "I guess. Uh, I just remembered something. I've got to...um...go to an appointment early in the morning. Ski lesson. Yeah, a lesson...because like I said, I really stink at the whole skiing deal. So I have to get up really early."

"But we haven't even ordered."

He stood up. "I'm sorry, I totally forgot about this lesson when I talked to Bev about meeting you today. So give her my regards when you see her, okay?"

Lisa stood up. "I will." When she called her friend and read her the riot act.

Jonah put on his coat and scurried out of the restaurant. It was quite possible that Lisa had set a new record for scaring off a man. The word "cancer" seemed to cause an unprecedented flight response. It was a good thing she'd sworn off men, since she seemed to have a unique ability to repel them.

Having lost her enthusiasm for Italian food, Lisa gathered up her purse, left a tip for the glass of water she'd had, apologized, and left the restaurant. She drove to the grocery store, picked up a to-go Caesar salad, and went to Bev's house.

She stalked from the sidewalk up the neatly shoveled walkway to the house and pounded on the door.

Bev opened it and her jaw dropped. She peeked around Lisa into the darkness. "Where's Jonah?"

Lisa walked past her and into the house. "I don't know. That little piggy went *wee-wee-wee* all the way home."

"What did you do?"

"I didn't *do* anything." Lisa dropped the salad on the kitchen counter. "Why do you always assume it's me? He left,

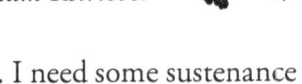

so I went to the store and got a salad. I need some sustenance before I kill you. That was the worst date *ever*. What were you thinking?"

"He was cute and seemed nice enough." Bev put her hands on her hips. "All right. What did you say to him?"

"Nothing! We were talking, and he mentioned that sometimes his allergies turn people off."

Bev slumped her shoulders. "Oh no. You didn't go all hypochondriac on him, did you?"

"I might have mentioned I wasn't feeling well." She shrugged. "And I might have mentioned the cancer."

"You convinced the guy you're at death's door and now you're wondering why he ran away?"

"He said I was *intense*. What's that supposed to mean?" Lisa looked around the kitchen. "You know, it's awfully quiet here. Where is everyone?"

"Kevin is at a meeting, and the boys are chained to their chairs in that bedroom until I say they can come out. We're having a homework situation." Bev snatched the salad off the counter. "That looks good. So, okay, spill your guts about the date. You know you want to."

Bev split the salad onto two plates and they settled into eating while Lisa described her short-lived evening with Jonah. By the time she was done, they were both laughing, and when Lisa left, she felt a lot better about her pathetic excuse for a date. She warned Bev not to fix her up again, but the admonishment would probably fall on deaf ears. Bev was determined to get Lisa out of the house and "into circulation," as she called it.

The next morning Lisa returned to the kennel to pick up Harley, who seemed no worse for the experience, but eager to join Lisa wherever she might want to go.

The owner of the kennel was considerably less lively. Kat looked like she'd hadn't slept at all. Was she wearing the same clothes she'd worn the day before?

Lisa took Harley's leash and cleared her throat to get Kat's attention. "Thank you for taking him. I hate to ask, but is something wrong?"

Kat jerked her head toward Lisa. "What did you say? I guess I was spacing out. I didn't get much sleep last night."

Lisa narrowed her eyes. Was this woman on drugs? If so, Lisa certainly didn't want to bring Harley here again. "Do you have insomnia?"

"Sleeping is no problem when I get the chance to do it." Kat motioned in the general direction of the house. "But I'm writing a book. I have a deadline and I stayed up most of the night writing."

"I should probably be going now and let you get back to it."

Kat bent to ruffle Harley's ears. "You still have one more free day of boarding. Let me know when you want to use it."

Lisa nodded. "I will." Writing all night? That sounded like something Cheryl might have said back in high school, during the Great Science Fair Project Crisis of 1994. Although Lisa's daughter had been a master at homework avoidance, it seemed procrastination didn't have an age limit.

After Harley left, Kat slowly meandered back to the house. Although Lisa had been polite, she'd given Kat a look like it would be a cold day in Neverland before she'd consider bringing Harley back.

Now even her dog-boarding clients were noticing that Kat was acting like a zombie. Great. This horrible book project was screwing up her business in addition to her home life. It wasn't a shock that she looked like death. Writing until three in the morning didn't do much for a girl's appearance. By that point, Kat had been writing so long that she could barely see straight and had staggered upstairs to bed.

The morning had not gone well. At the horrible buzzing of the alarm, Joel had leaped out of bed and slapped the button to turn it off. The air temperature had been something south of freezing, so Kat had nestled back down under the covers.

Because she'd been so focused on writing, Kat had failed to remember to put wood in the stove the night before, and that had led to waking up in a house that felt like an igloo. All they needed were some penguins to complete the arctic ambiance.

When she'd stumbled out to the kitchen, she'd been distressed to discover Joel wasn't around. Where was he? Where was the coffee? He always made coffee. After she descended the stairs and meandered through the sea of canines to Joel's office, she'd found him squinting at something on his computer screen.

Kat knew better than to interrupt the nerd when he was nerding, but the lack of coffee had made her unusually bold. Or stupid. So she'd tapped on the doorjamb lightly, smiled, and wished him a good morning.

He'd clicked something, pushed back the chair, and stood up. "I restarted the stove."

After a curt exchange about the lack of coffee and heat, Joel had stalked by her and gone upstairs. Kat hadn't been sure how to respond to his uncharacteristically surly mood, and when the kennel buzzer rang, she'd dashed outside to deal with Harley.

Because of Joel's earlier irritability, Kat was dreading the mood she was likely to encounter back in the house. Something odd was going on with him. She removed her jacket, wandered into the kitchen, and discovered he'd disappeared again.

She opened a cabinet and pulled down some coffee filters. Joel walked back to the kitchen from the bedroom and she waved a filter at him. "I'm sorry I forgot to put wood in the stove last night. I think my brain self-destructed from too much writing."

He took the filters from her and set up the coffee. "Yeah, there's been a lot of that."

"I know. Harley is already out of here, so today all I have to do is revise the new chapters, then send them off to the publisher in the morning. And after that, only one more deadline!"

"I've got to meet someone this morning, so I won't be able to do dishes and whatever." He waved a hand toward the mountain of dishes in the sink. "But by my calculations, I'm ahead by twenty-seven dish washing events, so I think I'm covered."

Kat raised her eyebrows. Okay, Joel was analytical by nature, but this was new. What was going on? "Do you actually keep track of when I do the dishes? Is there some spreadsheet you have that I don't know about?"

"Not when you do dishes; when you *don't* do them. It takes me three times as long to do dishes by myself versus when we do them together."

"Did you time it?" Kat pointed at the counter. "It wouldn't be a problem if we had a dishwasher. I'm not sure where we'd put one, but it would be great to have a modern labor-saving appliance."

"And of course, I'd have to install it, right?"

"I suppose so. Past experience has shown that it's better if you deal with construction projects. Would that be a problem? You've torn up these cabinets before. With all that practice, you should be good at it."

"Yeah, because of the dachshund that got stuck. I remember."

Kat narrowed her eyes and tried to read his expression, but it was impassive. When he was extremely upset or angry, he had this way of letting his face go blank and speaking in a controlled, reasonable voice. Although Kat understood that it was a defense mechanism, trying to argue with a monosyllabic robot could be frustrating beyond belief. "Is something bothering you? What's going on?"

"Nothing. I have to get ready to go." Joel grabbed a mug and poured some coffee into it. He gestured with the mug in the general direction of the stairwell. "Don't forget to put wood in the stove this time."

Kat clamped her mouth closed to prevent a snotty rejoinder from leaping out. Turning to lean against the counter, she stood motionless holding her mug as he disappeared down the stairwell.

Although she was probably asking for a fight, the curiosity was getting to her, so she followed him down the stairs. "Where are you going so early?"

He grabbed a book from his desk and threw it on a pile with a thump. "Town."

"I figured as much. Who are you meeting?"

"No one you know." He collected his wallet from a drawer and shoved it into the back pocket of his jeans. "Just someone I went to school with."

Kat leaned against the door. "Did I do something? You're being weird."

"No, I'm not." He downed the last of his coffee with a gulp. "I've got to go. I'm late."

Kat reached out and grabbed his arm as he went by her through the doorway. "Stop for a second. Why are you so angry at me? I know I haven't been much fun to be around because of the book and not sleeping. But that's not new. What happened in the last day? What is going on with you? I mean, even with everything we've dealt with since we've known each other, you've never been like this. Well, except maybe once."

He stopped and looked down into her face. "Like what?"

"Angry? Frustrated? I'm not sure. But you're the most patient person I know."

The hard look in his eyes softened slightly. "Thanks. It's nothing. Don't worry about it."

"You do realize who you're talking to, right? I worry about *everything*."

He gave her a quick kiss. "Don't. I have to go."

Kat watched him go up the stairs and pressed her hand to her stomach as the knot tightened. Whatever was going on, it definitely wasn't *nothing*.

∽

After Lisa got home with Harley, she settled into calling more contractors. She was striking out as far as finding anyone who wanted to work on this remodeling project. It was either too large, too small, they were already working on something else for the winter, or they weren't working at all.

Another issue was deciding on the new decor. Over the years, Lisa had made decorating choices for her own house, but because it was her house, she simply selected colors and fabrics she liked. It turned out that other people in Gleasonville shared her taste, so when she and Mike put the house up for sale, they'd had an offer within a week.

This remodeling project was going to involve redoing everything, and it wasn't her house. After Lisa had the ugly carpet ripped out, inevitably she would need to put something else down. There would be new paint, new counters, and new cabinets. Did Larry and her father really expect her to make all these decorating decisions herself? She didn't feel completely comfortable with the responsibility. If she made bad choices, the house wouldn't sell. Her mother was going to have a heart attack about the remodeling work, but if the house didn't sell, her father would be angry too.

She picked up the phone and called Larry at his office. Brigid answered the phone and quickly shuttled her off to Larry.

Lisa ruffled the fur on Harley's neck. "What is going on there?"

"I'm having a bad day," Larry said in a glum voice.

"It's only nine fifteen."

"Believe me, I'm aware of that fact." He paused and there was a muffled shout before he came back on the line. "Lisa, I just thought of something. You could really help me out here."

Lisa frowned. It was unlikely she was going to like this idea. "Actually, I called to talk to you about colors and flooring options. What does Dad want? Shouldn't we talk about this? It's his house and his money, after all."

"Anything you can buy through the hardware store is fine. Dad doesn't care. Could you do an errand for me today?"

"I suppose, but why me? You have an assistant."

"I have to file papers with the court and Brigid has a lot of cleanup to do here." He paused and then said more loudly, "And then she has to *take that dog out to the ranch*."

"Cleanup?"

"A dog vomited in one of the file boxes. I don't know how long it will take to deal with this mess, so I need you to take some papers to be signed at Snow Grove."

"I don't want to go there."

"Lisa, that was a million years ago. It's a big mountain with ski runs on it. You spent much of your youth there. I mentioned the possibility of you doing errands for me previously, and I need your help today. It's an emergency."

"All right, fine. I guess I can do that, if it's that important." Harley stood up and gazed at Lisa, looking concerned. "It's okay, Harley."

"Whatever you do, do *not* bring that dog into the office. That's the last thing I need. Listen, I'm late. Stop by here and Brigid will hand you the papers. You need to drop the package off with Sean Jenkins at the resort by noon."

"That's not much time to get all the way out to Snow Grove."

"You have plenty of time, if you leave now. I have to go."

It was unlike Larry to sound so upset about work, especially with her, so Lisa figured the errand truly was important. She somewhat reluctantly gathered her things and loaded Harley into the old pickup for the quick trip to Larry's office. If she was lucky, it was early enough that she might be able to get a parking place right in front of Larry's office, so she could keep an eye on Harley.

As she slowly drove down the main street, a car pulled out of a spot near the law office. Lisa did a reasonably competent job of parking the truck, but it was exhausting. The manual steering meant that parallel parking was quite the workout, reminding her that she really needed to get back into shape. Visiting the mountain would be a distressing reminder of how much she'd changed.

"Be good Harley. I'll be right back, and then we'll go visit a lot of snow." Harley wagged his tail and stood up on the seat, watching as she closed the truck door and walked around the vehicle to the sidewalk. Noting the anxious expression on the dog's face, Lisa shook her index finger at him. "Sit down. You'd better be good. No eating the truck!"

Lisa opened the door to the office and found Brigid at the desk, looking upset. She shoved a lock of red hair behind her ear, picked up a manila envelope off the desk, and handed to Lisa. "Here you go."

"Thanks." Lisa quickly stole a glance around the office. It didn't smell good in here, but the offending dog was nowhere to be seen. "Do you know when Larry will be back? I need to talk to him."

"Later this afternoon." She stood up. "I have to deal with a dog. Do you have what you need?"

"Yes, and Harley is outside in the truck, so I should go."

Brigid's tense expression relaxed slightly. "How is he doing?"

"Great, so far. I think he likes me. He follows me everywhere and loves sleeping on the foot of my bed."

"That's wonderful. I knew he would do better in a home environment." Brigid grabbed her coat off a hook and followed Lisa out the door. She waved at Harley, who had his nose pressed up to the passenger door window of the truck. "Look at that face! Thank you again for being such a great foster mom and for delivering those papers. I really appreciate it."

Lisa nodded and walked back to the truck. She felt like she was turning into a slacker. Everyone was so busy and yet she was unemployed, living in her parents' old house, and sleeping in her childhood bed. Somehow it seemed as if she were going backward in time, as if she'd never been a grown-up, contributing member of society with a husband and kids.

Harley stared at her expectantly through the window. Now Lisa's primary job was to be a foster mom to one slightly neurotic Labrador retriever. She opened the door of the truck and shoved Harley over to the other side. "Okay, let's go!"

The Snow Grove ski resort was located southwest of Alpine Grove and Lisa knew every inch of the journey. For years, she and Bev and other kids had carpooled to the mountain, their parents taking turns shuttling them up the winding road to the resort in the wee hours of the morning so they could practice. The kids had started competing in children's events at the age of six, then graduated to more and more competitive racing, gliding seventy-five miles an hour on skis pointed straight down the mountain.

The Snow Grove Ski Team, or SGST, competed in slalom, giant slalom, and downhill. The resort had let the ski team kids access the slopes early in the morning before general opening so the kids could work on speed training. Once Lisa had gotten a taste for going fast, it had become addictive. For years, she had dreams about flying through the slalom gates, the wind whipping her face. It was an adrenaline rush like nothing else she'd ever experienced.

Back then, she'd been completely fearless to the point that it was almost as if all those years of training and competition had happened to someone else. Now, Lisa was an extremely different person from that wild teenager who hadn't been afraid of anything.

~

Lisa turned off the highway and onto the winding road that led to the resort. It had probably been twenty-five years since she'd been on this road. She'd heard about some of the changes they'd made to Snow Grove, but had never seen them.

Lisa had gotten into skiing seriously not too long after they'd finally paved the road, which had been a big deal at the time. The resort had opened in the early sixties with one long double chairlift and a T-bar. By the time Lisa had been skiing competitively in the late sixties and early seventies, the owners had expanded the lodge, added six more chair lifts, another T-bar, and a rope tow for the bunny hill. The base area had a deli in the lodge and a small condominium building.

As Lisa got closer to the top of the mountain, the walls of snow alongside the road grew higher, and it was as if she were driving through a long white tunnel. The first notable difference at the resort was signage. Way back when, there weren't any signs because it was obvious where to go. The road up the hill simply dead-ended in the parking lot. Now signs pointed toward multiple roads leading off to condominium complexes and several different parking areas.

Lisa came to the disconcerting conclusion that she had absolutely no idea where she was supposed to find Sean Jenkins or his office. She hadn't even thought to ask, which had been a stupid oversight on her part. Places did tend to change over the course of multiple decades. She slowed the truck, studying the signs more closely. A car came up behind her and honked, so she opted to follow a road that claimed it went to "The Village at Snow Grove." That sounded promising. With any luck, the resort offices were located there.

She navigated to a parking lot that was jammed full of cars. Finally, she snagged a parking place by using the stalker approach of waiting for someone to pull out and then zipping in. After wedging the truck into the slot, she put on Harley's leash and got him out of the truck. Since she had no idea where she was going or how long it would take, he was going to have to go with her on this expedition.

If the parade of skiers was any indication, the village was toward the north. Lisa could see the ski runs rising up on the mountain above, but from this parking lot, it was quite a trek to where the old lodge had been at the bottom of the slopes. A six-story opulent-looking condo complex blocked the view, but presumably, the village was behind it.

Harley was excited about all the people carrying ski gear and eagerly yanked Lisa forward. She jerked back on the leash, "Harley, stop that! It's slippery. You're going to kill me, if you don't calm down."

Momentarily chastised, the dog slowed and glanced at Lisa as she gained her footing again. Once she was steady, he resumed his program of pulling her toward the buildings. Maybe he smelled food. Whatever it was, the dog was desperate to get to the slopes.

Seeing all the skiers happily chatting about their upcoming day of recreation on the mountain brought back memories of being here with Bev. On a clear day, from the top of Chair 1 you could see across the valley, all the way over to the lake. With chattering teeth, they'd turn in their chairs, hugging the backrest, so they could enjoy the stunning view during the long, slow lift ride up the mountain.

Along with the rest of the skiers tromping alongside her up the metal stairs, Lisa finally made her way around the tall condo complex. People were skiing or walking in a central courtyard at the bottom of the hill. Shops and restaurants ringed the huge area, their signs waving in the morning breeze.

The old lodge had been expanded and now sported a large outdoor balcony that faced the slopes. The balcony was dotted with skiers, resting and eating in-between runs. The old Chair 1 was gone, replaced by a high-speed quad lift that was swiftly spiriting skiers up the mountain. Although Lisa had received third-hand reports from her family and Bev about what the resort was like now, it was startling to see it all spread out in front of her. The slightly quirky Snow Grove she remembered from her youth had been replaced by a bustling high-end resort, and she suddenly felt extremely out of place. When she was young, she knew all the members of the Greenberg family and had skied with their kids. Presumably, those kids had been running the resort for a while now and they were the ones selling it.

A few people glanced at Harley with raised eyebrows or smiles. Were dogs allowed? Lisa hadn't even thought about the possibility that dogs might not be welcome, given that the place was so crowded. The dog seemed convinced that he needed to be somewhere, dragging her along the snowy ground. What was his problem? Most of the time, as long as he was with a human, he was reasonably mellow. If she'd known visiting the ski resort would turn him into some type of wanna-be sled dog, she would have figured out a way for someone to take care of him. This was ridiculous. She hauled on the leash, dragging him toward the buildings so she could see the signs. "Harley, cut it out! There's nothing *over* there, except more snow and a whole lot of skiers. We need to find this office."

Lisa wandered around the perimeter of the courtyard, looking at signs. Skiers coming down off the mountain intent on getting an early lunch zoomed around her. Snowboarders stomped by, the boards they had attached to one foot thumping on the ground.

The windows of the shops were filled with every possible form of colorful skiing and snowboarding gear imaginable. The low-tech equipment Lisa had owned back when she was skiing competitively would be laughable now. As a skier, Lisa found all the snowboarding accoutrements in the displays completely mystifying. Strapping both feet onto a board seemed like a bad idea, unless you happened to have a death wish.

At last, she found a sign for the Snow Grove offices, which were upstairs from a small cafe. She opened the door and manhandled Harley inside the narrow stairwell, which was difficult because the dog was insisting on going the other way. "Harley, we're going over here. *Come on!*"

She stomped her feet to remove the snow from her boots and pulled Harley up the stairs behind her. He continued his quest to go in the other direction. What was wrong with him? "Give me five minutes, Harley, then we'll get out of here. I promise."

Lettering on a glass door indicated she'd found the Snow Grove operations office, so she walked inside. A pretty blonde woman looked away from her computer monitor and smiled. "May I help you?"

Lisa pulled the manila envelope out of her bag. "I need to drop this off for Sean Jenkins. Can you get it to him? Larry Lowell asked me to bring it by."

"Oh yes, the lawyer. I'll take it; that's fine." She took the envelope and placed it on the desk. "Sean is in a meeting, but I'll make sure he gets it."

Harley was attempting to tie his leash into a knot around Lisa's legs. She bent over, pulled the leash away, and thanked the receptionist. It was definitely time to go home. This dog was acting like he was possessed by some type of alpine demon.

Once Harley realized they were leaving, he resumed his campaign of pulling, eagerly galloping down the steps, back to the ground level. Lisa struggled to keep him from dragging her head over heels down the stairs. When they were close to the bottom, the door opened and a man looked up in surprise at the dog barreling toward him.

Lisa shrieked as she stumbled and dropped the leash. Harley jetted past the man, down the last steps, out the door, and into the sea of skiers in the courtyard.

Lisa shoved by the man, yelling "Harley!" over and over.

She half-ran, half-slid out into the snowy central area, where Harley was galloping toward the ski slopes at full Labrador speed. What was he doing? As Lisa ran through the crowd, people turned to look at her and then at the dog she was chasing. Although she was yelling for someone to grab the dog, everyone was busy skiing. Most people ignored her and the people who did notice didn't seem to know what to do.

A few skiers made feeble efforts to slow Harley, but big bulky winter gloves weren't conducive to corralling a dog on a mission. Lisa was rapidly running out of energy and wanted to cry as skiers deftly skied around Harley. The dog galloped at full speed up the main ski run that dead-ended into the courtyard. Lisa had skied down Midway a million times, but she'd never tried to run *up* it on foot.

Gravity and friction were not on her side, and breathing heavily, despair settled in. Trying to ignore her burning lungs, Lisa continued slowly climbing upward, following the paw prints in the snow as the rapidly retreating yellow canine form grew smaller in the distance. Losing a dog after two days would probably win the Worst Foster Mom of the Year prize or something. Brigid was going to kill her, and Larry wouldn't be too happy either.

Lisa bent to catch her breath, placing her palms on her knees. With a sigh, she looked up the hill. Harley had disappeared into a copse of trees. She had to find this idiot dog and get him back home.

Chapter 4

Hero Dog

Wherever Harley was going, he was making a beeline to get there. Lisa continued trudging up the hill as more skiers whizzed by. A few jerked their heads to look when they realized she wasn't attached to skis or a snowboard. People didn't generally walk around on the slopes with no equipment. But by the time anyone realized, they were too far downhill to say anything. Only a fool like her would walk up a ski run.

A skier wearing a colorful joker's hat noticed her trekking upward, swerved, and tried to stop. Lisa turned her head to look as the young man flailed his arms, which launched his ski poles up into the crystal blue sky. He curled and began rolling like a boulder down the hill, skis and clothes hurtling away from him in a shower of alpine wear.

The man stopped rolling, sat up, and started laughing hysterically. Another skier shouted and waved his ski pole. "Billy Bob! That was one righteous yard sale, dude. You totally rocked it!"

Billy Bob continued laughing as his friends swooped by, picking up the paraphernalia scattered across the ski run. Other skiers whooshed by, yelling encouragement and support for the spectacular show.

Convinced that Billy Bob was fine and even pleased with himself, Lisa moved to the side of the run and resumed her trudge up the hill. The trail of paw prints left the groomed ski trail and went off into one of the out-of-bounds areas filled with deep snow that blanketed the huge trees.

A orange plastic snow fence marked the out-of-bounds area and Lisa could tell that Harley had shoved his way under the floppy material. She pulled the fence up and crawled under. The dog was nowhere to be seen and Lisa was already cold, wet, and utterly exhausted. Too bad Mom and Dad didn't have a hot tub at the house. If she ever made it down off this mountain, maybe she'd suggest adding one as part of the big remodeling project.

She stopped to rest again and turned at the sound of a demanding dog bark. Was Harley hurt? The bark had an urgent tone and Lisa hurried forward as fast as she could through the deep snow. It was packed down with a thick layer of new powder on top, so she had some footing, but it was slow going. At least Harley had blazed a trail for her.

Up ahead, Lisa could see the dog standing next to a tree. Harley's sharp bark had evolved into an insistent, repetitive woofing. At least he'd finally stopped running, so Lisa had a chance of finally catching this animal. Her lungs hurt from the unaccustomed exertion and puffs of steam surrounded her. If she survived this expedition, she was taking up an exercise program. No more excuses. This was pathetic. She was a former world-class skier and now she could barely even walk uphill.

As Lisa got closer to the dog, she spotted something in the snow near Harley. Was that a ski? "Harley, be quiet and get over here. I'm dying of exhaustion. What are you *doing*?"

Harley refused to move and continued to bark, so Lisa trudged on. She picked up the ski as she walked by, dragging it behind her. Someone would be really glad to get that back, although hauling it down the hill with her and Harley wasn't going to be a lot of fun.

A dark shape came into view behind Harley. What was that? Lisa hurried closer and Harley bounded toward her, then backward, encouraging her to move more quickly. As she approached, her stomach clenched when she encountered a trail of bloodstained snow and then a person's body. Kneeling down, she pulled off the skier's goggles and looped them over her arm. The man was unconscious and bleeding from the head. Even worse, one of his legs was contorted in a way that indicated it must be badly broken, possibly in multiple places.

The sight of the man's leg was all too familiar, but having her own little mental meltdown out here in the snow wouldn't help this poor injured skier. Lisa squeezed her eyes shut, trying to shove down her emotions.

Before she'd become the mother of twin girls, she'd been squeamish about many things. Now almost nothing could gross her out. Fortunately, she wasn't terrified by the sight of blood like her daughter Carol. Years ago, when Carol's twin Cheryl had fallen and needed stitches on her chin, Lisa was asked to remove Carol from the building, since the screaming wasn't helping anyone's stress level. Fortunately, Mike had been there to tend to Cheryl. Having a doctor in the family had been useful during emergencies like that one. Well, when he'd been around anyway.

Lisa opened her eyes and took a deep breath, pushing aside memories of her husband and kids. She needed to focus. Harley was lying next to the man, licking his face. Lisa rummaged in her bag. In one of the pockets she found an old silk scarf that had been her mother's. Mom sometimes used it to cover her hair when it was windy.

Lisa folded the scarf and wiped away the blood, pushing a clump of dark brown hair off the man's forehead, revealing the wound. Fortunately, the cut didn't seem to be deep. Maybe he'd been scraped up by the trees.

Lisa gasped when the man moved. He opened his eyes and shoved Harley's nose away from his face. She leaned over him and looked into his face. The color of his eyes was a startling blue, almost the same shade as the brilliant blue winter sky above them. She gently put her hand on his chest. "Don't try to move. You might have hurt your back."

He groaned and said in a raspy voice, "Leg."

"Yes, I think you hurt your leg. It looks like a type of injury I've seen before. Please try and lie still."

"Who are you?" He moved his hand feebly at Harley, "Where did this dog come from. Yuck—stop licking me, dog!"

"I'm Lisa and that's Harley. He found you. I need to get help. You're way out of bounds and no one can see you here from the ski runs."

He closed his eyes again and Lisa touched his shoulder. "What's your name?"

"Pete."

"Don't go to sleep, Pete. You need to stay awake."

"But I'm tired."

Lisa pressed the scarf to his forehead more firmly to get his attention. "*Pete*, look at me. Tell me what happened."

"I went the wrong way and then I caught my ski."

She moved the scarf and put her other hand on his cheek. "Pete, talk to me! What happened then?"

"It felt like I was rolling off a cliff or something. I don't know really. It's all kind of a blur."

Lisa had a good idea where he must have fallen and what had happened. "All right. We need to get you back to the village."

He moved experimentally and cringed. "Great idea. What are you going to do, carry me?"

"No, I'll get help. It will be faster if I use one of your skis." She looked around and spotted the poles nearby, and dug in the snow to find his feet. "Can you wiggle your toes or move this leg?"

He moved his leg toward her. "Yeah, that one is okay. I don't think I hurt my back. It's just the other leg..."

"Okay, that's good. Try not to think about it." At least he didn't appear to have a spinal injury. She dug around in the snow, undid the latches on his ski boot, pulled it off, and gently moved his foot into her bag. "This will keep your foot warm until I get back. Please hang onto Harley's collar and don't let go."

He raised his eyebrows in question, but did as instructed while Lisa began unwinding the plaid wool scarf from her neck.

Pete leaned his head back in the snow and closed his eyes. "What are you doing?"

"Don't close your eyes!" She shook his shoulder and went for her most stern mom voice. "I *mean* it. Don't you dare shut your eyes again."

"I'm tired. Why not?"

"Because I said so! Harley will keep you company while I go get the ski patrol. They'll come up here on a snowmobile with a toboggan to get you out of here. I promise it won't take long."

"Right. Though this be madness, yet there is method in 't.'"

She wrapped the scarf around her foot and paused to look at him. At least his eyes were open. Was he quoting Shakespeare? Maybe this guy was a delirious English teacher or something. "Pete, pay attention to me. Your job is to stay awake. Hold onto Harley's collar so he doesn't try to follow me, although he spent so much time trying to get to you, I doubt he'll go anywhere. But don't lose him or I'll be in big trouble."

He nodded. "What's with the scarf?"

Lisa finished wrapping the scarf around her foot, stuffed it into the boot, and latched it closed. She got up and limped around the area collecting the ski poles. "You have big feet. I don't know where the other ski ended up, so this one will have to do."

Pete moved and groaned slightly. "What are you doing?"

"I told you. I'm getting help the fastest way I can. Walking is too slow." Lisa jammed her booted foot into the ski binding and felt the familiar snap as it engaged. "Once I get back to the ski run, it will only take me about five minutes to get down the hill. After I find the ski patrol, they can get back to you in a few minutes on a snow machine. I'll be gone maybe twenty minutes, tops. So I need you to hold onto Harley's collar and stay awake for twenty minutes. Can you do that for me?"

"I guess. I'll talk to the dog. I like him."

"It's just twenty minutes. Remember, you *need* to stay awake."

He nodded again and Lisa pulled on the ski goggles and pushed off into the path she and Harley had made, back toward the ski run. It was so much easier and faster to slide and push than to walk. It was almost like cross-country skiing, minus one ski.

She ducked under the snow fence and worked her way back onto the official ski run. Stopping at the edge of the trail, she moved the goggles onto her forehead and scanned the village below. The old ski-patrol building wasn't there anymore, and now their office could be anywhere. Rather than wasting time trying to figure out where it was located, it was probably best to get down to the lift and ask the operator to call the ski patrol on the radio.

After readjusting the goggles over her eyes, she waited for a break in skier traffic, clearing her mind the way she'd done before a race when she was in high school. With a whoop, she pushed off and shot down the slope on Pete's ski, lifting up her unshod foot and balancing her weight on the single ski.

For a moment, it was like no time had passed, and she was eighteen again, her body shifting, reacting, and responding to the turns automatically. She didn't have a chance to be afraid and there was nothing except her, the mountain, and the need for speed.

~

At the bottom of the hill, Lisa swerved over toward the ski lift. She skidded to a stop, the single ski swirling up a curtain of snow that landed on a few of the skiers in the lift line.

Lisa stopped to catch her breath and suddenly the reality of what she'd done hit her. She started to shake from both the cold and some sort of emotional upheaval. She'd skied. How did that happen?

To be fair, she was cold because she wasn't exactly optimally attired. Beige dress slacks and a woolen pea jacket weren't ideal ski wear. She hadn't skied since that fateful day when she'd crashed so spectacularly and destroyed her dream of going to the Olympics. After months of painful rehab and physical therapy, she'd decided that she was done with skiing forever. Until now. She hadn't even thought about it. She was so worried about Pete that she'd skied down the hill without thinking and without any fear. After so many nightmares about the crash, what she'd just done felt like a miracle.

"Hey lady, no buttinskis! Get in the line like everyone else." The well-bundled snowboarder jerked his mittened hand behind him to emphasize his point.

A lift operator turned to look at her, gestured at his compatriot who was helping people into the quad chair, and walked down the line toward Lisa. "Can I see your ski pass?"

Lisa gestured toward the village. "I need you to call the ski patrol right now. There's an injured male skier up off Midway, in the out-of-bounds area they used to call the Cavern Chute. It's in the trees between the rocks."

"The Cavern? Uh, wow, man, I'm not sure...like...where that might be at."

"It's a steep chute, and I think he went off the cornice along Blue Ridge. I can show you, but you need to call someone now! They will need a toboggan—I think his leg is broken."

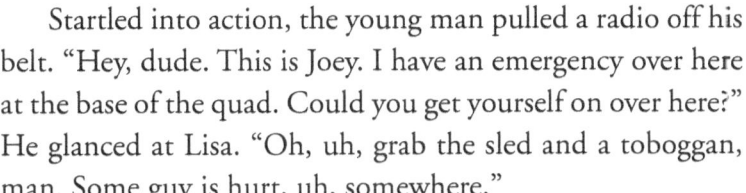

Startled into action, the young man pulled a radio off his belt. "Hey, dude. This is Joey. I have an emergency over here at the base of the quad. Could you get yourself on over here?" He glanced at Lisa. "Oh, uh, grab the sled and a toboggan, man. Some guy is hurt, uh, somewhere."

Lisa nodded, pleased that he seem to have conveyed some urgency. "Thank you, Joey."

"You're dressed kinda funny for skiing." He tilted his head. "Is that one of those cool monoskis like they have in Europe?"

"No." She held up her ski-less foot. "I'm wearing a regular ski with a boot that doesn't fit right."

"Whoa, that's gnarly."

They both turned at the roaring sound of a snowmobile approaching them at high speed. Clusters of skiers shuffled out of the way. The woman driving the machine stopped in front of them and Lisa was relieved to see that she appeared to be somewhat more mature than Joey, who looked like he was about twelve years old.

Joey lifted his gloved hand in greeting and pointed at Lisa. "Hey, Rose…this is the lady I told you about."

Lisa gestured up the ski slope. "The injured man is up there. Please hurry—I told him I'd only be gone twenty minutes and I'm worried he'll pass out again."

Rose turned in her seat at the sound of another snowmobile coming toward them. "That's Jim—he's bringing the toboggan."

A man in a red coat wearing goggles and a pointed red ski cap pulled his snow machine up next to Rose's. He took off his goggles and his eyes widened. "Holy cats! Lisa Lowell, is it really you?"

Lisa grinned. "Sweet Baby James! Who let you onto the ski patrol?"

Jim smiled. "Wow, nobody has called me that in a long time. I joined the ski patrol years ago. Now I'm in charge of it."

Lisa removed her ski and stomped over to hug Jim. What a blast from the past. When he'd been a liftie, he'd played James Taylor tapes on an endless loop, which led to his nickname. "You know Cavern Chute, right? That's where Pete is and I think he's got a bad break in his leg. His head is pretty scraped up too. I'm worried he has a concussion. We need to hurry."

"Throw that ski into the back and hop on. Let's go get him."

Lisa settled in behind Jim, put her arms around his waist, and he took off, jetting up the hillside. Skiers veered away from them, getting out of the way. Although the noise of the snow machine made conversation impossible, Lisa pointed a few times to indicate where they should go.

Lisa gestured at a spot at the edge of the woods where the path she and Harley had taken was visible in the snow. Jim stopped and they got off as Rose drove up. After a quick consultation with her, Jim hooked the toboggan up to himself, and they set off into the forested trail with Lisa in the lead, pushing along on her single ski.

When Harley barked sharply, Lisa smiled and turned back to Jim. "That's Harley. We're getting close."

"Harley? We have an avalanche patrol dog named Gracie. But I left her sleeping in my office."

"No, Harley is my dog. Well, sort of. I'm taking care of him."

"How did your dog end up on the slopes?" Jim waved a ski pole ahead of him. "Is he a search-and-rescue dog or something?"

"Definitely not. He's not obedient either. I had a little problem."

Jim shook his head. "Never mind, I don't want to know."

Pete was exactly where Lisa had left him, and when Harley jumped up, Pete turned his head to look at the group approaching him. He raised a hand in greeting. "What took you so long?"

Lisa stopped, removed the ski, and knelt down next to him. "This is Jim. He's on the ski patrol, and even though he used to be kind of an idiot, I think he's matured."

After detaching the toboggan, Jim got down next to Pete and began digging in the snow to assess the situation with Pete's leg. "Don't listen to her. I'm the best there is. But Rose is way cuter than I am, so focus on her."

Rose whacked Jim's shoulder with her mittened hand and settled into a spot in the snow. She removed her gloves and began pulling items out of her backpack. "Who's your favorite totally sexy actress in a movie?"

Pete made a wry face. "I don't know. Princess Leia was pretty hot when she wore that metal bikini thing."

Lisa said, "Who'd have guessed? You're a space geek!"

Rose continued, "Now pretend Jim is sexy Leia. He's gotta move your leg so we can get you out of here, and it's going to be uncomfortable."

Pete winced and twisted to see what Jim was up to. "What are you doing? That *hurts!*"

"Hey, I'm sexy Leia. Ignore me, or I'll hurt you more. If I can take out Jabba the Hutt, you're nuthin'."

"Some are born great, some achieve greatness, and some have greatness thrust upon them," Pete chuckled in spite of himself. "You guys are a little twisted, you know that?"

Rose nodded. "We know."

Having successfully moved Pete's leg, Jim continued his first-aid activities. "Hey, you should be grateful that you were found by someone famous. Not everyone could have gotten us up here so quick."

Pete ran his gloved fingers across the fur on Harley's head. "The dog is famous?"

"Not the dog." Jim pointed at Lisa. "This is Lisa Lowell. The pride of Snow Grove and an Olympic hopeful. She tore up the Giant Slalom back in the day."

Pete gazed up at Lisa. "You went to the Olympics?"

"No I didn't, and I'm certainly not famous. Don't listen to him. My old friend Sweet Baby James has always had a tendency to exaggerate," Lisa said.

"Hey, you were awesome," Jim said. "I had the biggest crush on you."

"That was a long time ago and I haven't been on skis since."

"That's surprising. The chatter on the radio was that some woman was tearing up Midway on one ski." Jim held up a roll of bandages and gestured toward the ski run. "I gotta say that's pretty hot. Sexy Leia's got nuthin' on you."

Lisa laughed. "Oh brother—give me a break. Pete's right; you guys really *are* twisted."

∽

As he and Rose moved Pete onto the toboggan and strapped him in, Jim continued his offbeat commentary. Discussing

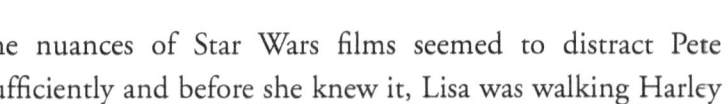

the nuances of Star Wars films seemed to distract Pete sufficiently and before she knew it, Lisa was walking Harley behind Jim and Rose back out to the ski run.

When they arrived, another member of the ski patrol was waiting for them with a toboggan that had been outfitted with a sky kennel. Jim had radioed for reinforcements to make sure Harley didn't try to run off again.

The parade of snow machines and skiers made their way back down to the village, where an ambulance was waiting for Pete. Lisa was impressed by Jim's actions during the entire rescue. He'd been such a bonehead when he was young that it was strange to see him behave so responsibly during an emergency. No wonder he was in charge of the ski patrol. It was good to see that Pete was in good hands.

After the ambulance pulled away, Jim stood next to Lisa, holding the handle of the toboggan. "So hey, you didn't say why you were here and running around the slopes with no skis, not to mention no ski pass."

"I didn't come here to ski. I had to bring some legal paperwork up here for my brother." She looked down at Harley. "Then he ran off. I don't know what possessed him to do that."

"Dogs are smarter than you might think. Maybe you can train him to be a rescue dog. I mean, you don't see dogs like that every day."

"He's not really my dog. I'm fostering him for the local rescue group."

"Okay." Jim shrugged and then looked into her eyes. "So tell me what you've been doing for the last twenty years or so. I mean, there was the horrible accident, but I never found out what happened, except when I stopped by the hardware store once, your mom said you got married."

"I did. And I have twin girls, Cheryl and Carol. They're in college now."

"So who's the lucky guy?"

"His name is Mike, um, Dr. Michael Ryan. I met him during my rehabilitation after the accident."

Jim smiled. "Hey, that's great. I'm happy for you."

"Well, I'm divorced now."

He raised his eyebrows. "Oh, well, uh, so are you…um… seeing someone? I wasn't kidding about having a crush on you."

Lisa gave him a coy smile. "Why Sweet Baby James, are you asking me out?"

"Yeah, I might be. Maybe dinner? I could drive over to Alpine Grove and we could go to that Italian place."

"That would be great." Lisa pointed at Harley. "But I have this dog problem. In addition to not being obedient, he hates being alone. I'm staying at my parents' house right now because I got roped into remodeling it so it will finally sell. How about if you stop by the house and I'll make you dinner?"

Jim grinned. "It's a date."

After exchanging phone numbers with Jim, Lisa walked Harley back to the truck. What a strange day. Bev would be so proud of her for agreeing to go out with Jim. She could hear her friend's voice in her head saying, "It's about time you rejoined the world!"

While Lisa drove back to Alpine Grove, Harley amused himself by staring out the window and panting as he watched the scenery go by, apparently oblivious to his earlier heroic deed. It was hard to imagine the goofy Lab being trained, much less a search-and-rescue dog. Lisa would need to make sure to tell his new owner about his big adventure though. Maybe Jim was right and the dog had undiscovered talents. Harley paused in his panting, looked thoughtful for a moment, and then belched loudly.

Okay, maybe not.

Lisa stopped by the deli in town and ran inside for a sandwich and newspaper. She parked right in front of the door, so she could keep an eye on Harley in the truck through the window. The newspaper purchase was just for the crossword puzzle, since the periodical wasn't good for much else. Finally she pulled into the driveway of her parents' house. It was such a relief to be home. At least for a couple more days everything would be quiet, then the deluge of contractors would begin. Which reminded her that she still had a few more phone calls to make. Oh boy.

She looked around the living room and came to the disturbing conclusion that the idea of Jim seeing the house in its current colorful glory was completely mortifying. The house had always been embarrassing to everyone, except Lisa's mother. Wanting to crawl into a hole and hide when people stopped by the house was nothing new, but what had Lisa been thinking when she invited Jim here? The only consolation was that Lisa would be able to explain that the hideous house was going be exiting its seventies-flashback mode soon.

Lisa had spent some time with flooring samples and brochures so she was starting to have a better feel for what the house could look like someday. If you ignored the hideous color scheme, the physical layout of the house was family-friendly and comfortable, with large rooms. And it was located on a large, beautiful lot close to town.

Once the place finally sold, it was likely her parents would earn back the money they'd have to spend to make the house more appealing to potential buyers. The fact that Larry had told her not to mention what she was doing to Mom remained worrisome though. He claimed that Mom was under the impression that Lisa was taking a little vacation in Alpine Grove and needed a place to stay. When it came to dealing with Mom, Larry could be such a wimp.

Lisa was settling into her late lunch and crossword puzzle when the phone rang. Harley didn't stir or even open an eyelid at the noise. Lisa groaned as she got up. Harley wasn't the only one who was tired. After the ride in the truck and sitting around the house, all of her long-unused ski muscles were seizing up. It would be a miracle if she could move at all by tomorrow.

An unfamiliar voice announced he was a reporter for the local newspaper. "Is this Lisa Lowell?"

"Yes." Lisa put her hand on her back and rubbed the sore muscles. What did the newspaper want with her?

"I'm following up on a story about a ski accident and rescue that involved a dog at Snow Grove. They said you found the skier and I'd like to ask you a few questions."

"Okay, that's fine I guess." Lisa stuck her tongue out at Harley, who was now sitting up and looking at her expectantly.

"The story I got from the ski patrol is that your dog found Peter Harmon, who was injured, and you put on one of his skis and went for help."

"Yes, that's true. Harley ran up the hill and I ran after him." She paused. "But he's not really my dog. I'm fostering him for a rescue group."

"What's the name of the group?"

"Um, I can't remember. But Brigid, the secretary at my brother's law office is the person who runs it."

The reporter paused. "So your brother is Lawrence Lowell, right? The lawyer working with the owners of Snow Grove on the sale?"

"Yes, Larry is my brother. I was delivering some paperwork to the resort and I brought Harley with me. He doesn't like being alone."

"I see."

Lisa wasn't sure what the reporter could "see," but she was starting to be a little worried that maybe some huge scandal would erupt if she said the wrong thing. The Alpine Grove newspaper wasn't widely known for its accuracy or journalistic integrity. She cleared her throat and tried to sound businesslike. "I was just in the right place at the right time. I hope Pete is okay."

"I talked to the hospital and he's out of surgery. It sounds like he'll be fine, although he's probably not going to be skiing again for quite a while."

"Oh, that's a relief. He seemed like a nice person."

"Based on what the ski patrol said, I did some research, and you are the same Lisa Lowell who was predicted to go to the 1972 winter Olympics, correct?"

Lisa rolled her eyes. Wow, this guy had actually gone to the effort of digging up all that ancient history? "Yes, that was me. But I didn't go to the Olympics. I had an accident that ended my skiing career."

"Yes, I read about that too. Well, I think I have what I need. Thanks for your help."

Lisa hung up the phone, still worried that she might have gotten Larry in trouble. If nothing else, her past was likely to come back to haunt her *again*. There might be three people left in Alpine Grove who actually didn't know or remember her failure to go to the Olympics. Apparently, those select few members of the community that hadn't known before were about to find out.

~

After taking a long and steamy shower, Lisa felt much better. Maybe her poor, exhausted body would survive the skiing ordeal after all. She really needed to get into better shape, but the idea of engaging in more exercise sounded inordinately unpleasant, so Lisa opted for a snack instead.

Wandering around the old kitchen in her bathrobe took her back to lazy afternoons in high school after she'd returned from practice on the mountain. She had the same slightly sore, relaxed, and hungry feeling she'd had after training all morning. But back then, the house was full of noise and activity as her siblings passed through foraging for food.

All of the Lowell kids had been hungry all the time. Lisa didn't remember her mother doing a lot of shopping, but keeping the house stocked with food must have been difficult. With four teenagers at home, Mom must have had to do a daily store run after work to keep everyone fed.

Lisa shook her head at the idea. Raising twins had been difficult enough. It was a miracle her mother had survived raising four active kids while running a family business. How exhausting. No wonder Mom hadn't wanted to deal with the house for so long. She'd had more than enough to do.

The phone rang and Lisa pushed her plate aside, got up, and grabbed the handset off the old wall phone. That hadn't changed either. She was surprised to hear Kat Stevens's voice on the other end of the line. "Hi Kat. How are you?"

"I'm fine, but the Alpine Grove dog-related grapevine is buzzing with Harley's exploits at the ski resort."

Lisa reached over to pet Harley. "Yes, at first I thought he was running away, but it turned out he had a serious mission."

"Brigid said there's going to be an article in the newspaper tomorrow. AGAA wants to capitalize on this PR opportunity."

"AGAA? What's that?"

"Alpine Grove Animal Adoptions. I'm in charge of PR and Brigid wants me to do a write-up about Harley for the newsletter."

"The reporter asked about that, but I forgot the name of the group. That seems like a good idea."

"I know. It's a huge opportunity. The newsletter is supposed to go out this week. I'm in between book deadlines, so I told Brigid I can write it up and redo the layout. We need to yank out another article and save it for next time, but this is a great chance to help get Harley a home and promote our foster program."

"Do you need to ask me questions?"

"I don't think so, but I really need a photograph of Harley. That's why I'm calling. Could you bring him out here? My dog walker isn't available tomorrow morning, so I have to be here."

"I suppose so. Doesn't anyone else have a camera?"

"Not a decent one, and I'm the only person who has a scanner. It would be great if we had a digital camera, but they're too expensive. Maybe someday. Joel has to go to town tomorrow, so if you come out early I can take pictures and he can drop the film at the one-hour photo place, then pick up the prints on his way home and give them to me. Then I can scan the photo of Harley, dump it into the newsletter layout. Then Brigid is going to pick up the newsletter files and take them to the printer. They're expecting them tomorrow afternoon."

"Good heavens. You certainly have this all figured out."

"My life is complicated at the moment. Could you get here around eight?"

"All right."

Lisa hung up the phone. What was wrong with her? Why did she keep saying yes without thinking? It was supposed to snow and driving all the way out to the boarding kennel was not what she had expected or wanted to do tomorrow. Why didn't she ever say no to anyone? Bev was right. She was a total pushover. Of course, with no real excuse she'd had no reason to say no, other than "I don't want to." And that wouldn't be fair to Harley. She was actually starting to like the dog, and it wasn't his fault he was homeless. He deserved all the free publicity he could get.

She leaned over to stroke his head. "Okay, Mr. Hero Dog, let's go to bed. You need to be well rested for your big photo shoot tomorrow."

Harley stood up, yawned, and stretched deeply. It had been a long day for everyone.

The next morning, Lisa took Harley out for his morning trip around the yard to do his business. When she stepped outside, she discovered to her dismay that as predicted, it had snowed overnight. The snow was the heavy, wet "mashed potatoes" type that skiers hate. Drivers weren't too fond of it either. Harley, on the other hand, was thrilled and cavorted through the sloppy muck with glee.

Lisa smiled as he leaped around, throwing snow and slush around with his paws and grabbing it in his mouth. "Maybe you have a future as an avalanche dog after all. You sure love the white stuff. Let's go inside, goofball. I have to get ready to go. We can't disappoint your adoring fans."

Harley finally focused on the task he was supposed to be dealing with in the great outdoors, and after that mission was accomplished they went back into the house. One thing that was nice about staying in a house that was about to be remodeled was that Lisa didn't have to worry about wet or muddy paw prints on the carpet because it was all going to be ripped out.

Given that the rest of her family had opted out of providing any input on the remodel, Lisa had to make some choices. She planned to replace the carpet with wood or laminate flooring because it would be easy to clean. Wood grain also never went out of style, unlike the jarring rainbow of hues that had graced the Lowell household for so many years.

After dealing with the morning routine and getting herself organized, Lisa loaded Harley into the truck for the drive north. It was no longer snowing, but the sky was dark with gloomy clouds that looked like they might want to spew forth more unpleasant forms of semi-frozen precipitation. It was a dismal day for photography. Kat said she had a good camera, but no camera was that good.

Lisa's mood darkened along with the sky as she got off the highway and onto the back roads toward the kennel. The plows had obviously not visited yet, and the heavy slop on the road was slippery. Although Larry's ugly truck had four-wheel drive, it could only do so much.

It began drizzling and Lisa stared at the road ahead, carefully navigating the ruts in the slush. About ten nanoseconds after she turned onto a side road, she realized it wasn't the right one. This wasn't the way to Abigail Goodman's...or Kat's...place. What was she thinking? Lisa cursed her stupidity as she slowed the truck, trying to find a place to turn around without getting stuck.

As the incline of the road increased, the truck started to fishtail mildly. Underneath the slush was a layer of ice, and because Lisa had slowed down, the vehicle had lost momentum. She clenched the steering wheel more tightly. There was no way she was going to make it to the top of the long hill. She slowly brought the truck to a stop and shifted it into reverse. Turning in the seat, she carefully backed down the hill and then into a driveway. The mailbox said "The Millers" and Lisa said a silent thank you to whichever Miller had plowed their driveway that morning.

She took a deep breath and looked both ways at the road. A car came over the top of the hill and Lisa could sense that it was going far too fast for the conditions. When it hit the downhill side, the little silver two-door car began swerving. The driver over-corrected, a tire hooked the edge of the road, and the little Hyundai shot off the road into a ditch just past the driveway where Lisa was parked.

The driver got out of the car and Lisa could tell from his wild gesticulating that he was using some creative language to describe his predicament.

Lisa shook her head. In Alpine Grove during the winter, slide-offs were not an unusual event, and yet people never seemed to learn to slow down. "Okay Harley, I need to go check on this guy. You behave yourself. I'll be right back." Harley wagged a few times and laid down on the seat, resting his head on his paws.

Lisa got out of the truck and reached down to press the seat release to determine what junk Larry had stashed back there. When Dad had owned the truck, he'd always carried a tow strap and jumper cables with him everywhere.

The good news was that amid the fast-food wrappers and other trash behind the driver's seat was the same heavy-duty yellow tow strap that had been there for as long as Lisa could remember. The bad news was that Harley was likely to be late for his photo shoot.

~

Holding the neatly folded tow strap in her hand, Lisa walked across the road to the car. The man was wearing a wrinkled brown suit and was younger than she was, although the scowl on his face made him look older than he probably was. He had a stocky build and the kind of white-blonde Scandinavian hair that women spent lots of money trying to achieve artificially with a noxious brew of peroxide-laden dyes. Lisa had tried the Marilyn Monroe look once long ago, chemically treating her hair to a crispy, crackly crunch. Never again.

She smiled and held up the strap in greeting. "My name is Lisa. Do you want me to pull you out?"

The scowl remained on the man's face. "How? This is such a nightmare. I can't believe I missed the turn. But that sign wasn't visible. Those people need to cut down that tree. How is anyone supposed to see that sign?"

Lisa was taken aback by his hostility. Usually people were grateful when you offered to yank them out of a ditch, since getting a tow was expensive and time-consuming. "If you prefer, I can call a tow truck for you when I get to my destination."

"Hey, I don't know how you think you can get this car out of the ditch, but be my guest. It's not my fault. I think the steering is screwed up on this thing." Apparently having a momentary bout of self-consciousness, the pinched look on his face relaxed and he said more mildly, "Uh, my name is Steve, by the way."

Lisa was regretting ever getting out of her truck. What a creep. "To answer your question, as you can see, I have a tow strap and my truck over there has four-wheel drive. I'll attach the strap to the front of your car and pull your car back up onto the road."

Steve glanced at the salmon-colored truck. "You think you can pull me out with that hunk of crap? Who paints a truck pink?"

"It's my brother's truck and technically, it's a salmon color." Lisa raised her eyebrows. "Obviously, you have a very, very small…*car*. And my brother's hunk of crap has pulled out a lot of cars a lot larger than yours."

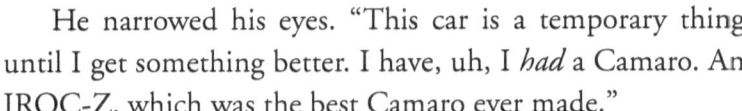

He narrowed his eyes. "This car is a temporary thing until I get something better. I have, uh, I *had* a Camaro. An IROC-Z, which was the best Camaro ever made."

Lisa wanted to roll her eyes. Given that Camaros had rear-wheel drive, the oh-so-fabulous IROC probably wouldn't have been good in the snow either. He just would have hurtled himself into the ditch more quickly. "Well, your car has the advantage of being small and light. After I've hooked up the strap, once you feel the pull, I'll need you to carefully give your car some gas. Don't gun it or you'll end up digging yourself deeper into the ditch."

Steve nodded and got back into the little car while Lisa attached the tow strap. She pulled the truck in front of the car and attached the strap. She slowly pulled forward and when the strap was taut, she waved out the window for Steve to press on the gas. There was a roaring noise and the tires spun. The car dug itself deeper and began moving forward down the ditch.

Lisa stopped, got out, and waved her hands at him. "Stop that!"

"What are you doing? You're dragging me down the ditch."

"Let the truck pull you out. Be patient. I'm going to end up going sideways, but it's on purpose. When that happens, turn the wheel so your tires can go back up onto the road."

Steve frowned, but nodded his agreement.

Lisa got back into the truck and pulled forward, so the tow strap was taught again. Maybe Steve would do a better job of following instructions this time. She slowly pressed the gas and the truck started going crab-wise down the road. The little car behind her moved forward a few feet, then as

Lisa had predicted, suddenly all four tires were on the road and Steve was motoring toward her. Lisa pulled over and he stopped behind her.

He waved out the window. "Hey, it worked."

Lisa got out, undid the ends of the tow straps, and walked up to him. "You're welcome."

"Uh yeah, thanks. I'm really late for a sales appointment. I've been trying to get the hardware store gig in this backwoods town for years and they won't go for it. It's nuts, since I have great prices. I mean, come on, everyone needs drywall—even out here in the middle of nowhere people build stuff. I don't know what their problem is."

Lisa smiled. "What's your last name, Steve?"

"Middleton."

"Good to know. By the way, my name is Lisa *Lowell*. My family has owned the hardware store for a very, very long time. It's been a real pleasure to meet you, Steve."

The expression on Steve's face changed to deep dismay as the realization of who he was talking to settled in. "Yeah, well thanks again."

Lisa waved as he drove by, pondering the upcoming chat she was going to have with her father about drywall. She got back into the truck and Harley sat up, ready for whatever was next.

Lisa gave the dog a pat. "Sorry about that. I guess today *I* had to be the hero. Lucky me." Harley wagged a few times in sympathy. Sometimes making someone else's day wasn't what it was cracked up to be, particularly when they didn't deserve it.

When Lisa arrived at the boarding kennel, Kat was walking from the house toward the kennel buildings accompanied by a huge, furry brown dog. She was wearing a remarkably ugly coat that appeared to be several sizes too large. As Lisa got out of the truck, the big dog strolled toward her and barked a few times without much enthusiasm. Kat waved in greeting as she approached.

Lisa unloaded Harley, who wagged happily, obviously pleased to see the gigantic hairy beast again. Lisa pointed at the pair. "I guess they know each other."

Kat nodded. "This is Linus. He lives here. I was starting to get worried about you two. Were the roads really bad out there?"

"It would have been okay, but I turned onto the wrong road and then stopped to pull someone out of a ditch."

"Joel has done that a few times. I guess that's what happens when you have a truck."

"Yes, although I have to say, people used to be a lot more gracious about being rescued than they are now." Lisa waved at the forest in exasperation. "Ugh, I sound like my mother. I'm not old enough to be saying something like that."

Kat laughed as she unzipped her coat and pulled out a camera that was hanging from a strap around her neck. "At least the weather isn't committing some horrible act of precipitation right now. Let's take the picture before the atmospheric gods have a change of heart."

"Where should we stand?"

"How about over in front of that wall? The newsletter is going to be black and white, and it's so dreary outside that any background will look crummy no matter what we do. I'll zoom in close, so everyone can see Harley's sweet Labrador face."

Lisa smiled down at the dogs. It was touching how much effort everyone involved with the rescue group was going to on Harley's behalf. Maybe Kat wasn't so bad after all. If the photo helped Harley get a good home, dealing with the repugnant Steve would have been worth it. But she still was going to have a chat with her father about who he should *not* use as his drywall supplier in the future.

Chapter 5

Advice

After Lisa left, Kat went back inside. Joel was standing in the kitchen eating a sandwich. Given the expression on his face, he was obviously still annoyed about how late Lisa had been for Harley's photo shoot.

Kat hurried to get the film out of the camera. "I know you have to go, but Lisa wasn't late on purpose. Hold on while I wind this back." She opened up the camera, pulled out the film roll, and put it in a canister.

Joel didn't say anything, but he raised an eyebrow as Kat capped the film canister.

A flush of anger washed over Kat like a wave. Maybe she hadn't been all sweetness and light lately, but she was tired of living with Captain Monosyllable. She thrust the film at him. "Here you go. Enjoy your trip to town. May you have a wonderful time with your friend."

He took the film from her. "Why are you giving me that look? I told you before, I went to college with Casey. It's not every day someone I know passes through Alpine Grove."

"I know. It's just that you've barely spoken to me in what feels like forever. It's starting to really get to me."

"I have a lot on my mind."

"Like what?"

"Can we not get into this right now? I'm really late."

Kat crossed her arms. "Fine. Maybe someday I'll get to meet this fabulous guy."

"Not this time. Casey is leaving tomorrow." Joel bent to give her a kiss. "See you later."

"I'll be here hanging out, waiting for FedEx to show up." Kat uncrossed her arms and let them flop at her sides as the door closed behind Joel. Had she been so wrapped up in her work that she'd managed to completely screw up her relationship with Joel? Was that what was happening?

After reading over her chapters for what felt like the thousandth time and packaging them up for FedEx, Kat was still upset about her recent non-conversations with Joel. She had three typical responses to upsetting situations: eating ice cream, reading a novel, or calling her friend Maria. She was too tired to read and calling Maria was less fattening than ice cream, so she picked up the phone.

Maria answered on the first ring. "Hey, girlfriend! How are you? I miss your voice. Are you finally emerging from your writer's cave?"

"I am! Or at least until I have to crawl back inside for the next set of chapters. FedEx is supposed to pick up my peerless prose soon. I'm tired of my office and feeling really squirrelly."

"It's Friday, and I think you are facing a serious TGIF situation. In fact, this may be the TGIF situation to end all TGIF situations. We need to do happy hour. Plus, Larry left me another message."

"Larry? You mean Larry the lawyer? Are you together again? I thought that was ancient history."

"It is. Or it was. He keeps asking me out and I've been making excuses because to deal with him and let him down gently, I need a wing woman, and you've been too busy. If you come to the Soloan with me tonight, I can get him off my case. The dark dive-bar ambiance might be good in case he gets all weepy or something."

"Well, I have to lay out a newsletter this afternoon, but after that I guess I could go. You really want to go there though? That's where Fred works."

"No big deal. Fred knows about my sordid past with Larry. And Fred and I broke up anyway, so it's none of his beeswax anymore." The muffled sound of Maria's voice came through as she covered the mouthpiece with her hand. "Girlfriend, I have to do the work thing, which is seriously disappointing. But your voice sounds sad. What's wrong? Do we need to talk? Can you get away for lunch?"

"I can't. Today is Mia's day off, so I'm on dog-walking duty. I have to wait around for FedEx and Joel took the truck, so I'm stuck here. He's dropping off film for me in town. I took a photo this morning of a dog that we want to feature in the AGAA newsletter."

"Well, that explains why I saw Joel across the street near the photo place. Who's that woman?"

"What woman?"

"The one he was walking with. I thought it was his sister at first, then I realized the woman was tall and blonde, but definitely not Cindy. I figured you'd know who it was."

"No clue. All he said this morning was he's meeting some guy he went to college with named Casey."

"Are you sure Casey is a male of the species?"

"I've never met a woman named Casey. I guess I assumed Joel was talking about a guy."

Maria was silent for a moment. "Maybe you should get some specifics about this friend, like which box he or she checks on the gender column. In the meantime, I'll keep my eye out the window and snoop when I can."

"You do have a front-row seat on Alpine Grove pedestrian traffic."

"Don't knock it. It helps me remain well informed about what's going on within our fine community."

Kat laughed. "No kidding. You always have all the good dirt."

"You know it, girlfriend."

After agreeing on a time to meet at the bar, Kat hung up the phone slowly. The slightly sick feeling in her stomach had returned. Had Joel ever mentioned that Casey was male? Joel had said so little over the last few days, you'd think Kat would remember.

She shook her head, exasperated by her swirling thoughts. The idea of Joel cheating on her was impossible. Even apart from the fact that he loved her, the man was many things, but stupid wasn't one of them. If he had something to hide, he wouldn't parade some girlfriend in front of the ad agency where Maria worked. Kat needed to talk to him. They'd clear everything up like they always did. After all, they were engaged and getting married in less than two months.

Kat crossed her arms on the table, laid her head on them, and closed her eyes. She was so incredibly tired all the time. The word exhaustion didn't cover it anymore. But only one more set of chapters and this awful book project would be over.

She started awake at pounding on the wooden front door and the resulting cacophony of barking from the downstairs hallway. Leaping up, she grabbed the package from the counter and ran to the entryway.

She opened the door and grinned at Marty, the FedEx man. "Here you go."

"Thanks." He grabbed it, handed her the form, and ran back down the stairs. "On my way."

Kat waved as the white truck whizzed down the driveway. Marty had to be the fastest delivery person in the West. One time, he'd somewhat sheepishly admitted that he'd trashed the suspension on multiple vehicles by exceeding the speed limit on the washboard-filled dirt roads that criss-crossed the rural county. His lead foot might be hard on his vehicles, but at least Kat could be sure her package was absolutely, positively going to get there overnight.

⁓

After FedEx left, Kat wrote the newsletter article about Harley, redid the newsletter layout, and tended to many dogs. By the time Joel returned, she was upstairs relaxing with a novel and a cup of tea. She got up and walked into the entryway to say hello.

He paused in hanging his coat in the closet to hand her the packet of photographs. "Here you go."

She took the package, walked back into the kitchen, and tossed them on the counter. Turning, she leaned back on the counter. "Thanks. I have a question for you."

"If it's about the photos, I didn't look at them. I picked them up and came home."

"How was breakfast?"

"That's your question?"

Kat shook her head. "I'm getting there. I can't believe I'm asking you this, but is Casey male or female?"

Joel looked startled for a second. "She's a woman."

"You never mentioned that, which is sort of strange, now that I look back on it. Which I have been for most of the day. Phrasing sentences with no gender-specific pronouns is tricky."

"It wasn't relevant."

"*Relevant?* You didn't correct me when I called her a *guy.* That isn't relevant?"

Joel tilted his head slightly. "Okay, so maybe I didn't want to have this conversation."

"What conversation? You mean the conversation where I point out that you lied to me?"

"No, the conversation where me going to breakfast with an old friend who happens to a woman is an issue."

"It's not an *issue.*"

"Good." He turned to go downstairs. "I should get to work."

Kat followed him down the stairs and through the gate, shoving aside the crowding dogs. "Wait a minute! I want to talk to you."

Joel sat down at his desk, leaned back in the chair, and crossed his arms across his chest. "All right."

Kat stood in front of him. "What is going on with you?"

"Nothing."

"You said you had a lot on your mind. So what is it?"

He looked away from her and out the window. "I'm not sure how to explain it."

"Does it have to do with Casey?" Kat took a couple of steps closer to him. "Talk to me. What happened?"

"Casey and I were in a bunch of the same classes in college. We ran across each other again on an alumni forum online, and we started sending emails. It's no big deal."

Kat's eyes widened. "So she wasn't just passing through Alpine Grove. She came to see you."

"I suppose so."

"Should I be worried about this? Because I'm starting to feel like I want to throw up. What is happening here?"

Joel rubbed his palms over his eyes. "Don't get all insecure on me. Nothing is going on. *Nothing*. She's going through a divorce, and she needed someone to talk to. So we talked."

"I'm not being insecure." Kat reached over and clasped one of his hands in both of hers. "But I don't understand why you lied to me."

"I didn't lie. I omitted a few facts, but I didn't lie."

"Wow. Okay, if that's how you want to play this, fine. If there's one thing I've learned about you, it's that when you don't want to talk, you don't." Kat dropped his hand and quickly wiped an errant tear from the corner of her eye. "Obviously, you're not going to tell me what's really going on in your head."

He shook his head. "I don't want to talk about this right now. I have a lot of work to do."

"I'm going to walk dogs. Then I'm going to town, so I need the truck. Maybe by the time I get back, you'll be in more of a mood to talk." Tears began welling in her eyes, but Kat was *not* going to cry in front of him. She whirled around and scuttled out of his office, across the hall into hers, slamming the door behind her. Flopping face-first onto the bed, she hugged the pillow to muffle her hot, angry sobs.

A loud bark from the hallway woke Kat. Her face was salty and sticky where she'd smashed it into the pillow, and now in addition to being angry and sad, she also had a headache. The idea that sometimes you "needed a good cry" was idiotic, since afterward you usually felt like you'd been run over by a semi truck.

She glanced at the clock. The dogs were probably barking because it was time for their afternoon excursion through the forest. Oops. Sorry guys. Dragging herself up off the bed, she quickly scanned the photo of Harley and finished up the newsletter layout.

Afterward, she went out to the hall and leashed up the canine gang. The door to Joel's office was closed, which was fine. She didn't want to see him until he was ready to talk to her about…whatever it was they weren't talking about. Somehow they'd managed to have a fight about almost nothing.

Once her dog-walking duties were complete and she'd handed off the newsletter to Brigid, Kat got into the truck and drove to town. Joel had remained sequestered in his office and she was glad to have an excuse to get out of the house. It had been too long since she had been anywhere. Book deadlines had made her life miserable for what seemed like forever.

To avoid the horrors of parallel parking the curmudgeonly old vehicle, Kat parked the truck in the lot at Maria's apartment complex and walked the two blocks to the ad agency where Maria worked. She waved at her friend through the plate-glass window and went inside.

Maria gathered up her purse and coat and made a shooing motion toward the door. "Let's go, girlfriend, before someone thinks of something else I'm supposed to do. It's Friday after five, and they need to accept the fact that nothing more is happening until Monday."

Kat turned and they hustled back outside into the cold evening. Maria had donned her huge fake-fur coat, which, with the matching fur-trimmed boots, gave her an unfortunate resemblance to Grizzly Adams.

Maria took Kat's arm and looked around to peer into her face. "Girlfriend, what happened to you? Have you slept at all? You look like death."

"I took a nap this afternoon."

"I'm a fan of naps, but yours didn't do the job. I think we need to have a conversation about concealer. Because those dark circles under your eyes are not attractive at all."

"You know I hardly ever wear makeup. And certainly not to go to the Soloan."

"I suppose you have point. No matter what you do, the flickering neon of the beer signs isn't going to be flattering."

They walked down the street until they got to a sign that said Mystic Moon Soloan. The bar was referred to as the "Soloan" thanks to the misspelling of the word saloon on the sign. Given that no one had ever gotten around to fixing the sign for forty or fifty years, it was unlikely to change anytime soon. Kat yanked on the huge wooden door and they went into the dimly lit bar.

Larry Lowell leaped up from his bar stool and made a beeline for Maria, who gripped Kat's arm more tightly.

"Don't you dare leave me, girlfriend," Maria whispered to Kat as she smiled demurely at Larry's approaching form.

Kat nodded as she settled into a bar stool next to Maria. She waved to the bartender. "Hi Fred. I'll have some tonic water with lemon."

He nodded and raised his eyebrows at Maria, who said, "The usual, please."

Fred turned away to make the beverages as Larry settled onto a bar stool next to Maria and began whispering urgently.

Kat tried to stifle a sigh and picked up the cardboard coaster in front of her. She put it on end, holding it upright with her index finger. With a flick of her fingers, she watched as it spun briefly and fluttered down to the bar. It was going to be a long evening.

~

After Fred delivered the drink, Kat had a straw wrapper and napkin she could use to amuse herself in addition to the cardboard coaster. After a few false starts with the straw wrapper, she settled on a complicated origami-like zig-zag folding. Moving on to the napkin, she was tearing small holes to create a snowflake while Maria continued to listen to Larry's monologue. It was odd for Maria to be so quiet. Maybe she was waiting him out. No one could talk forever, although Larry *was* a lawyer, so his speech could take a while. Kat hunched over her drink and expanded and contracted the origami straw wrapper.

Kat looked up from her paper projects and smiled as Lisa sat down next to her. Even though Lisa might not be her best friend, at least Kat knew who she was and it was good to see a familiar face. "I didn't know you frequented the Soloan."

Lisa said, "I try not to, but I need to get Larry to sign something for me because a contractor is coming tomorrow."

"I try to avoid this place too, but my friend dragged me here to keep her company. You have a contractor working on a Saturday? That's remarkable."

"It's complicated and you don't want to know. I've had a long day of talking to people. Brigid sent me here and Larry shushed me. He told me to wait while he talks to his friend Maria over there, which he *knew* would piss me off. Sometimes I wish he was still in elementary school so I could beat him up. But I left Harley in Larry's truck, which is the next-best thing. The longer it takes for him to sign this, the more likely it is that Harley will start chewing. It will serve Larry right if Harley eats his way out of that old truck."

Kat opened up her ratty-looking napkin snowflake and made a face. "Harley would never do that."

"You and Brigid were right when you said he doesn't like being alone."

"When Harley visits me, he gets to stay in the extra-special, industrial-strength kennel."

"That reminds me—I was so focused on getting Harley to sit still for his photo, I forgot to ask. Could I use my other day of free boarding tomorrow? I know it's really late notice."

Kat glanced at Lisa. No kidding, late notice. Was there an open kennel? The basset was leaving in the morning, so it should work. "I guess so. Is it only for one night?"

"Yes, I'm going out again. I mean, well, someone asked me out. I was going to have him come to the house, but the place is too embarrassing and I can't face it. Ugh. I sound like I'm in junior high school, blabbing about how a boy likes me and worrying about what he thinks about my parents' house."

"If it's just one night, it's fine. I have more dogs coming in next week." Kat tried to smile reassuringly. Lisa looked so mortified at her romantic confession that Kat wasn't sure what to say. "But if you have a date, that's good, right?"

"Maybe. At least I know this guy a little. Or I did a long time ago. If Harley's not around, we can meet at a restaurant. That would be so much better than making him dinner. I don't know what I was thinking. At least this date has got to be better than the blind date I went on the last time Harley stayed with you." Lisa smacked her hand on the bar. "I don't know what's wrong with me. When it comes to my friends and family, I can't think of an excuse to say no, so I say yes. My friend Bev says I'm a pushover and she's right."

Kat put down the napkin. This was getting more interesting. "You went on a blind date in Alpine Grove? I haven't lived here long, but that's unusual, isn't it? Everybody knows everybody else."

"It turns out he was a tourist, which Bev didn't mention. And now he thinks I'm about to die. It was a nightmare." Lisa heaved a big sigh. "Ugh, enough about me. I think about myself and my life and it's all so boring. When did you move here?"

"About a year and a half ago when I inherited my aunt's house."

"After leaving here, I vowed never to return, but here I am. That was another time I said yes when I should have said no. I don't know what is wrong with me."

Kat took a sip of her water. "Why did you come back?"

"Larry talked me into it by playing the family card. I couldn't say no. Now I'm working on fixing up my parents' house, so they can sell it. That's another nightmare."

"Why?"

"It just is. Family stuff makes me crazy."

"I can understand that. I'm sure there are things you missed about Alpine Grove though."

"Well, it's still pretty here. Beautiful, actually. But I hate everyone knowing everything about me. It's different if you grew up here. No one ever forgets *anything*. Maybe it would help if I put my wedding ring back on."

"You're married?"

"No, I'm divorced. You're probably the only person in Alpine Grove who doesn't know that. And contrary to what Jonah may think, I'm not about to die either."

"I don't know Jonah, but that's good. I'm sorry about your marriage though." Kat paused, trying to decide if she was nosy enough to ask what she wanted to ask. What the heck? "This is probably too personal, but I'm getting married soon and, uh, I'm curious why you got divorced."

Lisa glanced at her quickly. "I suppose that's not a secret either. We got married young and over time, we grew apart."

"You mean you didn't love each other anymore?"

"That wasn't really it. I'll always love Mike in some way. It was more like we ran out of things to say to each other." Lisa gazed up at the bottles of liquor behind the bar. "He's a doctor and I was a stay-at-home mom. Once the kids grew up and left the house, Mike and I had nothing to talk about anymore. Nothing in common."

Kat put her elbows on the table and rested her chin in her palm. The idea of not having something to say to Joel anymore made her want to cry. "That's so sad."

"The fact that I got sick didn't help either. That's a whole different issue. But I'm hoping it's all behind me now. When is your wedding?"

"March."

"Are you asking me this because you're worried about getting married?"

Kat tore another piece off her napkin. Was she really that transparent? "Maybe. I wasn't worried at all when we got engaged, but my fiancé has been behaving really oddly lately. I'm worried he's regretting having met me."

"Have you talked to him about it?"

"I tried, but it didn't go well." Kat frowned. That was an enormous understatement.

"Try again. The only way to work out problems is to talk about it. Mike and I stopped doing that. When we lost interest in trying, that's when we knew it was over."

Kat stopped fiddling with her napkin snowflake and laid it down on the bar. "You're absolutely right. I need to go home."

"Me too. Shall we break up the negotiations over there?"

"I've been trying not to eavesdrop, but I don't think Larry is ever going to shut up and Maria isn't stopping him." Kat turned away from Lisa and gripped Maria's arm. "I've got to go. You're on your own."

Maria looked at her and hissed, "Don't you dare leave me!"

"I need to talk to Joel."

"Now? Why now? You've been here two minutes."

"I just do." Kat got up from the bar stool. "Your wing person is flying away."

"Oh, come on. You promised! What did the engineer co now? You can't just leave me, girlfriend."

"Sorry, but this is important. I have to get home."

Lisa walked around Kat and Maria and thrust some papers in front of Larry. "I've had a long day of dealing with the members of the Alpine Grove building community and if you care about the welfare of your old truck at all, you need to sign these now."

Larry bent to scribble his name and as she put on her coat, Kat smiled at Lisa and mouthed, "Thank you."

Lisa nodded. "Harley and I will see you tomorrow."

Kat spent most of the drive home trying to figure out what she was going to say to Joel that wouldn't immediately irritate him and cause him to retreat into his office again. Sure, he hadn't ever been an overly talkative person, but he was taking taciturn to a new and more hostile place. On the one hand, she could walk into the house and nonchalantly pretend they hadn't just had a big fight about virtually nothing. Or she could go for the confrontational approach and try to *make* him say something about whatever was bothering him. Neither idea seemed promising. She was going to have to wing it.

The worst part of it all was that she was agonizing over talking to someone who was one of the only people she'd ever met who actually understood her and the sometimes bizarre way her mind worked. Talking to Joel had always been so easy, almost from the moment they met. Now she felt like she was in danger of losing the best friend she'd ever had.

Although Maria was a great girlfriend with a wonderful sense of humor, she was hard to deal with in large doses. Joel was someone Kat wanted to be with all the time. It wasn't only that she loved him, which she did. When she was around him, Kat felt like she was the best version of herself. Nobody else had ever had that effect on her. She clenched the steering wheel with one hand and rammed the old green truck into second gear as she rounded the corner into the driveway. She was going to fix this...whatever it was.

When she walked into the house, she was greeted by the typical canine festival of barking. After the dogs realized who the interloper was, they lost interest and resumed their regularly scheduled napping. Kat went into the kitchen and through the living room into the bedroom to change her clothes. Joel was lying fully clothed on the bed with his arm over his eyes. He sat up as she walked in and Kat kicked off her shoes and crawled onto the bed next to him.

Snuggling herself up alongside his body, she stretched an arm across his chest. "I'm sorry."

Joel stroked her hair and kissed the top of her head. "Me too."

She moved her head to look into his eyes. "I've been trying to think up what I should say, but all I came up with was 'I'm sorry.'"

"No third degree?"

"Nope." She moved closer, placed her cheek on his chest, and closed her eyes. "I'm going to lie here and listen to your heart beat for a while, if that's okay."

Joel didn't say anything, but he continued running his fingers across her hair, so Kat figured she didn't have to move.

At the moment, she was pretty sure she'd like to stay right in this spot forever.

After a few minutes, Kat was starting to doze off when Joel said, "I'm not mad at you, you know."

"I didn't know."

"I'm not."

"That's good. I'm not mad at you either." Kat shifted her position so her ear wasn't on his chest and she could hear better. If he was going to reveal what was bothering him, he was going to have to spit it out because she wasn't asking again. "I love you."

"I love you back."

Kat pulled the corner of the blanket up over her. "I missed being here with you. Writing all night has been awful."

"It was lonely for me too." He curled a hand under her blouse and laid his warm palm on her back. "When I was trying to go to sleep, I kept wondering if this is what the rest of my life is going to be like."

Kat propped herself up on her elbows. "That sounds ominous."

"It spiraled down from there."

"The book is almost done, so things should return to normal. Or as normal as normal ever is around here."

"I know—I mean, intellectually I know that. But things aren't like they used to be."

Kat readjusted herself and placed her palm on his chest. There was no getting away from it. She was going to have to ask a question now, whether he liked it or not. "What things?"

"When we first met, we couldn't keep our hands off each other."

Kat smiled. "I know. That was great."

"You realize you just used the past tense, right? That's what worries me. We've hardly spent any time together and you're always exhausted. Then I started wondering if all the jokes about marriage are true—that you get married and never have sex again."

"I hope not."

"Me too, particularly since we're not even married yet. When Casey got in touch with me and we were emailing back and forth, she mentioned she was getting divorced, and I was curious why."

"You're kidding. I just asked Lisa the same thing an hour ago. She said they grew apart."

"Okay, it's not just me then. Things have changed, haven't they?"

"I suppose in a way they have. I mean, after you live together for more than a year, it's not like that first intoxicating rush of infatuation and adoration when everything is brand new. We know each other now. But it seems like I love you more the longer we're together."

"That's a relief."

Kat sat up and looked down into his face. "Were you honestly worried about that?"

"I guess not. I mean I know you love me. But I didn't want to talk to you about what I was thinking."

"I noticed." Kat raised her eyebrows. "And I can't say I'm not more than a little disturbed that this person Casey now knows way too much about our sex life. Or lack of one."

"I didn't mention it. I just wanted someone to talk to."

"So you're saying talking to her was easier than talking to me?"

"In a way. We met in a programming class. If you think I'm analytical, believe me, I'm nothing compared to Casey. I figured if anyone could be objective about the realities of marriage and divorce, it would be her."

Kat scowled. "Okay."

"Don't give me that look. You were busy writing and dealing with deadlines. I knew you'd be pissed off and it would be like that movie where the guy says men and women can't be friends. But Casey and I really *are* just friends. When we met in college, she was already engaged to the guy she's now getting divorced from."

"Well, now you're talking about the friend amendment. In *When Harry Met Sally*, Harry says that men and women can't be friends unless they're involved with other people. But it doesn't really work because the person you're involved with—i.e. *me*—doesn't understand why you'd need to be friends with Casey. That something must be missing in our relationship. So it comes back around to men and women can't be friends because the sex always gets in the way."

"How many times have you seen that movie?"

"Too many. Let's just say I know my romantic comedies. But you get my point. Do you think something is missing from our relationship?"

"Other than sex?"

Kat tried not to roll her eyes. Now she knew what all this was really about. "Yes, other than that. Once I finally get to sleep regularly again, I'm sure I will be more amorous and affectionate. I don't feel sexy when I'm too tired to think straight."

"Are you going to write more books?"

"Maybe, if they ask. I'm not sure." Kat glanced toward the window. "Forever, my dream was to write a book, and it turns out it's been one of the most awful work experiences I've ever had. I mean the writing is okay, but all the arbitrary deadlines, rules, and convoluted writing templates from the publisher have made my life miserable. I just want the whole thing to be over."

"Part of my spiraling thoughts was that this is what our life will be like forever."

Kat took his hand and straddled his body so that she was looking down at him. She leaned over so her face was close to his and smiled. "So what you're telling me is that you're worried that you'll have a bleak future in which you never have sex again, and that you are doomed to a life of austere celibacy because I'll be so busy writing books that I'm never going to touch you until death do us part."

"Well, when you put it like that..." He grinned. "Hey, I'm a guy. We think about sex every seven seconds."

Kat bent to kiss him. "And that's not a bad thing. I love you and I'd be delighted to jump you right now. Just promise me that you'll talk to me the next time you're upset about something."

Joel pulled her down into his arms. "I promise."

Chapter 6

Visiting

The next morning, Lisa loaded Harley into the truck for his journey back out to the kennel. She'd spent most of the night tossing and turning after the argument she'd had with Larry in the Soloan. Maria had bailed out about five minutes after Kat had left the bar.

A wiser person would have seen the handwriting on the wall and fled after the other two women, but Lisa was too slow. Larry had cornered her and launched into a long and tedious lecture about how Lisa had to go visit Aunt Betty at the nursing home. To hear him tell it, he'd been having to do everything and it was her turn to step up to the plate when it came to Lowell family matters.

Lisa thought that being tasked with remodeling the house should count for something, but Larry insisted at length that she needed to call their mother and deal with whatever was going on with Betty.

When Lisa had called Mom she was busy at the store, but had said that whatever Betty wanted might have something to do with jewelry. She suggested dragging an old jewelry box down to the nursing home so Betty could find whatever it was she wanted. Before hanging up Mom had added, "Let her take anything. She can have all of it, for all I care."

The contractors weren't starting until Monday, so Lisa had no excuse not to visit her great aunt. Most of her Friday had been spent dealing with the primary contractor Craig Maddox, who would be overseeing a number of subcontractors for flooring, painting, and various other tasks. Most building contractors took the winter off, so finding anyone in the greater Alpine Grove area willing to work at all was a huge accomplishment. Larry had no idea how many phone calls she'd had to make to find this guy Craig.

The only problem with visiting Betty was that the woman was completely off her rocker. When Lisa was growing up, Betty had always been the oddball aunt, which was cute and funny, especially when Lisa was little. Now Betty was totally nuts. There had been a slew of doctors and diagnoses, but in the end, it seemed like Betty reveled in her nuttiness. Being nutty gave her a free pass to do whatever she wanted, including telling corny or dirty jokes to anyone who would listen. She refused to follow any instructions or take medications, and when forced into doing things she didn't like, stopped talking or went on a hunger strike.

After Betty had taken a few unscheduled naked strolls around downtown Alpine Grove, it was clear that she shouldn't live alone anymore, so the suggestion of moving to assisted living was gently put forth. Everyone in the family knew it was time for her to receive more care, but no one wanted to bring up the topic. In the end, all the worries about her reaction were for nothing because Betty was all over the idea. Having people around to entertain her and tend to her every whim sounded like a good deal to her.

Lisa glanced over at Harley, who was looking official, sitting in the passenger seat, riding shotgun. The night before, he'd only managed to gnaw on the driver's side door lock a little, so Lisa figured Larry got off easy. It was an old truck and no one would notice a few extra tooth marks. She reached over and ruffled one of Harley's silky yellow-gold ears. "Hey, don't look so serious. At least you don't have to go see Betty with me. You get to visit all your dog friends at camp again."

Harley leaned in for a little more affection and panted happily. He probably would like Aunt Betty. The two had a lot in common. They both appreciated being the center of attention, not to mention running off and not coming when called.

Lisa pulled into the driveway and parked in front of the kennel. Harley seemed pleased to be back and eager to get out of the truck. Lisa got out and unloaded him from the cab. She looked up just as Kat opened the kennel door and walked outside. The woman looked completely different. The dark circles under her eyes had faded and she looked relaxed. Maybe she'd finally gotten some sleep.

Kat said, "Welcome back. Harley looks ready for his walk."

"He's always ready."

"So did you get Larry to sign whatever it was you needed last night?"

"Yes, although I got a lecture about how I'm not being a good sister. Most of the Soloan now knows that I need to visit my aunt Betty, who is in assisted living. So that's what I'll be doing today before my date."

Kat smiled. "Family stuff can be fun like that. My fiancé and I are sort of wishing we could skip the whole wedding thing and go straight to the honeymoon."

"I guess you talked things over?"

"Yes. Thanks again for your advice last night. I feel so much better." Kat spread her arms wide. "I've been so upset, and now it's like this dark shroud of gloom has lifted."

Lisa laughed. "I'm glad to hear it. When I was driving back to the house last night, I was thinking about how difficult it is to sustain a marriage over time."

"How long were you married?"

"Twenty-one years."

"It's disturbing to think about things falling apart after so many years together. I hope Joel and I don't get divorced in 2018."

"There's no way to know what will happen." Lisa looked down at Harley, who was lying at her feet, chewing on a stick. "But I think one advantage you have is that you are older than I was when I got married. My husband—or rather ex-husband—was an intern when I met him. I was only nineteen and had just had a terrible accident and was in the hospital, then rehab. Over two decades many, many things changed, including me and Mike."

"I suppose that's true. I'm different than I was at nineteen. *Way* different."

"I'm told that falling in love with your doctor or therapist is common. He seemed so much smarter and wiser than I was, and I fell head over heels for him. Then almost as soon as I'd recovered from the accident, we had kids. We stayed together for years because of the twins, which also is common." Lisa sighed. "I probably shouldn't be telling you all this. It's got to be horribly depressing to someone who is about to get married."

"It's okay. In fact, it's helpful. I should think about these things and talk to Joel about it. When you sign up to get married, you know it's supposed to be forever. But what if it's not? Forever is a long time and no one ever talks about how things might change as you get older." Kat shrugged her shoulders. "I mean, the divorce rate is fifty percent, right? Why is that? I'm sure there are a lot of reasons."

"I think when you're head over heels in love, you don't think about the fact that living with someone day in and day out for years can be challenging. The happy couple is convinced marriage will be nothing but flowers, candy, and romance all the time. But being married requires compromises every day. You do thousands of little things because you're paying attention to the other person's feelings. When you let resentments creep in and you stop caring, that's when things start to fall apart. Or at least that's how it was for me."

"I guess that makes sense."

"I've probably spent far more time going over all this in my head than I should have. I remember that I used to think of my little family as a garden that needed tending. I was completely focused on keeping my girls happy and everything running smoothly. Looking back, I ignored problems with Mike, thinking they were temporary and would go away. They didn't, which became obvious when the girls left for school and I got sick."

"You mentioned you were sick before. What happened?"

"Cancer. Although Mike and I did okay with the for-richer-and-poorer part, the sickness-and-health clause didn't work out as well for us. I'm fine now though."

Kat moved forward two steps, stretched out her arms, and gave Lisa a hug. "I'm glad. Thanks for telling me all this. I'm sure it isn't easy to talk about."

"I hope it helps." Lisa returned the hug and rested her head on Kat's shoulder. Telling people about her divorce wasn't so terrible anymore. Maybe she finally *was* moving on at last.

~

After returning to the house and getting some lunch, Lisa collected the jewelry box, got back in the truck, and headed south toward the Alpine Grove Care Center, where Great Aunt Betty was staying, probably permanently. The facility was a relatively new complex made up of multiple buildings that provided a wide range of medical services. The medical campus had physical therapy and rehabilitation, hydrotherapy, assisted living, outpatient services, and more traditional long-term care for people who were ill or incapacitated.

Back when Lisa had her skiing accident, the medical services in Alpine Grove were more limited, so she'd been hospitalized and spent her initial recovery in Gleasonville. It was odd how your entire life could change in an instant. Sometimes Lisa reflected on the fact that if she hadn't crashed so horribly that day, she would never have met Mike or had Carol and Cheryl. The past two decades would have unfolded completely differently.

She couldn't imagine not having her girls in her life . Since she'd been in Alpine Grove, it had been all she could do to not call them every single day. When the twins started college, both Cheryl and Carol had made it clear that they didn't want their mother calling them constantly. After they'd both been so kind when Lisa was sick, she'd done her best to respect their wishes.

They formulated an agreement that Lisa would only call them once a week on Sunday. Over time, it had gotten easier for Lisa to let go, leave the girls alone, and let them live their lives. But it didn't mean she didn't wonder how and what they were doing about three hundred times a day.

Sundays had turned into Lisa's favorite day of the week because she could finally catch up on everything she'd missed with her daughters. Even though she always thought of them as her "girls," the reality was that Cheryl and Carol had grown into incredibly smart, funny women. Lisa was so proud of their accomplishments and loved to talk with them and hear about the trials and tribulations of classes and college life.

Lisa pulled the truck into the parking area in front of the large brick building where visitors had to check in at the care center. It had been some time since she'd seen Betty, and the report from Mom didn't sound promising. Maybe if the jewelry box contained whatever it was Betty wanted, everything would be fine.

She grabbed the box from the passenger seat and went inside. The lobby had a muted beige and pastel color scheme that was typical of medical facilities everywhere. The receptionist greeted Lisa warmly and reminded her how to get to Betty's room. As Lisa wandered down the carpeted hallways, she felt a bit self-conscious about being able to see into the rooms. In some ways, it felt like a terrible invasion of privacy, like going through a hotel where all the doors were open. When she'd been in rehab, she'd always felt like she was in a fishbowl. Today, no one seemed concerned, however. In fact, many of the residents were fast asleep.

Betty was definitely not asleep. Lisa recognized her aunt's voice booming from the room before she reached the doorway.

"What do you call a snowman on a hot day?" Betty announced to a group of older women sitting around the small table in her room.

Lisa stood in the entryway and responded, "A puddle."

Betty looked up and put down the cards she was holding. "Linda!"

"No, I'm Lisa. My sister is Lynn, not Linda."

"Close enough. Your mother had a real fixation with the letter 'L,' so how am I supposed to remember?" Betty got up and ushered the other women out of her room. "Everybody out. I need to talk to Linda."

Lisa sighed and stepped aside so the women could shuffle by. Today it seemed she was going to be Linda. She walked over and hugged her great aunt. "How have you been?"

Betty crawled onto her bed. "Those old biddies are trying to steal from me again. I know they are. You can't trust any of them. I make sure to play cards with them every day, so I can keep an eye on them. Canasta is a good cover."

"No doubt." Lisa set the jewelry box on the small table. "Mom said you wanted to look at something in this jewelry box."

Betty waved her hand dismissively. "No, that's all junk. I want to see the other stuff. *My* stuff!"

"Mom took all of her good jewelry with her when she moved. I don't know if any of it was yours." Lisa pulled out a drawer in the jewelry box and went over to the bed to show it to Betty. "She said you wanted to see something inside this box. It's all the old costume jewelry we used to play with when I was little."

"Why do you think I want a bunch of pop-it beads? They're plastic crap. I'm not a four-year old, you know!"

Lisa set the drawer down on the bed. "What do you want then?"

"Hey, here's a question for you: what do a bungee jump and a hooker have in common?"

Lisa knew better than to answer. When the topic of the joke turned sexual or scatological, it was best to ignore the question and pretend it had never happened. "Betty, I brought you the jewelry box. Do you want to look through it?"

Betty raised her hand and moved her fingers in a gimme gesture. "Only if there's something good. Those beads were tacky in 1954 and it's not like pink plastic gets better with age."

Lisa carried the box to the bed, set it down, and pulled out the drawers. "This drawer has clip-on earrings. Is that what you want?"

"I'm betting a man invented those. Maybe the same guy who invented the girdle. That's another thing that pinches and hurts you in the name of making you prettier."

"Maybe. I think high heels fall into that category too."

Betty lifted a gaudy pink jeweled earring, held it in front of her eyes, and dropped it back in the drawer. "Yuck. Did Natalie really wear this junk?"

"I don't remember it, but I wore them a couple of times when I played dress-up. They do hurt your ears."

Betty grinned. "Told ya! So how did Burger King get Dairy Queen pregnant?"

"If it includes the word whopper, I don't want to know."

"Okay, I guess you heard that one." Betty shrugged off the rebuke and pushed the drawer away. "This isn't what I want."

"What *do* you want?"

"The stuff in the house."

"Larry said that he made up something that you signed. I promise I'll tell you what I'm planning to sell before I do anything." Lisa mentally cringed at the idea of having to come back here regularly with lists of furniture. She held up a drawer filled with gaudy bracelets. "So you're sure you don't want any of these things, right?"

"This is a bunch of garbage. I don't care what you do with it."

"All right. I guess I should be going then."

Betty reached out and grabbed Lisa's forearm. "Did you ever notice that bald eagles only have one eye?"

"No."

"You never see both their eyes in pictures. Always profile. I think it's a government plot."

Lisa tried not to laugh. "A plot relating to the national symbol of the United States?"

"Yes. It's because there are two kinds of eagles. Bald eagles are either left-eyed or right-eyed. The government doesn't want us to know that because it affects the image on our currency. Like they say, he who has the gold makes the rules."

"Okay, well, ah, that's interesting. I really should be going now, Betty."

"It was good to see you Linda. Come back soon!"

Lisa leaned over to hug her aunt. "I will."

After collecting the jewelry and putting the drawers back in the box, Lisa left the room. Conversations with Betty were always confusing. Maybe in the process of going through thirty or forty years of detritus in the house, she'd finally run across whatever it was Betty wanted. Talk about a needle in a haystack.

As she was walking down the hallway, a male voice called out, "Hey Lisa!" and she turned to look back at one of the rooms. Pete was lying on a bed with his leg elevated and encased in a complex knee brace. He waved at her to encourage her to come into his room. She'd only seen him bundled up in heavy ski gear and it was intriguing to find out what he looked like, particularly since as it turned out, he was remarkably attractive. Who would have guessed? The main thing she'd remembered from their prior encounter was the startling sky-blue color of his eyes and, of course, the blood on his face, which she would have been perfectly happy to forget.

She stopped in the doorway, trying to look nonchalant. Her heartbeat had sped up, which was a little pathetic. You'd think she'd never seen a good-looking man before. Maybe Bev was right. She needed to get out more. At least she had a date tonight, for a change, but right now she needed to get a grip. "You look a lot better than the last time I saw you."

He scratched at the small bandage on his forehead. "I feel better. What are you doing here?"

"My aunt is a resident." Lisa shook her head. "It's a long story."

"I've got time. Lots of time. Nothing but time. I'm bored and the Saturday morning cartoons are over, so the TV is switching to religious programming. I could lose my mind in here. Could you stay and talk to me for a minute? I'll listen to any story you have."

Recalling how desperate she had been for visitors after her own accident, Lisa walked in and sat on the edge of the bed, setting the jewelry box down beside her. "Okay, but just for a minute. I have to get back home and get ready for an appointment later."

"Hot date?"

Lisa's eye's widened. How did he know? "That's a good guess, although I don't know how hot it's going to be."

"That ski patrol guy was drooling all over you. He asked you out didn't he?"

"For someone who was severely injured, you certainly didn't miss much."

"I've got eyes. Although right now, I'm so doped up on painkillers, my crime-fighting skills aren't what they used to be."

Lisa wasn't sure what he meant. Maybe he'd watched too many cartoons this morning. "How is your leg?"

"I had surgery, and the doctors have talked to me about physical therapy and rehab. I trashed my knee and it's a mess. I had no idea joints could be so complicated."

"I know. I had a somewhat similar accident when I was eighteen."

"That explains why you gave me that look."

"What look?"

"Like my leg was totally screwed up and you knew I'd be hating life once I got off that mountain."

Lisa felt strangely uncomfortable. How could he possibly recall something that specific? When she'd found Pete, he'd barely been conscious and she'd figured he wouldn't remember much of anything. "Well, yes, I was afraid you were badly hurt."

"You'd seen it before."

"Yes." How did he *know* that? Had she told him? She couldn't remember. Lisa moved to get up. "I should really get going. It was nice to see you again."

"Have fun on your date. And hey, I don't think I said it before, but thank you for saving my life. I could have frozen to death out there if you hadn't found me."

"I think Harley is the one you need to thank."

"You're right! Are you going to come visit your aunt again?"

"Yes, I promised her I would."

"Great! Bring Harley. People bring dogs to visit all the time. No one will mind. How about tomorrow? If the religious programming is this bad today, imagine what TV is going to be like tomorrow. On a Sunday, it will be all televangelists all the time. I may have to throw myself out the window."

"I'm not sure. On Sundays I make phone my calls."

"You're on the telephone all day? Who are you talking to for that long?"

"My kids. I suppose it doesn't take all day." At the imploring look in his eyes, Lisa smiled. "All right. I'll check with the staff on my way out to make sure it's okay to bring Harley here. He isn't good about being left home alone."

Pete shot both his arms up in the air. "Yes! A visitor under the age of eighty-five."

Lisa laughed. "Get some rest. Harley and I will be back soon."

∽

After taking her own dogs for their afternoon walk with Joel and a couple of the boarding dogs, Kat went back outside to round up the rest of the boarders for their turn. She went into the kennel building and Harley jumped up on his kennel gate, barking eagerly.

Kat put leashes on a shepherd mix named Velma and a small dog whose heritage was anyone's guess. Marvin was some type of gray terrier with short legs and wiry hair. He undoubtedly had quite a few breeds lurking in remote branches of his family tree. The two dogs ran around in the walkway in front of the kennels while Kat got Harley out and put on his leash. Finally, everyone was leashed and ready to head out into the forest.

Kat opened the door and the dogs rushed outside, eager to get on with the walking program. Marvin wasted no time taking care of his personal needs while Harley sniffed everything within reach. The Lab obviously had a serious sense of smell.

As she walked, Kat went over the topics for her upcoming book chapters in her mind. Her dog-walker Mia would return from her days off the next day and Kat was determined to get back into writing as soon as possible.

If Kat were brutally honest about it, she knew her own incessant procrastination was a big part of the reason she'd ended up down to the wire in submitting her previous book chapters. Her failure to suck it up and write had led to the sleepless nights and resulting surly attitude. But she was determined to do better and meet her final book deadline with grace and ease, instead of pain and agony this time. She'd promised Joel that even though she'd probably be stressed and anxious about the book, she'd try harder not to make his life miserable.

Kat was jerked from her ruminations by Harley yanking on his leash. Suddenly the end of the leash dropped to the ground and Kat was left holding the handle and watching Harley bolt into the trees. The other two dogs were startled to see their compatriot having more fun than they were and began whining.

After a moment of stunned paralysis, the reality that the dog was no longer attached to the leash in her hand hit Kat and she ran toward the trees shouting Harley's name, dragging the other two dogs after her. Marvin immediately fell behind, his stubby legs not up to the task of hurtling through trees at high speed. Kat stopped and looked down at the dog, who was clearly annoyed and committed to being small furry dead weight. They weren't far from the kennel, and losing one dog was bad enough. Losing three was even worse, so she hustled the dogs back to the kennel as fast as she could and put them back into their cages.

She ran up the driveway to the house and around to the back door. Slamming the door behind her, she ran inside and stopped at Joel's office door, panting, "Help! I need help!"

He looked away from his computer monitor at her and jumped up out of his chair. "Are you okay?"

"I'm fine. Harley…got away…I don't know what…his collar…leash. Something broke and he ran. I need help."

"All right, let me get my coat."

Kat clipped a leash on Tessa and handed it to Joel. "Tessa has a nose like no other dog I've ever seen. Hang onto her and maybe she can help us track him down."

Tessa, who was hyperactive on a good day, was beside herself with joy, leaping around them, ecstatic at the thrilling concept of getting an extra walk. Generally, she went for walks harnessed to Linus because he was huge and Tessa was almost impossible for any human to tire out. Kat called Linus the "boat anchor" because he weighed about four times as much as the slight golden retriever, which helped to keep her exuberance in check.

Kat called Linus and opened the door to let the large dog out. She waved the other three dogs back. "You have to stay here. It's just Linus and Tessa this time."

Tessa dragged Joel out the door and headed for the forest trail. Kat said, "Okay Tessa, I need you to find Harley. Let's go."

One good thing about having soggy muddy snow on the ground was that it was easier to follow Harley's trail. It was obvious where he'd left the dog-walking path and headed off into the trees. His tracks weren't obscured until they got deeper into the forest, where bare patches had opened up under some of the larger cedars after the recent thaw and rainy weather. Tessa seemed to be inspired, her nose snuffling along the ground, following the scent of something.

Kat looked up at Joel. "Do you think she's following Harley or a deer?"

"Who knows? As you've pointed out before, she has the attention span of a fruit fly."

"I know. Brigid is going to kill me if I lose Harley. How awful is it to lose a dog that's already homeless?" Kat turned her head, scanning the forest ahead. "I hope you know where you are, because I'm going to end up lost too."

"I know where we are. We just passed a spot where I cut firewood last fall."

"At this rate, we're going to end up on the national forest land, if we aren't already. Where the heck is Harley going?"

"Don't ask me. It is the land of many uses. Maybe Harley thought up a new one."

Kat smiled at him. "I'm glad you're retaining your sense of humor, even in the face of disaster."

"Last night left me in a good mood."

A bark came from somewhere ahead of them and Linus ran from Kat's side toward the noise. Kat ran after him, shouting "Harley!" as loudly as she could, followed by Joel and Tessa.

Kat stopped at a break in the trees where Harley was standing in front of something and barking madly. Joel and Tessa came up alongside her and he said, "What *is* that?"

Kat shook her head and took a few steps forward. She said quietly, "Harley, shhh, come here, buddy. Let me help."

Harley looked over at her and wagged his tail, but refused to move from where he was standing. Kat got closer and realized he was standing over what looked like an old white laundry bag. The bag moved and Kat leaped backward, crashing into Linus. Placing her hand on the dog's back to steady herself, she turned to Joel and pointed at the bag. "It moved!"

He made a face. "That can't be good."

"You know I'm way, *way* too big of a chicken to see what's in there."

"All right. Hang onto Tessa for a second."

He handed Kat the leash and walked closer. When he was next to Harley, he crouched down near the bag. "Hi, Harley. So what do you have there?"

The bag moved again and Joel grabbed the drawstring, dragging it closer to him. A mewing noise came from within and Harley stretched his nose closer to sniff. Joel carefully lifted the end of the bag and opened it slightly. A hissing sound came from the bag and after closing it, he gazed up at Kat with a despairing look in his dark green eyes.

"Oh no, is it awful, scary, gross? What?" Kat said, "Why are you looking at me like that? What's in there?"

"I think Harley found a friend. How do you feel about adopting another cat?"

"We already have more than our fair share of felines." Kat stepped closer. "There's really a cat in there? You're saying someone left a cat out here in the middle of the forest? Who would do that?"

Joel stood up, gathering the bag in his arms. "I don't know, but this kind of thing makes me sick. We need to get him or her back to the house."

"You're right. The poor thing must be freezing."

He tucked the bag to his coat, snuggling it close to his chest. "Let's go."

∽

After she returned to the house, Lisa was feeling extra glad that she'd asked Jim to meet her at the restaurant. She was nervous enough as it was. Why hadn't she suggested coffee? It had been so long since she'd even thought about asking someone out, she'd forgotten the traditional dating hierarchy. First coffee or drinks. If that experience wasn't completely horrible, then and only then do you graduate to dinner out. If and only if there was any attraction at all, maybe you'd consider cooking for someone.

After the adrenaline rush she'd had following Pete's rescue, Lisa's brain clearly hadn't been operating at full capacity and she'd jumped three steps by asking Jim over to the house.

Maybe Jim had realized that too. When he called to return her message, his voice didn't sound upset when she listened to the machine play it back.

Now Lisa had to get dressed up again. Maybe this time the date would last longer than fifteen minutes. It was like déjà vu all over again as she drove to the Italian restaurant. She said a silent plea to the universe that a different hostess would be working that evening and that Larry wouldn't be there.

As she entered the restaurant, she quickly scanned the room. Apparently the universe was feeling generous, because the hostess was a brunette and Larry hadn't arrived for his dinner yet. Thank heavens. The hostess seated Lisa at the same table near the fireplace and handed her a menu. Before Lisa had a chance to look at it, Jim walked up and sat down across from her.

He took a menu from the hostess and leaned forward to smile at Lisa. "It's great to see you. How's my favorite heroic skier today?"

Lisa laughed, pleased that he'd broken the ice. "I'm not feeling heroic at the moment. Just hungry. And still sore, which is embarrassing."

"You said you haven't skied since you had the big accident way back when. Never once in all those years?" Jim shook his head. "I can't imagine you *not* skiing."

"Well, for a while I was focused on moving my legs, then on walking. It felt like it took forever. Rehab was rough."

"At first, people said you were paralyzed. Everyone was totally freaking out. A few people even said you were dead."

"Obviously I wasn't dead, but I was paralyzed for a while. Fortunately, it wasn't permanent. Those rumors probably floated around when I was in the trauma-care unit. The doctors didn't know if the paralysis was permanent or due to swelling. Fortunately, it was swelling and the sensation came back. But I had multiple leg fractures, including my knee, so I had surgery."

"Yeah, I'm sure that guy Pete you saved had to go under the knife too. His leg wasn't looking too good."

Lisa gestured toward the door. "I saw Pete again today. I had to visit my aunt at assisted living and he's recovering there."

"Is he doing all right?"

"He seemed to be in good spirits. Certainly a lot better than I was after my accident."

"What do you mean better?"

Lisa gazed at the flame from the votive candle on the center of the table. "I was kind of a mess after the accident."

"Well, you did get pretty badly hurt."

"It wasn't only the physical part. Rehab was hard, but I also felt like I'd let everyone down. You remember what it was like. The whole town was excited about me. Then the story went national and the whole country was talking about me as the great hope of the United States women's ski team. There were all those articles and so much attention. After the crash, I wanted to crawl into a hole and die. I felt like my life was over."

"I had no idea."

Lisa smiled. "Well, it's old news now. Like I said, Pete seemed fine. Maybe a little bored, but he seemed to be in a good mood. He said he wants me to bring the dog who found him when I visit."

"That's cool." Jim checked out the waitress who was at the next table before looking back at Lisa. "You know, it's strange, but I can't imagine you depressed."

"You should be glad you missed it. I think it was one of those things I needed to go through. To grieve for the future I'd lost, I suppose." Lisa took a sip of water. "So enough about me. Tell me what you've been doing."

He glanced at the waitress again. "Same old, same old. I ski in the winter and work on Snow Grove maintenance crews in the summer."

Lisa reached across the table and touched his hand to get his attention. "Do you know that waitress?"

"I hope she's not serving our table."

"Why?"

"Well, uh, I might have been married to her for a while."

Lisa raised her eyebrows. "Oh, really? You didn't mention you were married. I'm assuming you're not now."

"Well, uh, I'm sort of in the process of a divorce right now."

"From the waitress?"

"No, she was number two. I'm getting divorced from Terri now."

"How many times have you been married?"

"Terri was number five." He raised his palms toward the ceiling and shrugged. "I don't have much luck with marriage because eventually my wives figure out what I'm like and kick me to the curb. Terri said I was an untrustworthy flake."

"You rescue people for a living. That seems trustworthy and not flaky at all."

Jim's shoulders slumped and he mumbled, "Oh crap," as the waitress walked up to the table.

The tall woman tilted her head, swishing her long mahogany ponytail behind her back, and smiled sweetly. "Why Jim, how nice to see you again."

"Hi Monica," he said as he handed her a menu.

Monica turned to Lisa. "Are you ready to order?"

Lisa could sense the animosity oozing off the waitress and hurriedly passed off her menu. "Yes. I'd like the fettuccine, please."

"Ravioli for me," Jim said.

Monica turned, her ponytail whipping behind her. Jim made a wry face. "Sorry about that."

"It's Alpine Grove. Inevitably, the person you would least like to meet will show up when you least would like her to."

"I suppose. I didn't know she was working here now."

Jim seemed unsettled by seeing his ex, and Lisa racked her brain for something to say. "So, other than skiing, what do you do? Do you have any hobbies?" She cringed inwardly. Hobbies? That was the best she could come up with?

Jim reached down into his pocket and popped some pills into his mouth. "Nothing much. Sometimes I paint or maybe write some poetry."

"I didn't know you were an artist. That's wonderful."

"I'm not really an artist. Most people think I'm goofing off. I probably am."

"I don't understand. Why would creating art be goofing off?"

"You don't think painting is me screwing around being irresponsible?"

"No, why would I?"

He pointed at a small wood-framed painting of a mountain on the wall. "Well, that's a painting of mine over there."

Lisa turned to look. "It's lovely. Obviously, you were inspired by Snow Grove."

"Yeah, you've probably seen that view a million times."

"It's something I've missed. I'd forgotten how beautiful it is up there on the mountain until I went back."

"I don't feel alive, except when I'm skiing."

"Well then, you have the perfect occupation." Lisa picked up her fork and turned it over. His eyes had an odd unfocused look. What was in those pills he had taken? "How lucky that you can do what you love."

"I guess. Most people think I'm a loser for living off my family since, well, forever."

"I didn't know you were related to the Greenfields."

"How do you think I could live there? I could never afford one of those condos myself. Lifties don't make the big bucks, you know."

"Are you upset the Greenfields are selling the resort?"

"It doesn't matter. I got the condo and the job years ago, so I think I'm safe." He grabbed more pills from his pocket and gobbled them down. "I'm not sure why I'm telling you all this. I mean, I've been living this lie for years. Heck, some of my wives didn't even know what a freeloader I really am. But we were probably too busy partying, I guess."

"I see." Lisa was starting to wonder why he'd ever been attracted to her. "I've never been much of a partier."

"Yeah, you were hard core, always training. So after the accident, did you ever think of killing yourself?"

"What? No, of course not!"

"Just wondering, since you said you were depressed. I've thought about it sometimes."

"Why on earth would you want to do that? You have an enviable life."

Jim glanced back at the waitress. "I don't know. I don't envy it. Freeloading off my family's money and failing at so many relationships for so long...I feel like a failure. All the parties and the drugs. I mean, I kept thinking 'yeah, that party is gonna do it. That's gonna make me happy.' But then I wasn't. Sometimes everything seems...I don't know... pointless, you know?"

"Why are you telling me this?"

"Why not?" He grinned. "I try writing poems, but that only takes you so far. Gotta let these feelings out somewhere, right?"

"I think you should be grateful. And if you don't want to live off your family's money anymore, you can always stop."

"Stop? Are you nuts?"

"Well, it might be scary at first. Maybe you need to face up to that fear."

"You mean give up the job and the free condo?"

"See? You know what you're afraid of. If you don't like what's going on, you can do something else." Lisa mentally chastised herself for not taking her own advice. She was one to talk. Here she was in her forties for heaven's sake, and completely lost, unsure and afraid of what might lie ahead.

Jim shook his head, "I don't think so. I'm sure things will be better once I get through this latest divorce. Don't mind me. I'm just going off on a bunch of stupid tangents. It's what I do."

The rest of the dinner passed reasonably uneventfully, but it was clear that no sparks were going to fly. Lisa also was worried about what might be in the pills Jim was chowing down like candy. At the end of the evening, there was a halfhearted, "I'll give you a call sometime" gesture from Jim, but that was it. He seemed as relieved as she was for the date to be over.

By the time Lisa got home and crawled under the ugly plaid bedspread in her childhood bedroom, she had renewed her promise to herself to be done with men. No matter what Bev might say, all the awkwardness and uncomfortable situations inherent in the whole awful spectacle of dating simply wasn't worth the effort.

~

The next morning after she talked to her daughters, Lisa was eager to pick up Harley to distract herself from the inevitable post-call letdown. After hearing about her daughters' slew of exciting new experiences, her status as former housewife seemed even more dull and pedestrian.

The house seemed too quiet without Harley's goofy presence and Lisa was surprised to find she missed the dog. He deserved the perfect forever home. Lisa needed to talk to Brigid about letting her be involved in the adoption-screening process. Sure he needed some training, but Harley was too special to let just anyone adopt him.

After breakfast, Lisa got into the truck for the trek back out to the kennel. As she drove, she went over the conversation with Jim in her mind. He'd seemed like such a happy-go-lucky person out at the mountain, which showed you never knew what was really going on with people inside their head.

At least she'd been able to deflect any questions about her nebulous future by asking him to recite some of his poetry. The poems weren't bad, although he wasn't kidding that they revealed his dark side. With any luck, those pills were anti-depressants. He could certainly use some.

Lisa had been trying to shake the sulky mood she'd been in since last night, but it wasn't working. Maybe Harley's exuberance would cheer her up. She'd spent some time looking around the house and had found another pile of old costume jewelry in a dresser drawer that she could show to Betty. After talking to her aunt, Lisa wasn't completely sure jewelry was what she was after. Maybe today she could get a few more answers to clarify what Betty *did* want from the house.

When Lisa drove up to the kennel, Kat was walking down the driveway with the big hairy dog Linus. The beast seemed to follow her around in much the same way Chewbacca trailed Han Solo. Kat lifted her hand in greeting, and Lisa waited next to the truck as she approached.

"Welcome back," Kat said. "How was your date? Better than the last one I hope."

Lisa shook her head. "Well, not exactly. Just because you knew someone twenty-five years ago doesn't mean you should date him. People change. Or maybe they don't change enough. I'm not sure. It was unsettling, and thankfully, it's over. I'm planning to more fully embrace my single status now. Dating is too confusing and I've had enough of men to last me for while—a *long* while. How's Harley?"

"He's great." Kat paused in front of the kennel door. "So how do you feel about cats?"

"I like cats. Why do you ask?"

Kat shook her head as they entered the kennel, since any further conversation would be drowned out by barking. She extracted Harley from his enclosure and he leaped around the walkway, sharing his joy and delight at seeing Lisa.

When they were back outside, Kat answered the question. "Harley did the hero thing again."

Lisa looked down at the dog, who was sitting quietly next to her, slowly wagging his tail in the gravel. "What do you mean? Was someone hurt?"

"No, but he ran off. I think I clipped the leash onto his collar wrong or something. Suddenly, I was standing there holding a leash, but no dog. We tracked him through the forest."

"I'm so glad you were able to find him." Lisa crouched down next to Harley and put her hands on both sides of his neck. "Listen here—you have *got* to stop running away like this!"

"It turns out he was on a mission. He found a young cat. Really a kitten still—maybe six months old, I'd guess. He or she is currently confined in my bathroom. Unfortunately, we only have one bathroom in the house, so it's not an ideal situation. I don't suppose you'd like to foster or adopt a cat, would you? A really pretty long-haired gray tabby?"

"I'm not really in a position to do that because of all the work being done on the house. What do you mean *found?*

You're saying Harley ran off and happened to discover a cat wandering around in the woods?"

"The cat was in a drawstring bag. I think someone dumped it." Kat gazed off at the trees. "Someone once told me that the reason my aunt had so many critters was because they ended up here. I'm starting to understand how that might have happened."

Lisa stood up. "That's horrible."

"I know." Kat ran her hand across the fur on Linus's broad head thoughtfully. "Joel told me he ended up with his dog more or less the same way. Someone dumped Lady out near his cabin."

"I guess it's been that way for a long time. People didn't talk about it when I was a kid, but I think you're right about Abigail. She always had lots of animals out here. There wasn't any type of animal shelter or animal control back then, and I think she helped find new homes for lots of animals. From the sounds of it, she was a one-woman foster-care program."

Kat laughed. "That's easy to imagine. It's why I loved visiting when I was little. Abigail always had some new dog or cat for me to play with. And every one of them had a story. I'm guessing she might have cleaned up the tales a little to avoid scaring her wimpy little niece though."

"She was one of the kindest and most compassionate people I've ever met." Lisa opened the passenger door of the truck. "I should get going. I promised Pete I'd bring Harley by his room at the assisted-living place later today."

"Pete? You mean the guy you rescued?"

"Well, technically the guy Harley rescued, but yes. It turns out Pete is recuperating at the Alpine Grove Care Center where my aunt is staying."

Kat watched as Harley hopped into the truck cab. "I bet Harley will have fun."

"I'm more concerned about the other residents of the facility putting up with Harley."

Kat gave Harley a final pat. "You behave yourself. With any luck, no one needs rescuing there."

After returning to the house and eating lunch, Lisa threw the costume jewelry into a bag, collected Harley, and got back into the truck. For someone without a job or kids, she certainly did a lot of driving. Now, instead of driving her girls all over Gleasonville to get to soccer practice or music lessons, she was driving one slobbery Labrador around Alpine Grove. Larry probably wasn't going to appreciate the sheen of Harley's drool all over the passenger-side window when she returned the truck, but it was Larry's fault she was here in the first place, so she wasn't going to lose any sleep over it.

She parked and went inside the facility with Harley, stopping at the reception desk to remind everyone that they'd approved the dog's visit the day before. Harley got a few pats and treats from staff members, which seemed to improve his already exultant mood. When he wasn't off keeping the world safe, Harley was an unusually happy creature.

Lisa stopped by Pete's room first because it was closer to the lobby. Harley launched into the room, yanking the leash from Lisa's hand. He jumped up, placing his front paws on the bed. The expression on Pete's face went from surprise to pleasure at the sudden visitor. "You brought him!"

Lisa picked up the leash and pushed Harley back to the floor. "They were really nice about it. I guess a lot of the residents have canine friends who visit them."

Pete scooted over to the far side of the bed and patted the bedspread. "Come on up, buddy."

"Be careful!"

Harley got onto the bed with a surprising degree of grace and lay alongside Pete, who ruffled the dog's ears. "Remember what we talked about, okay?"

Harley looked unusually thoughtful and Lisa smiled. "Is this some secret I don't know about?"

"Just a little male bonding over blood, gore, and snow."

"How are you feeling today?"

"All right, I guess. They cut back my drugs, so now I hurt and am noticing even more how unbelievably bored I am."

"You have physical therapy, right?"

"Twice a day. Then there are meals. But there's a lot of time in between when it's me, myself, and I doing a lot of nothing and having way too much time to think. So I'm trying to focus on my breathing instead."

"You *must* be bored. Unless you're dead, breathing happens pretty much automatically. Don't they have anything for you to read or anything?"

"I meant meditation. They say there's a little library down the hall, but I'm not particularly mobile yet. The drugs make it hard to concentrate, so I return to the breath."

"You meditate? Are you a monk?" He did have a lovely, low, slightly gravely voice.

"Not even close."

"What do you do? Other than ski."

"You mean ski badly?"

Lisa laughed. "I didn't say it, you did!"

"But you thought it." He stopped petting Harley and pointed at her. "You know you did."

"I told you my accident wasn't terribly different, so apparently we both are terrible skiers."

"Not according to the ski-patrol guy. That reminds me. How was the big date?"

"I don't want to talk about it. You dodged my question. What do you do?"

"I'm retired."

Lisa gave him an appraising gaze. He couldn't possibly be even close to sixty-five. "You look awfully young to be retired. What did you do before you retired? Make millions in the stock market? Sell some big company?"

"Nope. I took early retirement from the police force. I was a cop."

Lisa looked down at Harley. Interesting. That explained the solving crimes comment and his controlled, calm, almost stern presence. Even lying in a bed, he exhibited a quiet strength that was a little unnerving, but was probably invaluable during a crisis. "What kind of police work did you do?"

"Narcotics mostly. The K9 partner I had was the most amazing drug dog I've ever seen. I got really lucky with him."

"What was his name?"

"Lakota, which means 'friend' or 'ally.' And he was."

"I'm sure. Is Lakota retired too?"

"Yes, he lived with my old partner, Tom."

"So he's gone?"

"Yes, but Lakota had a great retirement. Tom's family loved that dog to pieces."

"I see why you like Harley so much." Lisa smiled. "Once a dog person, always a dog person, right?"

"This guy just needs a little training, that's all." Pete stroked the dog's head. "Check it out. See what a good boy he's being?"

"Harley is available for adoption. I could put in a good word for you."

Pete shook his head as he ruffled Harley's ears. "No, I can't handle having another dog."

Given the tone of his voice and the heartbroken look in his eyes, Lisa wasn't about to argue. "Okay, but the offer stands if you change your mind."

∼

Bringing up his canine partner seemed to dampen Pete's mood, but he was still obviously enjoying petting Harley. After a slightly awkward lull in the conversation, Lisa said, "I need to go show some old jewelry to my aunt Betty. Would it be okay if I left Harley here with you for a few minutes?"

Pete's expression brightened. "Sure. We'll hang out."

"Thanks. If it's like yesterday, she won't remember who I am or what she wants, so I should only be a few minutes."

"Take as long as you need."

Lisa encouraged Harley to stay out of trouble and left the room. The hallway, like the rest of the facility, was generic, with pastel-colored carpet and walls. Everything was clean and new, and yet still institutional. Various scary-looking pieces of stainless steel equipment were scattered along the walkway in stark contrast to the artwork on the walls, which featured peaceful meadows and colorful flowers. She pushed the chrome handle on one of the double doors to enter the section of the building where Betty was located.

Once again, Lisa heard Betty before she entered the room. Her aunt's voice echoed down the hallway. "A lot of deer get hit by cars on that spot on the highway near the Enchanted Moose. Why did they put the deer crossing there? They need to move that sign."

Lisa stopped in the doorway, and the three other women looked up. The last time she'd seen Betty holding court in her room, Betty had thrown the women out before Lisa could even say hello to them. "Hi Betty. I'm sorry to interrupt, but I brought by some more things for you to look at."

Betty said, "Interrupt what?"

"Your conversation with your friends." Lisa smiled at the women and put her hand to her chest. "My name is Lisa. It's nice to meet you."

A woman with a tight gray bun protruding from the back of her head said, "I'm Doris, that's Alice, and over there is Bernice."

Betty said, "Get out, Doreen. And the rest of you too!" Doris moved uncomfortably and adjusted her pink housecoat. Alice narrowed her eyes and gave Betty a death glare.

Lisa frowned. "It's okay with me if they want to stay."

Betty repeated her command and the women shuffled out. Alice turned her head for a final icy glance as Lisa sat down on the edge of the bed. "They really didn't have to leave."

"Yes, they did. I don't want them to see my stuff. You brought it, right?"

Lisa pulled the bag off her shoulder and reached her hand inside. She pulled out a clump of heavy bead necklaces and chains. "I found these in a dresser."

Betty snatched one of the chains and held it up in front of her face so that it was almost touching the purple frame of her glasses. "I don't care about this. Why are you bringing me this crap?"

Lisa pulled out more jewelry and laid it on the bed. "I thought you wanted the jewelry. Isn't that what you said?"

"I want the stuff in the house."

"Mom said you wanted jewelry and this *was* in the house. What do you mean by *stuff?* I can't exactly bring the furniture, you know."

Betty gazed out the window. "Is it dinner time yet? I think they are stealing my food."

"They are not! You're not going on another hunger strike, are you? I promise I'll try to bring whatever you want."

Betty turned to look back at Lisa. "What do you call two jalapeños getting it on?"

"Stop that, Betty. I'm not falling for it. I need to know what you want me to bring to you."

"You are just like your mother, Linda. Never listening. I remember when I stayed there that Thanksgiving, she got all over my case because I went for a walk. I *told* her I was going for a walk."

"Was that when you were gone for two days?"

"I don't remember."

Lisa slumped her shoulders. She was getting nowhere trying to talk to her aunt. The woman switched topics faster than a politician. And time was passing. Lisa needed to get back to Pete's room before Harley got too squirrelly. "Okay, I'll look around for more *stuff.* Is it jewelry? Could you at least give me a hint?"

"I told your mother about the box. And your grandpa too. Why does no one ever listen to me? Where is my dinner?"

"Okay, I'll look for a box. I promise." Lisa wasn't sure if Betty remembered that Grandpa had been dead for a long time. She gave her aunt a hug and hustled out the door and down the hallway back to Pete's room.

She peeked inside where both Pete and Harley were fast asleep. Pete's arm was around Harley's shoulders and the dog had his muzzle resting on Pete's chest. The scene was utterly adorable. Pete absolutely had to adopt Harley, because these two clearly needed each other. She vowed to convince Pete that he should have another dog.

As she walked closer, Harley lifted his head and thumped his tail. Pete opened his eyes and readjusted himself so that he was sitting up straighter. He smiled. "I totally passed out."

Lisa sat down. "Your body is healing and you need rest. I'm glad Harley was helpful. I was worried I'd been gone too long and that he'd pull another Lassie move and run off to find Timmy in the well."

"The conversation with your aunt didn't go well, huh?"

Lisa pursed her lips. "I didn't say that."

"But it didn't, did it?"

"Not really. She loses focus and it's hard for me to keep up. Half the time she's telling a dirty joke or recounting a distorted memory. I find it incredibly frustrating." Lisa flopped her hands on the bed in exasperation. "That probably makes me a bad person."

"You can always just smile and nod."

Lisa looked down and ruffled Harley's ears. "Well, yes, there's a lot of that. But she keeps saying she wants something in my parents' house, and I have no idea what it is. It's about to be remodeled and I need to figure out what she wants before my parents list the place for sale again."

"You seem upset about selling the house."

"Not at all. It's where I grew up, but I know it's the right thing to do."

"Really?" Pete put his hand under Harley's chin, raised the dog's nose off his chest, and pointed it toward her. "You wouldn't lie to the hero dog, would you?"

"I'm not lying! Okay, maybe I am a little. Sorry, Harley." Lisa returned to petting the dog's head as he closed his eyes and fell back asleep. "You must have been extremely good at interrogating people."

"I had my moments. But this isn't me interrogating. I'm curious. It's hard to lose your childhood home with all those memories."

"I suppose, but it's time. Past time, really. My parents moved out a year ago to an adorable little cottage in town, so they can walk to the hardware store. The old house refuses to sell, which is why I've been tasked with tearing it apart and remodeling it."

"You don't look excited about the project."

"I'm not. But I'm in transition, I guess you'd say, so my brother took advantage of the fact that I didn't have any excuse to say no."

"Transition from what?"

"Being a stay-at-home wife and mother. Now I'm divorced with no skills and no career. Larry knows that and he ran with it."

"Why are you discounting being a wife and mother? That's a lot of work."

Lisa tilted her head. "I think you're the first person who isn't a mom to ever say that to me. Are you married? Kids?"

"I was married once back in the dark ages, but fortunately we didn't have kids. She discovered pretty quickly that being married to a cop wasn't quite what she'd envisioned. I think she liked the uniform better than she liked me."

"I'm sorry. Did you enjoy your career in law enforcement?"

"In the beginning I did. I think I was trying to prove something. Cowards die many times before their deaths; the valiant never taste of death but once."

"Is that Shakespeare? High school English classes were a long time ago."

"Yes, from Julius Caesar. After I left the force, I read a lot of it. I found it comforting, somehow, to discover that human beings haven't changed much in the last five or six hundred years."

"What were you trying to prove?"

"That I wasn't a coward. I was supposed to go to Vietnam, but I didn't."

"I think that makes you lucky, unless you ran off or dodged the draft somehow."

"I certainly agree with you about the luck factor now. But I was eighteen in 1972, and I got a low draft number. I had mentally prepared myself to go be a brave soldier and serve my country, even though I didn't necessarily understand or agree with what was happening. I was called to report for induction, but then there were no new draft orders in 1973. I felt like I'd chickened out or that I should have felt differently about the war." He raised his hand with his thumb and forefinger an eighth inch apart. "I might have been a teeny bit screwed up back then though."

"You and everyone else." Lisa smiled. "I think I'm the only person in my generation who wasn't on drugs."

"Well, you and Bill Clinton. As I recall, he didn't inhale."

Lisa laughed. "So were you able to tell he was lying too?"

"No comment."

Chapter 7

Time Capsule

The next morning, trucks rolled up to the house, and Lisa spent a lot of time talking to contractors and attempting to keep track of Harley. After catching him heading for the front door, she kept him on a leash. The last thing she needed was for him to decide someone in the neighborhood needed rescuing.

Once the workers set to their tasks, the noise and dust level rose dramatically. Ripping out ancient carpet apparently required a lot of yelling and power tools. An air compressor came on intermittently. The sudden drone followed by sharp whacking noises caused Lisa to want to jump out of her skin. Harley also felt compelled to bark at the noise every time he heard it, which didn't help.

Before she'd left the assisted living facility the day before, Pete had begged her to bring Harley back for another visit. She'd hesitated and ultimately said no, but now she was rethinking her choice. At least it was quiet there. Plus, the fact was that Betty was still looking for something, and it was up to Lisa to figure out what.

Betty had mentioned a box. Maybe she was looking for some type of decorative box or knickknack, not jewelry. It was worth a try. And it would get Lisa away from the mind-numbing racket. She grabbed a cardboard box and wandered around the house, throwing a little wooden box, candlesticks, figurines, and a vase inside. If she collected a wide range of items, maybe something would trigger a memory and Betty would finally divulge exactly what it was that she wanted.

Lisa flagged down Craig Maddox, the general contractor in charge of the crew, to let him know she'd be gone for a couple of hours. He gave her a salute and told her they'd still be there when she returned, but quite a bit of the carpet wouldn't be. She smiled and thanked him before grabbing Harley's leash and her box of knickknacks and fleeing the premises.

Once she and Harley were settled within the blissfully quiet truck cab, Lisa breathed a sigh of relief. She reached over and patted Harley. "I probably shouldn't be leaving those guys alone, but I didn't think about how noisy this process would be. I hope Craig knows what he's doing."

Harley thumped his tail a few times in sympathy, but didn't seem to have any other suggestions, so Lisa started the truck for the trip back to the care center. Although she'd tried not to dwell on it, being around Pete made her uncomfortable. It reminded her of all the time she'd been in rehab after her accident.

Although he seemed like a nice person and she was certainly sympathetic to his situation, it seemed like she was being confronted by her past after years of trying to avoid ever thinking about that time in her life . In many ways, returning to Alpine Grove was even more upsetting than she'd expected it would be. Maybe she'd just visit Betty and take Harley for a walk somewhere, instead of visiting Pete.

Lisa parked the truck, unloaded Harley, and they followed the well-shoveled sidewalk inside. She stopped at the reception desk and placed the box of knickknacks on the counter so she could sign in. Harley was tugging on the leash and she yanked him back toward her, looping the leash over her arm while she tried to fill out the sign-in form. She mumbled "Just a minute!" under her breath, hoping the receptionist couldn't hear her quietly chastising the dog. Were obedience classes available in Alpine Grove? Harley needed to attend some type of intensive doggie boot camp.

With a mighty lurch, Harley yanked the leash off Lisa's arm. She turned and watched as he galloped down the hallway and skidded to a stop next to a man in a wheelchair. A nurse was holding crutches in one hand and helping the man stand up. He turned, looked down the hall, and grinned at Lisa. She raised her hand and waved slightly. So much for not seeing Pete.

She picked up the cardboard box and walked down to the group. Harley was wagging so hard that his entire body was wiggling at the joy of seeing his favorite human. Whether he liked it or not, Pete was going to *have* to adopt this dog.

With the assistance of the nurse, Pete somewhat ungracefully maneuvered himself onto the crutches as Lisa bent to grab Harley's collar to get the dog out of the way. She looked up at Pete. "Sorry about that. As I mentioned, he's not the most obedient dog."

The petite nurse moved the wheelchair out of the way. "Are you okay? Make sure you don't put any weight on that leg at all."

Pete nodded, moved the crutches, and took a few steps. "No problem."

Lisa grimaced inwardly, recalling how painful those first few steps had been for her. "Don't try to be a hero. If it hurts, say something."

Pete gave her an icy look and said, "It's fine."

Lisa shook her head. "I can tell it's not. Don't overdo it. That will only make it worse."

The nurse put her hand on his upper arm and said, "I think she's right. That's enough for now. We just wanted to get you up on the crutches today, not run a marathon. Let's get you back to your room."

Lisa followed with Harley as Pete got settled back into bed. Given the expression on his face, she could tell that he was annoyed. Lisa probably shouldn't have interfered, but she knew how it felt to walk with crutches for the first time after spending days in bed.

After the nurse left, Harley jumped up next to Pete and settled in for some affection. The tense look on Pete's face relaxed somewhat as he began petting the dog. Lisa set the box on the nightstand and sat on the foot of the bed. "As you figured out, I've been through this type of recovery and I know how hard it is."

Pete stopped petting Harley for a moment, letting his hand rest on the dog's back. "I hate being here. The doctor said I can't put any weight on this leg for weeks. *Weeks!* I'm going to go completely stir crazy."

"It's a tibial plateau fracture, isn't it?"

He looked up in surprise. "You certainly know your knee injuries."

"I can easily imagine what happened. That type of fracture often happens when you have a bad landing. You shot off that ridge, then *smash, crunch, ouch.*"

"It's all kind of a blur, but yeah, that sounds about right. Some snowboarder cut me off and I swerved to avoid him, went through a mess of trees, and the next thing I knew I was airborne. Then the crunch and the ouch."

Lisa smiled. "I wiped out pretty spectacularly too. My rehab took more than a year."

"I don't want to hear that. I thought I'd get a cast and in a few weeks be walking again, no problem. But from what they're saying, this is going to take months and months to heal." He moved his hand from Harley and flopped both palms on the bed in exasperation. "It's not like I can go home either. I can barely even walk on crutches yet."

"Where do you live?"

"Phoenix."

"Do you have family there? When I had my accident and later when I was sick, I really depended on my family's help, especially my mom. I don't know what I would have done without her."

"Nope. I already had this conversation at the hospital. That's why I'm trapped here."

Given the look on Pete's face, Lisa wasn't going to touch that topic. "I see."

"All I wanted was a ski vacation. That turned out to be a dumb idea."

"You must have skied before if you were on that trail. It's not a beginner run."

"Sure I have. I love to ski and I wanted to get out of the city and see some real seasons. At this rate, I'm going to end up seeing every season Alpine Grove has to offer."

"Winter is pretty, but I'm afraid mud season isn't a big tourist draw."

"I guess I'll find out."

Harley uttered a snorfly snore and moved his muzzle closer to Pete's chest.

Lisa grinned at the expression of canine contentment. "Are you sure you don't want a dog? This guy has completely fallen in love with you."

"I don't think so. Weren't we discussing the fact that I'm trapped here and I can't walk?"

"I know, but he's so completely smitten with you. Could you watch him for a minute again? I have to take this box to Betty and see if it spurs some memories this time."

Pete ruffled Harley's ears and smiled. "All right. I suppose I can do that."

~

With more than a little trepidation, Lisa walked down the hallway with her box of knickknacks. The last two visits with her aunt had been confusing and mostly made her feel like a rotten niece for not understanding what Betty wanted her to salvage from the house. And now the place was being torn apart, so it wasn't going to be any easier to find whatever it was Betty was so desperate to have.

Betty was Lisa's grandfather's sister. Grandpa had died of cancer when he was only in his sixties, so apparently Betty got the family genes for longevity. At this point, she was probably in her early nineties, although no one was completely sure, least of all Betty. Lisa's mom always said Betty was too weird to die.

Lisa remembered that when she was little, Betty often wore yellow because, as she said, it was a "happy" color. Her love for laughing loudly and often was why she spent so much time telling jokes and watching old comedy movies. Back in the days when Betty was a little more clear about who Lisa was, she used to refer to her as "baby doll." Although Lisa was never sure why Betty had given her the nickname, her obnoxious brothers never let her forget it.

When she reached the doorway to Betty's room, she found her aunt lying on the bed, curled up and facing the wall, away from the doorway. Maybe she was asleep. Lisa tapped on the door lightly and Betty shot straight up into a sitting position with a small yelp.

Lisa smiled weakly and held the cardboard box out in front of her. "It's me again. I have some more things for you to look at. Is it okay if come in?"

"Linda, why did you have to scare the stuffing out of me?"

"Lisa."

"Well, whatever your name is, come over here. What's in the box?"

Lisa walked to the bed and placed the box in front of Betty. "I thought maybe you'd be interested in looking at these. They're a few things I found around the house."

Betty peered into the box and pulled out a blue and white Delft candle holder, clasping the little round handle with two fingers as if it had a communicable disease. "I hate this kind of crap. Why use candles when we have electricity? That was a good invention, you know."

"Yes, I'd have to agree."

Betty dropped it back into the box and pulled out a small silver elephant figurine. "So why did the lifeguard kick the elephants out of the pool?"

"It has something to do with trunks, I assume."

"Okay, you heard that one before. But any joke that includes dropping your pants and mooning people is a good one!"

"If you say so." Lisa picked the wooden box and a miniature ceramic pony out of the box and held them up in her hands. "How about these?"

"Why would I need want a little wood box? To store toothpicks?"

"Um, you said…"

Betty grabbed the pony. "Or this homely clay thing. Does it have a cough?"

"What?"

"He sounds a little hoarse." Betty chuckled and pointed at Lisa, "Oh, come on. Get a sense of humor, Linda. Don't you get it?"

"Betty, could you please focus for a minute? I need you to really look at this stuff. The contractors are there ripping out carpet today. I'm going to have to start selling and donating the things in the house soon. I need you to tell me what you're looking for in the house, so I can give it to you. Time is running out."

Betty dropped the pony back into the cardboard box. "You're a party pooper. And you know what that means."

"Stop. No poop jokes. I mean it."

"Fine."

"What do you want from the house?"

Betty peered down into the box. "None of this crap. Your mother has the most hideous taste."

Lisa wasn't going to argue that point. "What do you want me to bring?"

"How many times do I have to tell you, Linda? I want the stuff in the house. I put it there so it would be safe."

"*What* stuff? The house is full of stuff! Furniture, kitchenware, everything! Half the toys we had when we were kids are still in those closets. What do you want? You have to be more specific. I can't bring *everything* out here for you to look at."

Betty seemed to curl up into herself. "You never listen. I'm tired of talking to you. Go away."

Lisa reached out to touch her shoulder, but Betty shrugged off her hand as she slumped back down onto the bed and mumbled, "Get out."

Not sure what else to do, Lisa picked up the box. "All right. I'll bring some more things by soon."

Betty rolled over and faced the wall again. She was done talking. Lisa left the room and went back down the hall to collect Harley from Pete. She felt as if she'd been cruel to her aunt, but she was getting nowhere and she wanted to scream. Maybe in the process of drafting the documents, Larry had figured out what Betty was talking about. It was time to give her little brother a call and get some answers.

Lisa glanced at a painting of perky yellow sunflowers on the wall. Was Betty of sound enough mind for any of that paperwork to hold up under scrutiny? That might be another question to ask Larry. If he didn't have answers, she was running out of ideas. Betty was going to have to live out the rest of her days without her mythical stuff.

Lisa stopped at the doorway to Pete's room and found that he and Harley were almost exactly as she had left them. Harley raised his head and thumped his tail a few times in greeting. Pete set his book aside and smiled at her. "How'd it go?"

Lisa set the box on the floor and sat in the chair near the bed. "Not well. This is absurd. I have contractors tearing apart the house and there's no way I'm going to figure out what she wants before I have to start clearing things out."

"What are they doing?"

"At the moment, ripping out carpet, I hope. And some task that involves an unbelievably loud air compressor. It's awful."

"Don't you have to get rid of the furniture first?"

"They said they could work around it for a while, since I'm living there. I can't get rid of everything yet." She slumped down in the chair. "I've been avoiding going through all the old stuff. I could say I've been too busy, but to be honest, I'm having trouble forcing myself to do it. Every time I open a closet door, I feel overwhelmed and close it again."

"You also had a big date, as I recall."

"Don't remind me."

"So it didn't go well? You never said."

Lisa crossed her arms and glared out the window. "No, and I don't want to talk about it. Suffice it to say I have given up on dating and sworn off men entirely. It's not worth it."

"Swearing off an entire gender is significant, and I'll try not to take it personally. Okay. New topic. You said the house is big. Does it have a bathroom downstairs?"

"Yes, there's a full bath next to my father's office. It has possibly the ugliest wallpaper ever made. Why do you ask?"

"Well, while Harley and I were hanging out here, I had an idea."

Lisa turned to look at him. "About the house? Or Betty?"

"Not exactly."

"Then what?"

"I'd like to hire you."

Lisa leaned forward, resting her elbows on her knees. "Hire me? To do what? I already told you I have no skills."

"This would involve skills you already have."

Lisa sat up and leaned back in the chair, flopping her hands onto the armrests. "I've just spent the last half hour trying to extract information from my aunt, and I'm not in the mood for riddles. I have no idea what you're talking about."

"Rent me a room in your huge house, feed me, and drive me to my physical therapy appointments. And if I trip over something, please call nine one one. I'll pay you, and as a bonus I can help keep an eye on Harley so he doesn't get in the way of the contractors."

Lisa was so surprised she didn't know what to say. "You want to move into the house? Are you crazy? It's a mess."

"I don't care. I have to get out of here or I'll go insane. You already seem to know everything about my injury. If you could handle raising twins, feeding and driving an old gimpy guy around should be no problem."

"I guess that's true, but I barely know you. And you don't know me either."

"Roommates never know each other at first. You can help me, and I'll do what I can to help you." He pointed at the box. "I could help you go through the stuff in the house. That doesn't require walking. Park me in a chair and I'll sort through anything you want."

"You'd really pay me?" Lisa said, trying to read the expression on his face. He did look sincere. The idea of not having to ask Mike about money for a new car was appealing. With her own source of income, maybe she could save enough to get a used car and avoid ever having to talk to her ex about the demise of the Volvo. It wasn't like she could drive Larry's piece-of-junk pink pickup forever. Eventually she was going to have to deal with her sad automotive situation.

Pete said, "How much does it cost to rent a room in Alpine Grove?"

"I don't know."

"Find out and I'll double it. Plus food. I'll pay for you to do a background check or credit check or whatever you want, so you can find out everything you ever wanted to know about me. Because I was a cop, I've been fingerprinted by every agency out there. Please?"

"I'm not sure about this. Shouldn't you talk to your doctors? The house is being torn apart. It's going to get a lot worse before it gets better, and I doubt it's good for someone recovering from surgery to be living in a construction zone. It's horribly noisy and dirty."

"Like I said, I don't care about that if it gets me out of here."

Harley woofed once to show his support and Lisa laughed. "I guess Harley likes the idea."

Pete thrust his fists in the air. "I'm free!"

～

The next day, Lisa and Harley returned to the Alpine Grove Care Center to confer with Pete's doctor about the idea of him staying with her. Lisa couldn't decide how she felt about it, but she had to admit that she was lonely out at the house. Every member of her family had made it clear they wanted nothing to do with the remodeling project, so she felt trapped with a lot of memories she didn't want to deal with alone. Having Pete around would help her to go through all the old stuff that she'd been avoiding. He was right about that. She was getting nowhere trying to do it on her own.

Lisa and Harley walked into Pete's room, but it was empty. She sat down in the chair near the bed and Harley sat in front of her, looking up at her expectantly.

Ruffling the fur on his neck, she bent down and whispered, "Don't worry. Pete couldn't have gotten far. He's too slow." Harley wagged his tail and slid down to the floor to wait. Lisa grabbed a book off the nightstand. Othello? Apparently Pete wasn't kidding about his affection for the Bard.

She flipped the book open and riffled through the pages. That was a whole lot of footnotes for one play. How could anyone stand to read this stuff when every-other word required a footnote? The petite nurse wheeled Pete into the room, and Harley jumped up to greet him. Lisa hurriedly closed the book and placed it back on the nightstand.

After helping Pete back into bed, the nurse said, "The doctor will be in to talk to you in a few minutes."

Harley eagerly jumped up to join Pete on the bed, who shrugged at Lisa. She folded her hands in her lap, trying not to be nervous. Somehow talking to doctors always made her feel like she was being sent to the principal's office for bad behavior. To Lisa, it felt like doctors looked at her extra pounds and lack of muscle tone with a critical eye. Yes, it was irrational, but it didn't make talking to medical professionals any less anxiety-inducing.

A man in a white coat walked into the room. He bore a striking resemblance Dustin Hoffman, except he was much taller and skinnier. An involuntary rendition of Simon and Garfunkel's "Mrs. Robinson" ran through Lisa's head and she bent her head, repressing a smile. Why did her brain turn to mush around doctors? No wonder she'd ended up married to one.

"Mrs. Ryan? How nice to see you again. It's been a long time."

Lisa looked up. "What?" Who was this guy?

The doctor put his palm on his chest. "Roger Burgmann. We met at the orthopedic conference in San Diego back in 1993. Listening to your husband discuss erythrocyte sedimentation rate after total hip arthroplasty was a real highlight of the event for me."

Lisa didn't remember meeting someone who looked like Dustin Hoffman, but she'd been so bored and met so many doctors that weekend, maybe she'd blocked it from her memory. "Of course. San Diego."

"How is your husband?"

"Fine, although Mike and I aren't married anymore. He lives in New York now. I'm single and planning to stay that way." Lisa gave herself a mental head slap. Why did she blurt *that* out?

"Oh, ah, I'm sorry. I suppose we should talk about Mr. Harmon."

Pete lifted his hand off Harley's back and raised his palm as if he were in grade school. "So can I move out of here? Like I told you yesterday, I *really* want to leave."

"Well, I need to discuss the medical issues with both of you. If she's going to be taking care of you, Mrs. Ryan needs to be apprised of your condition."

Imitating Pete, Lisa raised her hand. "It's Lisa Lowell now. Please call me Lisa."

The doctor looked down at the clipboard in his hand and focused his attention back on Pete. He cleared his throat. "At this juncture, your leg appears to be healing well. But I showed you the x-rays yesterday, Mr. Harmon, so you know what we're dealing with here. You suffered a significant impact injury."

"I know. My leg is full of screws and plates. I'm trying to forget about the fact that you put things that look like railroad spikes into my body," Pete said.

"It's imperative for the next six to eight weeks that you put absolutely no weight on your knee and leg. That means you will need to use a wheelchair or crutches at all times," the doctor continued.

"I know," Pete said, looking glum. "That's why I want to hire Lisa. I can't cook anything while I'm on crutches or do much of anything else."

The doctor turned to Lisa. "So you've talked about this and you understand what's involved?"

Lisa nodded. "We have. When I was eighteen I had a similar accident, so I know what the recovery is like. My mother took off work to take care of me. Back then, we converted my father's office into my bedroom because it's on the first floor near a bathroom with a walk-in shower. Pete can stay there like I did. We just need to move the desk out and rent an adjustable hospital bed. I'll need a complete list of Pete's medications and an outline of his physical-therapy protocol."

Dr. Burgmann flipped through the sheets on his clipboard. "All right. I can get that for you."

As the doctor droned on and on, Lisa remembered why she hated attending those medical conferences with Mike. No wonder she didn't remember Dr. Burgmann. MDs had a fondness for using long, complicated medical terms that were hard to follow, so the doctors all blended into a blur of Latin monotony. It was so much easier to talk to nurses, who tended to focus on how someone was actually feeling.

When the doctor left, Pete flopped back onto his pillow, which caused Harley to stir from his slumber. Pete said, "I feel like a science project. And not one of the fun ones like building a working model of a volcano. I thought he'd never leave."

Lisa chuckled "At least Harley got some rest."

"Lucky him."

"That's one issue that could be a problem. I didn't want to bring it up in front of your doctor, but all those contractors are really loud and your body needs rest. I know you're going to be tired and will want to sleep, but there's no way you can nap while those guys are busy working."

"I'll sleep at night." Pete sat up again and looked out the window. "They'll probably take a lunch break some time during the day, and I can nap then if I'm tired. It's no big deal."

"I'm still not sure this is a good idea. It would probably be better for your recovery if you stayed here."

"Maybe it would be better for me physically, but not mentally." He ran his thumb and forefinger down one of

Harley's soft ears. "I learned the hard way that being injured can lead to depression, and I'd prefer to avoid going through that again. Getting out of here will help a lot."

Lisa turned to look at him. "I wish I didn't know what you were talking about, but I do. I suppose the worst thing that could happen is that you'd decide you can't stand staying in the house and you move back in here."

Pete extended his arms wide. "Hey, how much worse could it be than *this*?"

"I don't suppose you're color blind, are you?"

"No, I can see color fine."

"That's too bad, unless you happen to have a peculiar fondness for magenta."

"Magenta?"

Lisa grinned. "You'll see."

~

Lisa made arrangements to come back the next day and pick up Pete, then she and Harley returned to the house. The contractors were packing up their things, getting ready to go home. Craig waved at her to get her attention. She walked into the living room and looked down at the kelly green carpet, which was still right where it had been for decades.

She pointed at the furniture, which was stacked and jammed into the hallway. "What's going on? I thought you were ripping out the carpet today."

Craig frowned. "We moved to the upstairs because I wanted to talk to you about this room. The pad underneath has completely disintegrated. It's literally turned to powder, which is gonna create a huge dust storm when we yank it, so I wanted to check with you first. The room is huge and that carpet-pad dust is going to get all over everything on the first floor. We can't open the windows either. That's why people usually do this type of thing in the summer."

Lisa tried not to roll her eyes. She was tired of getting lectures from this guy. His condescending tone made her want to slap him. She gave him a tight smile. "I know. You keep telling me that, but the timing of this project is not my decision."

"So what do you want us to do?"

"If you can't do this carpet yet, you can't. Put the furniture back and continue with the upstairs. I have a roommate arriving tomorrow and I need to get him settled. He'll be staying in the office. I need you to move the desk out because a bed is being delivered tomorrow from a medical-supply company."

Craig gestured toward the hall. "The roommate is staying in the office down there?"

"It's a long story. His name is Pete and you'll meet him tomorrow."

"That desk is gigantic. It's gonna take four of us to lift it and tilt it to get it out through the door. Where do you want us to put it?"

"In here. If you move the couches and coffee table down, there's room along that back wall. It will be fine for the time being."

"All right. I'll tell the guys to do it first thing."

"Thank you." Lisa motioned toward the front door. "Have a good evening."

"Yes, ma'am. We'll see ya tomorrow."

Lisa watched as the parade of workmen tromped out of the house. After everyone was gone, she was able to walk around in peace and evaluate what they'd done without Craig's incessant commentary. Although he was perfectly pleasant and professional, something about him rubbed her the wrong way. She was trying her best to be polite, but sometimes she wished he'd just shut up.

Lisa had grabbed a sandwich from the deli on the way home. Since Harley had been living with her, she'd only been to the grocery store once, while he was staying at the kennel. The cupboards were completely bare, with the exception of a bag of stale potato chips she hadn't finished and had subsequently forgotten about.

Once Pete was living at the house, he could stay with Harley while she did a major store run. That would be liberating. She could take the truck out without the addition of her drooly copilot. After eating by herself for so long, it would be nice to cook for someone again. When the girls were still living at home, if someone had told her that she'd miss cooking, she never would have believed them. But she truly did.

After feeding Harley and cleaning up the kitchen, Lisa went upstairs to her room and discovered that the orange carpet was gone. Now there was just grayish-brown plywood subflooring filled with rows of holes where the workmen had pulled out the tack strips. The room seemed oddly muted without its brightly colored carpet and the awful brown, orange, and gold plaid bedspreads looked even worse in isolation.

The house had been built in the early sixties, so Lisa was unlikely to unearth a lovely surprise like hardwood flooring when the carpet was removed. The home-improvement shows on TV tended to focus on old houses that had been built in the era of fine craftsmanship. Sadly, at the Lowell family home nothing pretty was lurking under all that hideous carpet.

Lisa spent most of the next morning supervising the furniture moving and the installation of the hospital bed in the office. It was more than a little jarring to see the room set up as a sleeping area again. She'd spent a lot of hours staring up at that ceiling, analyzing her pain and range of motion. Not to mention obsessing about her attraction to Mike and feeling sorry for herself. Lisa wanted to give herself a shake. She needed to stop thinking about that ancient history and focus on the present. It was time to load up Harley and pick up Pete.

At the care center, Lisa found Pete more than ready to leave. He was poised for departure, parked in a wheelchair with his suitcase packed and paperwork signed. All he needed was to be rolled out of the building.

Lisa smiled as she handed him Harley's leash. "Ready for some fresh air? It's cold out today."

He leaned over to pet Harley. "You have no idea."

"All right, let's go." Lisa pushed the wheelchair down the hallway. "You're going to have to help me figure out how you're going to get into the truck."

"No problem." As they approached the salmon pickup, he looked over his shoulder at her. "This is your truck?"

"It's my brother's. I'm borrowing it."

"Why is it pink? Does he sell makeup?"

Lisa giggled. "No, he's a lawyer, but I have to remember that the next time someone asks. I'll tell them Larry won it as a prize for selling the most lipstick. To be fair, he'd tell you in a stern, lawyerly tone of voice that it's *salmon*, not pink."

"Well, that makes all the difference then."

Lisa opened the passenger door and Harley leaped up into the cab. She turned to Pete. "You're next."

She looked at him for a moment, trying to figure out what to do. Finally, he reached out to take her hand and then leaned toward her as he stood up on one foot. She put her arm around his waist, which was more than a little awkward. Being so close to someone she didn't know was uncomfortable and seemed far too intimate, but nurses probably had to deal with this type of thing all the time. She needed to suck it up and try to behave like a professional. Underneath that coat and baggy shirt, Pete had some nice stomach muscles. He was deliciously warm, and whatever soap or shampoo he used smelled incredible.

Lisa struggled to return her attention to the task at hand and maneuver him closer to the truck so he could reach the passenger handle on the roof of the inside. He let go of her and dragged himself up into the cab next to Harley, who gave him a slurp on the cheek in greeting. Pete wiped the drool away. "Thanks for the moral support, buddy."

Lisa folded up the wheelchair and put it in the back of the truck along with Pete's suitcase and crutches. She came around to the driver's side, got in, and glanced at Pete, who was peering down at the floor.

She leaned over to see what he was looking at. "Don't worry. That's paint. This was my Dad's truck before it was Larry's. For years it was the hardware-store truck, and it turns out red paint doesn't come out of floor mats. Ever."

"Wow, I thought there'd been some type of ritual sacrifice right here in the salmon Dodge."

"The trucks of Lowell's Hardware have led strange and difficult lives."

"I guess so."

~

At the house, Lisa pulled into the driveway. The workmen had been instructed to park on the street because she needed to get Pete as close to the front door as possible. The walkway had been shoveled and because the sun had been out for a few days, the concrete was completely clear. Thankfully it wasn't slippery anymore, but the next time it snowed, it could easily turn into a skating rink. Lisa wasn't sure how she was going to deal with getting Pete out of the house when that happened, but she'd cross that icy bridge when she got to it.

Getting Pete out of the truck and into the house was complicated by Harley's enthusiasm about being back home. Lisa put her arm around Pete, helping him navigate the crutches while she held Harley's leash. Finally, Pete pushed her away and held onto the door handle of the truck while he balanced on his good foot. He took the leash from her and flicked it once. "Harley, sit."

The dog look startled, but slowly put his rear end on the ground and then wagged his tail a few times.

Lisa turned to look at Pete. "How on earth did you do that? He *never* sits."

"He knows the command, but he also knows you don't know that." Pete handed the leash back to her. "Make sure he keeps sitting while I get my act together."

"Okay." Lisa looked down at the dog. "You heard him. I'm wise to your game now."

Pete slowly made his way along the walkway and up the steps to the house. Lisa opened the door and he thumped inside, staring intently at the ground. Lisa knew how he must feel. Using the crutches still had to be painful and unnatural for him.

Taking a deep breath, he leaned against the wall to rest, and then turned his head to look around. "Holy shi..., I mean, this place is...I can't even think of the right word to describe it."

A crash came from upstairs and Lisa smiled. "I think the adjective you're looking for is *hideous*."

"No, that's not it at all. This house is remarkable...it's almost like a time capsule." He put the crutches back under his arms and went into the living room, taking in the carpet and curved couches with their elaborate matching kelly-green vine print. "I haven't seen a place like this since the sixties. It's like a childhood dream come to life."

"*Alice in Wonderland* has nothing on the Lowell family homestead."

"I can't believe you grew up here." He turned around and raised his eyebrows at her. "So where am I staying?"

At another banging noise from above, Lisa looked at the ceiling, then gestured toward the den. "My father's office is this way."

Pete dutifully followed her through the doorway. The huge old desk had been removed, replaced by an electric hospital bed, which was an odd modern anachronism in the ornate wood-paneled room.

Pete clumped over to the bar that ran the length of one side of the room and leaned against the cream-colored leather padding. "I have my own bar? You didn't mention that. This is like walking onto the set of a Rat Pack movie. I expect Dean Martin or Frank Sinatra to hunker up next to me and hand me a whiskey."

Lisa shrugged. "All I know is the contractors are worried about being able to get that gold watered-silk wallpaper off the wall. I guess that type of moiré wallpaper is coated and it doesn't want to leave quietly. Most of the rest of the wallpaper in the house is like that too. It's made to withstand The Apocalypse. The guys tried removing a little test patch in the hallway and they found out it only comes off in teeny-tiny pieces if you use a scraper. They're going to try a steamer next, but they're a little cranky about the whole thing. They wanted to just paint over it, but you're not supposed to paint wallpaper, so I told them no."

Pete moved behind the bar and looked up at the wall. "The mirrored backsplash over here is incredible."

"I'm glad you're having fun. Since you're staying in this room, the work on it is being back-burnered. You get to enjoy it in all its Rat Pack glory for a while."

He pointed to the opposite wall. "Look at all those books!"

"Don't get too excited. The bottom shelves are full of ancient hardware catalogs, but my mom's decorator bought some pretty leather-bound classics so the shelves would look more literary. I'm not sure they've ever been read. You could be the first to crack the bindings."

Pete made his way across the room and around the bed to examine his new library. "*Robinson Crusoe, The Count of Monte Cristo, Swiss Family Robinson*, and check this out, appropriately enough, we have both *Alice's Adventures in*

Wonderland and *Through the Looking Glass* on this shelf over here."

"There's also a TV behind the doors in that cabinet over there if you get tired of reading."

"After being trapped in a nursing home, I've had enough of TV for a while." Pete turned to look at her. "I can't believe how much better I feel already, being out of there. Thanks for letting me stay here. This place is great."

Lisa grinned. "Well, you are paying me rather handsomely. And I think you may be the first person to say nice things about this house in twenty years. It's very kind of you. I know this house is kind of strange, but it's home. Part of me feels sort of sick tearing it all apart, even though I know it's the right thing to do."

Pete went over to the bed, set his crutches aside, and sprawled out. A repetitive thumping began upstairs and he pointed at the ceiling. "I see what you mean about the noise."

"At least they're working." Lisa sat on the edge of the bed. "You look tired."

"I guess I am. I should have grabbed one of those books before I crash landed."

"Which one do you want?" Lisa walked to the shelf. "Alice, the Count, or something else?"

"The Count would be great."

Lisa handed him the book and sat down again. "I have to go to the store, so I need you to watch Harley. I'll close him in here with you, if that's okay. I'm sure he'll be fine, since he adores you."

"Sounds good." He glanced at the window. "I was too busy wrangling crutches outside and didn't notice it before, but that's a massive tree."

"It goes near the roof off my bedroom. My sister Lynn and I used to climb it to sneak in and out."

Pete looked back at her. "It must feel strange living here again."

"I've been trying to focus on the remodeling work, but to be honest, staying here has been a little overwhelming. It's like nostalgia overload. Everywhere I look I imagine younger versions of me or my brothers and sister running up and down hallways, or climbing that tree, or sneaking out the back door to do something we weren't supposed to do."

"It sounds like you had a great childhood."

"I guess I did, although I worked hard to forget everything about this place after my accident."

"Well, now you've been given the opportunity to remember before it's gone."

"I never thought of it that way."

"I'm sure I'll like it here. I mean, look at this room! It's the ultimate man cave."

You're right." Lisa chuckled. "No wonder my dad spent so much time in his office."

Chapter 8

Adjustments

Lisa went off to the grocery store gloriously free of Harley. It was so liberating to be able to drive somewhere without the dog. She'd had her doubts, but maybe this arrangement with Pete would work out okay after all. When she'd left, he'd seemed perfectly content reading his book with Harley curled up on the bed by his side.

The Save-a-Lot grocery store looked almost the same as it had when Lisa was growing up. The lack of competition was the not-very-secret entrepreneurial secret to business longevity in Alpine Grove. Certainly, Lowell's Hardware benefited from the fact that you had to drive a long way to find another store that would sell you a screwdriver. When you really needed something specific like a Phillip's head screwdriver, nothing else would do, and you'd pay whatever it cost to get one. All those small-town residents with unrelenting hardware needs had supported Lisa's family for a long time.

Lisa pushed her cart toward the produce section and began picking through limp-looking heads of lettuce in search of something that didn't look like it had been sitting in the bin for two weeks. She thought fondly of the gigantic, shiny white grocery where she'd shopped in Gleasonville. Maybe if she put the lettuce in the sink with some water, it would perk up a little.

She methodically continued down every aisle collecting supplies and pantry staples, stocking up so she had enough food to last a while. Unfortunately, she'd forgotten to ask Pete about his dietary preferences. She was supposed to be focusing on his recuperation, so he was going to have to eat healthy whether he liked it or not.

Grabbing a can of diced tomatoes, she put it in the cart and noticed Kat, who was arguing with another woman down by the seafood display. It looked like Maria, the woman Larry had been talking to at the bar when Lisa had waited around for him to sign the contracts.

Behind the two women, Bernie the singing butcher was happily conferring with Mrs. Sharpe about the merits of scallops, interspersing his commentary with a stirring rendition of "Octopus's Garden" by the Beatles. Lisa wasn't up for dealing with Bernie today. Maybe she'd skip the seafood.

Kat turned away from her friend and headed toward Lisa, who waved hello. Kat pushed her cart up next to Lisa's and parked it next to the canned goods. She picked up a can of garbanzo beans and gestured her greeting with the can. "Hi Lisa. How's Harley?"

"He's enjoying a nap at the moment." Lisa smiled politely at the woman with Kat, who threw a Twinkie into Kat's cart so forcefully that it bounced over a box of wine.

Kat gestured toward the other woman, who was wearing a skin-tight dress that was almost the same shade of pink as the curtains in the kitchen back at the house.

Kat said, "Lisa, I'm not sure you've met officially, but this is my friend Maria."

Maria flipped her long curly hair over her shoulder and put out her hand. "You were at the Soloan, weren't you? Kat is trying to get me to adopt the cat your dog found in the woods."

"I forgot Harley did that," Lisa said. "Is the cat okay?"

Kat said, "The vet says he's fine. We named him Quincy. Currently, he has broken out of his confinement in my bathroom and is probably fighting with my cat Tripod for space under my bed."

"She's just cranky because the cat is putting a crimp in her love life," Maria said.

Kat glared at Maria. "My love life is not the issue here. The problem is that Quincy and Tripod hate each other quite passionately and loudly. When I added Murphee into the feline mix at my house it was difficult, but that was nothing by comparison. These two cats want to kill each other. You, on the other hand, only have one cat. I think Scarlett needs a friend."

"She certainly doesn't need a *male* friend. If I can't have a boyfriend, neither can she."

"Larry wants to be your boyfriend," Kat said.

Maria put her hand on her hip. "You know that's not happening."

"I don't blame you," Lisa said.

"See what I mean! She should know." Maria said, pointing at Lisa.

Kat rested her arms on the cart. "I have to get back to work. Do you have what you need?"

"We can't go yet. I still need to get the party supplies we talked about," Maria said.

Kat said, "They don't sell that kind of thing here and I'm vetoing it anyway."

Maria turned to Lisa. "Do you want to come to Kat's party? It's going to be a huge blowout. I haven't been able to plan an event since I quit my last job and I'm going to pull out all the stops."

Lisa wasn't sure if she should say yes. "I, well, appreciate the invitation, but I'm not sure…"

Kat looked up. "You're more than welcome to come, although it might be a little, uh, I don't know how to put it…"

"The word you seek is *outstanding!*" Maria gave Lisa a knowing look. "Kat is a recluse, and if it weren't for me, I don't think she'd ever leave the house. Half the women in Alpine Grove are going to be there. I'm putting all my party-planning prowess into action and it's going to be incredible. You don't want to miss it."

Lisa said, "When is the event?"

"Saturday, February twenty-second, at the Enchanted Moose. We're booking a room in the convention area because I need space to do what I want to do. And it gives Kat a month to recover before the wedding."

"It may take that long," Kat said, leaning more heavily on her cart.

Maria widened her eyes at Lisa. "So are you in? Shall I add you to the invitation list?"

"Thank you. That sounds nice," Lisa said. "I should still be here in town then, unless an offer for my parents' house magically falls out of the sky."

"I'll provide the details on the invitation. In the meantime, start thinking about your costume," Maria said.

"Costume?" Lisa said.

Kat dropped her head onto her hands on the cart and groaned, "Nooo."

"I've been thinking about a sci-fi and fantasy theme. Robots, spaceships, aliens, and maybe a few elves and dwarves too," Maria said. "I looked at some book covers and some of those Viking ladies really know how to work a suit of armor. I could look seriously hot in one of those outfits."

Kat stood up straight. "No! There is absolutely no way I am dressing like some axe-wielding woman on a sexist Frazetta poster that you'd find hanging in some horny teenager's room. Absolutely no way."

Maria whispered to Lisa, "We're still fine-tuning a few little party details."

"I said no costumes and I *mean* it!" Kat said.

Lisa said, "I should get back to Harley. It was nice to see you. Good luck with the party planning."

"Did you leave Harley alone?" Kat asked. "Does that mean he's over his separation anxiety?"

"No, I left him at home with Pete. They are best buddies now. It's really sweet," Lisa said.

Maria pulled a can of cranberry sauce off the shelf and threw it into the cart. "Waitaminute. Who is Pete?"

Kat put the cranberry sauce back on the shelf. "He's the guy Harley rescued at Snow Grove."

"And this guy Pete is *living* with you?" Maria threw her arms in the air in a gesture of exasperation. "How long have you been in Alpine Grove? Two weeks? And you boarded your dog with Kat, right? I don't believe it. This has to be some type of new record."

Lisa shook her head. "I'm not sure what you mean. Pete is renting a room from me while he recovers from his knee surgery."

Maria shook her head and turned around, mumbling something that sounded like unbelievable, but with a few extra syllables added.

Kat smiled as Maria walked down the aisle away from them. "Don't worry about her. I'm glad Harley and Pete are doing okay."

"I guess I'll see you at the party."

"If you can find a way to get me out of it, I'd be grateful."

Lisa laughed. "Sorry, but as the guest of honor, I think you're on your own."

∼

Lisa returned to the house, where rolls of old carpet were sitting in the snow in the front yard. The flooring-removal program was obviously proceeding and the ugly wall-to-wall was being ripped out of the upstairs bedrooms.

She grabbed a few grocery bags and went up the walkway to the house. She opened the door and was greeted by ferocious barking as Harley came around the corner and skidded to a stop in front of her, wagging happily. She lifted the bags away from his nose as she went toward the kitchen. "Sorry, not for you."

In the kitchen, Pete was sitting at the table with two of the workmen. They all looked up at her and Pete raised his beer bottle toward her in greeting. It was suspiciously quiet in the house, and she narrowed her eyes at the group. "Where's Craig?"

"He had to go home," Pete said, then tipped the neck of his beer bottle toward the man next to him. "Luke had beer, and we all agreed that it must be happy hour somewhere."

Lisa tried to remember what the doctor had said about Pete's pain killers in combination with alcohol. You weren't supposed to mix them with alcohol, were you? Trying to rein in her irritation, she said evenly, "Luke, Rod, since you're both able bodied, why don't you help me bring in the rest of the groceries?"

Pete said, "Harley, come!" and the dog trotted over to his side. Pete leaned over to praise Harley effusively for his incomparable brilliance while Lisa and the two men went outside to collect the food. After loading herself and the guys down with many bags, Lisa returned to the kitchen and placed her groceries on the counter. In less than a day, Pete had somehow managed to teach Harley to come when called. Sure, *now* the dog was finally obedient.

After helping Lisa, Luke and Rod seemed to realize that their impromptu beer fiesta was over, so they quietly gathered their things and scuttled out of the house. Pete peeled a strip of the label off his beer bottle, curling it around his finger.

Lisa continued putting away groceries in silence while Pete sipped his beer. The more she thought about it, the more she was convinced there was no way he should be drinking while he was on medication. What if he was an alcoholic? She'd never thought about that. What if he'd left the police force because he had some terrible drinking problem? Maybe that's why his wife divorced him too. She was such an idiot, taking in a stranger she barely knew. Compassion was one thing. Being completely stupid was another.

From behind her, Pete said, "What are you upset about over there?"

Lisa put a box of pasta into the pantry with a thump. "I'm not upset. I'm putting away food. What do you want for dinner?"

"Nobody puts away food that loudly unless they're pissed off about something. What is it?"

"I'm not pissed off."

"Yes, you are."

Lisa turned around. "Okay, fine. I'm worried that you shouldn't be drinking while you're taking fistfuls of drugs every couple of hours."

"I was being social."

Lisa shook a can of beans at him. "But you shouldn't be doing that. It's bad for you. Didn't you read all the warning stickers on those bottles of pills?"

"Hey, I'm off the hard-core stuff and Luke offered me a beer. What was I going to say? No?"

"Yes, of *course* you should have said no!"

"I didn't want to act like a jerk. I have to see these guys here every day."

"Well, they should be working, not drinking beer with you." Lisa threw a bag of frozen corn into the freezer, where it landed with a thud. "Do they always do this when Craig leaves?"

"How should I know?" Pete ruffled the fur on Harley's neck. "I think you're overreacting a little."

"No I'm not! It's my house. And I don't want to have to call nine one one because you've keeled over from a drug interaction the first day you're here."

"That's not going to happen, and it's not what you're really worried about, is it?"

Lisa stashed the last of the vegetables in the crisper drawer and sat down at the table across from him. "I suppose not."

"What's eating you?"

"You're not an alcoholic or addicted to something, are you? Because if you've got some huge problem I don't know about, it would be good to find out about it now."

"I had two sips of beer, Lisa. I don't think I need to enter a treatment facility yet. It's fine."

Lisa placed her palms on the table and leaned forward. "I'm supposed to take care of you while you recover. I'm responsible for you."

"I'm responsible for me. You're not my mother, and I promise I won't die on your watch or even operate any heavy machinery." He handed her the beer bottle. "You can have the rest. But if I decide I want to have a beer to improve interpersonal relations with the construction crew, you need to not lose your shirt about it."

"Lose my shirt? Are you saying I should strip? What are you talking about?"

"Subtract a letter."

"Huh? Oh, all right. I get it. Very funny." Lisa took a sip of the beer. "Yuck. This stuff is awful."

"I didn't say it was *good* beer. You really should relax a little. What do you do for fun?"

"Fun?"

Pete twirled the bottle cap on the table. "Yes, fun. It's that thing that sometimes happens when you're having a good time."

"I don't know. What do you do?"

"Don't you have hobbies?"

"Not really. I've been too busy dealing with other things. Do you? How would you respond to that question?"

"I'm working on it."

"What do you mean working on it?" Lisa put down the bottle. "Who works on fun?"

"I do." He pointed at her. "After I retired, I was just like you. I'd spent all my time working and I had no hobbies. I had absolutely no idea what to do with myself once I had no job. So I decided to work on having more fun."

"How?"

"I tried new things to see where I might find some fun. You never know where fun might be lurking."

"What new things?"

"Well, I got up to 's,' which was skiing, and we all know how that turned out. It was fun at first, and then it wasn't fun at all."

"What do you mean you got to 's'? Are you saying you alphabetized your fun?"

"Sort of. Rather than agonize over figuring out what to do or prioritizing what to do first, I made a list of twenty-six things, starting with 'a' and going to 'z.'"

Lisa leaned forward and tilted the mouth of the beer bottle toward him. "Okay, now I'm dying of curiosity. What did you do for 'a'? Become an acrobat? An astronaut?"

"Do I look like an acrobat?"

"No, but I can't think of anything. Fly an airplane?"

"I'm not that ambitious and it wasn't a big deal. I took an art class, if you must know."

"Really?" Lisa took another sip of beer and set down the bottle. "So you're an artist?"

"Nope. I found out I'm even worse at painting than I am at skiing. I'm terrible, but the experience was still fun."

"I suppose taking an art class could be kind of fun."

He grinned as he balanced the bottle cap on his index finger. "Having fun doesn't have to be hard. You should try it sometime."

"Maybe I will." Lisa drank the last of the beer and stood up. "But first, it's dinner time. I'm looking forward to cooking, so the letter 'c' is handled, at least for tonight."

"You're going out of order."

"My liking the idea of cooking again benefits you."

"Good point. Only twenty-five more letters to go."

~

The next morning Lisa got up, let Harley out, and ate breakfast. No noise had come from her father's office all morning and she was starting to wonder if Pete was okay in there. What if he had fallen out of bed or tripped? On the other hand, maybe he was a night owl who slept in late. How would she know? It was his first night at the house. So far all she knew was that he wasn't a great artist and he liked spaghetti.

Lisa couldn't decide if she should interrupt his privacy or not. This situation was so strange. When her kids were growing up, she'd had no problem barging into any room at any time. It was her house and her kids. But roommate etiquette was more complicated than that and she wasn't sure what to do.

She looked over at Harley, who was slowly wandering around the kitchen with his nose to the floor, making sure no kibbles of dog food had magically leaped out of the cabinet while he wasn't paying attention.

Lisa looked up at the clock on the wall. The workmen were going to be arriving soon, so Pete was about to be forcibly awakened before too long. Maybe she'd check to see if he wanted some breakfast before the endless pounding on the ceiling began.

She tapped lightly on the door and didn't hear anything. Harley looked up at her and tilted his head. Turning the knob as quietly as possible, she opened the door and peeked inside the room. Harley shoved the door open with his nose and ran over to the bed. The curtains were shut so there wasn't much light, but Pete was lying with his leg elevated on pillows. He reached down to pet Harley's head. "Hey, you."

Lisa walked to the bed. "Are you feeling okay?"

"Yeah."

"You don't look okay." She noted the dark circles under his eyes and the tightness of his jaw. There was no doubt he was in pain. "Did you get any sleep last night?"

"Not really. Everything started to hurt."

"Didn't you take your painkillers?"

"Yeah, but my leg was stiff and achy. It felt like my knee was swelling up. Then I felt hot and sweaty, so I grabbed pillows from the couch and went to the bathroom to splash water on my face. I did the whole elevating-my-leg thing, but I couldn't get comfortable. This brace is horrible." He closed his eyes. "Doing anything is so complicated and takes forever."

Lisa reached over to place her palm on his forehead. "I don't think you have a fever. That's good."

He opened his eyes again and gazed at her intently. "Who put in all those handles?"

"My dad. After my accident, he was desperate to do something to help. When you own a hardware store, you have access to a whole lot of handrails. My mom said he went overboard. She was a little annoyed about how many he put in, but I thought it was sweet."

"I can't tell you how much I want to take a real shower."

"When I was recuperating here, I used to love to sit in that shower for ages, letting the warm water run over me. I'll dredge up the shower stool. I'm pretty sure it's still in the garage."

He shut his eyes again and took a deep breath. "I'm never going to be able to run again, am I?"

Lisa rearranged the pillows under his knee. "You need to ask your doctor about that. Everyone is different."

"I did a half marathon last year."

"Was that for 'h' or 'm' or something?" Lisa stroked the top of his foot gently. "I'm sure your feet will be back in running shoes before you know it. Or at least walking shoes."

"I've always been active, but now there are all these things I never even thought about before that are now a huge deal. Showering. Stairs. Pants. Scratching the itch on the bottom of my foot." He gestured toward her. "You said you haven't skied since your accident."

Lisa sat down on the edge of the bed and looked into Pete's face. He really needed a shave. "That wasn't because I couldn't. It was because I didn't want to."

"Why? All I can think about it all the things I might not ever be able to do again. Like never skiing again? That idea makes me so furious I can barely stand it. I want to punch that snowboarder who cut me off."

Lisa put her hand on his. "I understand how you feel."

"Last night, I was lying here staring at the ceiling getting more and more angry. It's not fair."

She squeezed his hand and smiled. "I thought you were Mr. Meditation and all that."

"Sometimes it doesn't work. I finally came to terms with having to retire by knowing that I could enjoy the rest of my life finding fun and interesting things to do."

"Why did you retire early if you didn't want to?"

"Medical reasons. I was shot during a drug bust. It's a long story." He moved his hand, indicating the hospital bed. "Suffice it to say, this isn't my first contact with the medical community. My insurance paperwork could fill a room."

"I didn't know about that, but you said you already know that a big part of recovery is mental. It sounds like you had a positive attitude about your retirement."

"Eventually, I guess. It took a while and I'm certainly no saint. But this is different because I might never be the same as I was before." He looked into her eyes. "That's why you never skied again, isn't it?"

"I've never put it exactly that way, but I guess so. It's not so much that I was badly injured at Snow Grove, but that I felt like I'd lost most of the person I had been. One day I thought I was going to the Olympics, then the next I thought I was going to be a paraplegic without any mobility at all. Obviously, that turned out not to be the case, but I still lost the life I expected to have, so I did everything I could to try to forget about what might have been."

"You were paralyzed?"

"Temporarily, but going through that experience completely changed who I was. I had to readjust and reconsider how I was going to live and how I was going to approach everything for the rest of my life."

"I guess that's a lot to deal with at that age."

"It was, and I definitely didn't handle it well. But I recovered, and you will too." Lisa put her hand on his again. "As long as I have any say in it, which I do, since you're a captive audience."

His mouth curved into a half smile. "Yeah, I'm too slow to escape."

"The first few weeks are going to be awful. But I promise it gets better. Just do your physical therapy exercises religiously."

Pete moved his foot in circles in both directions. "Okay, this is me strengthening my ankle."

The front door slammed and Harley stood up and barked a few times to acknowledge the interlopers. Lisa smiled at Pete. "I was going to ask you if you wanted something to eat before they got here. Too late."

"That's okay. I'm glad you stopped by." He struggled to sit up straighter. "I'll eat later. Now I think I'll try to figure out the shower. That should take up most of the rest of the morning."

"You know you're not supposed to get your incision wet, right?"

"I know."

"I recommend plastic wrap. I bought a huge new roll of it yesterday." Lisa stood up. "I'll go get it and find that shower stool for you."

"Thanks." Pete waggled his eyebrows suggestively. "Those guys are going to really wonder what kind of kinky stuff you're up to with all that plastic wrap."

"Don't worry. I'll never tell."

~

Over the next two weeks, Lisa adjusted to having a roommate and adapted to the routines required to care for Pete. She fed him, retrieved things he needed, helped him with difficult articles of clothing, did laundry and other household tasks, and took him to his physical-therapy appointments.

The day of his first appointment, the pretty winter weather decided to take a nosedive, so she and Pete had a snow-versus-crutches adventure. The effort to get him into the Alpine Grove Care Center building involved a lot of slipping on Pete's part and clutching on Lisa's part, just to keep him upright.

By the time they finally made it inside unscathed, Pete was laughing. "I'm glad I don't know anyone here. That was humiliating."

"Sure, it's fine for you, but *everyone* knows me." Lisa waved at a woman in a wheelchair who was pointing at her from the end of the hallway. "That's my third-grade teacher, Mrs. Louden."

True to his word, many days Pete sat and helped Lisa go through copious amounts of Lowell-family memorabilia. She set some items aside to take to Betty so she could look at them while Pete was at physical therapy. The last two visits with

Betty had been just as frustrating as the others, and Lisa was running out of ideas and patience with her aunt. And Betty was more interested in talking to Harley than explaining to Lisa what she wanted from the house.

Lisa had put classified ads in the newspaper to begin selling the furniture, so some large items like the living room couches and her father's desk had gone to new homes. The house seemed strangely empty without the larger furniture, but it did make it easier for Pete to maneuver around on crutches.

Finally the day arrived that the carpet in the living room had to come out. Craig hung huge sheets of plastic on the doorways in an effort to mitigate the inevitable dust storm from the horribly decayed carpet pad. Lisa, Pete, and Harley hung out in Pete's room, hiding from the filth. Harley napped while Lisa and Pete read and played cards.

Lisa put down her hand. "Gin. Read 'em and weep."

"At least we're not playing strip poker. I'd be naked by now."

"Not to mention cold."

Pete got up, collected his crutches, and went to the bookshelf. "I'm tired of getting whupped by you in cards."

"You must be running out of classics to read. I've never met such a voracious reader in my life."

"The hardware catalogs are starting to look pretty good."

Lisa got up and walked across the room to stand next to him in front of the faux-leather-bound books. "Are you feeling up to a trip to the Alpine Grove library?"

He turned to look at her. "You mean a real library?"

"Yes, we do have books in Alpine Grove." Lisa smiled and pointed at his bare legs. "But you might have to wear pants."

He followed her gaze downward. "But shorts or sweatpants are so much easier with the brace."

"I know, but you'll feel better being out and about in normal clothes."

"I like being comfortable."

Lisa picked a pair of shorts off a chair and threw it into the laundry basket. "The first time I was able to wear high heels again after my accident, I felt so much better. You'll see."

"Sorry, but I draw the line at heels. Is that why you have so many shoes?"

"Lots of women like shoes, and I'm no exception."

Pete stared at her without blinking or saying anything. A muscle in his jaw twitched and he was obviously trying not to smile.

Lisa tugged at her earring. "Okay, maybe my shoe fetish got a little out of hand. Mike used to call me the Imelda Marcos of Gleasonville."

"I guess you've got the letter 's' pretty well covered with shoe shopping."

"Very funny." Lisa picked up a sock and threw it into the basket. "That reminds me, you said you made it to 's,' but what were you going to do for the letter 't'?"

"Tae Kwon Do, but that's out." He shrugged. "I haven't thought of anything yet."

"You could make a terrarium."

"Why would I want to do that?"

"It's fun. That's the whole point of the list, right?"

"The word terrarium is not one I've ever associated with the word fun."

"Hey, setting up a terrarium was fun when I was in elementary school. Maybe we can pick up a fishbowl on the way back from the library."

"Where are you supposed to get plants in February?"

"Hmm, that's a good question. We might have to work on that."

"If I have to put poor, unsuspecting plants under glass in the name of fun, you need to at least start a list. You have twenty-five letters unaccounted for at this point."

"I'll get around to that sooner or later."

Pete went over to his bed and rearranged the pillows for his leg before settling in. "Are you happy?"

"I'm fine."

"That's not what I asked." He waved his hand at her. "Why are you picking up my clothes? You don't have to do that."

"Well, you can't, and I don't want Harley chewing up any more of your socks." She glanced over at the dog, who was wagging at the sound of his name. "Yes, I'm talking about you."

"He's working on it. The chewed sock was when he got a little too enthusiastic." Pete snapped his fingers to get the dog's attention and pointed at a t-shirt hanging off the closet door knob. "Harley, go get it."

Harley strolled over, grabbed the shirt in his mouth and ambled to the bed. Pete took the shirt and gave the dog a treat. "Good boy."

Lisa put her hand on her hip. "I don't understand why I can't even get that animal to sit, and you're the magic dog trainer."

"We've spent a lot of time together. While you're dealing with contractors, errands, and all the other house stuff, he's in here with me."

"I guess I haven't spent as much time with him as you have." Lisa sat down on the end of the bed and looked down at Harley. "Is he sharing his secrets with you?"

"Giving him lots of treats would be secret number one," Pete said. "Harley, sit."

The dog sat politely and wagged his tail a few times. Lisa glared at Pete. "He doesn't sit when I say sit."

"That's because he knows you don't mean it."

Lisa frowned. "But I *do* mean it."

"It doesn't sound like it. You can't just say 'Harley sit' in that wishy-washy tone of voice and expect him to believe you. It sounds like you're asking a question, not telling him what you want him to do. Plus, he's not stupid. He knows you don't carry around treats, so he has zero motivation to do what you want. You aren't going to follow through with your command and correct him or reward him when he does something right."

"I suppose."

Pete pointed at her. "You didn't answer my question though. Are you happy?"

"Why do you keep asking me that? I'm probably as happy as anyone else." She glanced at Pete, who was giving her one of his skeptical 'I'm not buying it' looks. "Okay, maybe not. I miss my kids, but I promised I wouldn't call them more than once a week."

"On Sundays. I know. You plan your whole day around it."

"The thing is I'm thinking about them constantly. It's like this little nagging voice in my head that won't shut up. I'm either worrying about them or wondering what they're up to. It drives me nuts that I don't know what they're doing every day anymore."

"Maybe you need to find more stuff of your own to think about."

Lisa glared at him. "Is this where you tell me to make the list again?"

"Hey, if you're happy, you don't have to worry about the list. If you're not, maybe you should stop putting it off. It's not like I have a lot to do, so I can help or go places with you, assuming you don't go in for things like acrobat, of course."

Lisa giggled. "Do I look like an acrobat?"

"Getting away from the noise and dust here wouldn't be so bad either."

"You do seem to be feeling better. I guess we could go to the library and do whatever my 'a' thing is." Lisa made a wry face. "I can't think of anything that begins with 'a.' This always happens whenever I try to think about it. It's like my mind goes blank. Or I think of things like going on an African safari, which is something that, while fun, I can't realistically do at the moment."

"True. I'm talking about smaller things. How about make an aquarium? You can have my fishbowl and then we won't have to worry about plants. Just a goldfish."

"I don't want a fish. And where would I get one in Alpine Grove?"

"Yeah, I suppose that doesn't work. I suggest we veto the fishbowl entirely. You help me come up with a new 't' idea and I'll help you with 'a.'"

"Okay, 't' is for train a dog, which you've already done."

"Well, training is never done, but I suppose that having a tibial plateau fracture counts as more 't' activity. Even though that wasn't fun, it led me to being here with you, which is fun. So I can move on to 'u' without feeling like I'm cheating."

Lisa looked at him. "You think being with me is fun? Really?"

"Sure I do. You've also been sympathetic, even when I'm being a big whiny baby."

"Nobody has ever said I was fun before. Well, except maybe Bev. But she's known me forever, and most of the time she says I'm a stick-in-the-mud, not fun."

"I'd like to meet her sometime. Maybe she can be part of 'b'. In the meantime, how about buy an anklet for 'a'? Those are kinda sexy."

Lisa twirled a lock of hair around her finger and gave him a sly smile. "A beaded one would be pretty, particularly with the right shoes."

"I'm sure you can find something in your vast collection."

"For 'u' how about we walk in the rain with an umbrella? Spring is coming, so it won't be long."

"Okay, but you'll have to hold the umbrella."

"All right. It's a deal."

Chapter 9

Solving Problems

The next day after lunch, Lisa took Pete to the library, telling him she would wait with Harley in the truck for as long as he wanted to browse. Lisa pulled up in front of the building, which was a two-story brick edifice built in the twenties with cast-concrete decorations around the arched doorways and windows.

Lisa turned off the truck and glanced at Pete. "I forgot about the steps." She pointed out the window at the two long sets of concrete steps that went up to the huge wooden doors.

"I'm not sure I'm up for that. And if there's any ice at all, I'm doomed."

"There's got to be another way inside for deliveries. I've never gone around back, but the building is kind of set into a hill." She patted Harley's chest. "Wait here with Harley for a minute. I'll be right back."

Lisa got out, ran up the steps to the library, and went inside. A woman with curly reddish-blonde hair sat amid piles of books. She smiled politely at Lisa. "May I help you?"

"Do you have any way to get into the building that doesn't involve stairs? My, um, friend, he's on crutches and needs something to read."

The librarian stood up. "Yes. Technically, the building is considered accessible because you can get in the back door and we have an elevator if he wants to go downstairs."

"That's perfect. How do I get to the back?"

"Go around the block and then go down the alley. It dead-ends at the building. There's not really any parking back there, but you can drop him off and I'll open the door for you." She paused. "He doesn't have a problem with dogs, does he? My dog Rosa likes to sleep back there in my office. She's very friendly though."

"Pete loves dogs. He's sitting out there in the truck getting drooled on by my dog, Harley."

Lisa ran back out to the truck and got in. "You're in! There's a sneaky back entrance. I had no idea!"

"When was the last time you went to the library?"

"I don't know. I've been busy."

"So you've said."

She started up the truck and said. "I guess you'll need to get a library card too. Maybe I'll take Harley for a walk, so he doesn't get too squirrelly."

"At least one of us won't be squirrelly."

"You're being impatient again. Look at how much better you're doing than you were two weeks ago. Before you know it, you'll be walking Harley." Lisa parked the truck behind the library and waved at the librarian, who was holding the back door open.

Lisa got out, grabbed the crutches from the back of the truck, and helped Pete get settled on them. "Have fun. I'll see you in a little while."

"Take your time. Once I've found enough books, I'll hang out and read."

The librarian held the door open for Pete. "I'm Jan. I'd be happy to show you where everything is."

Lisa watched as they disappeared into the building, feeling suddenly alone. She turned to Harley. "It looks like it's just you and me again. Let's find a place to park and take a stroll around town. Maybe I'll let you annoy Larry too." Harley wagged his tail to indicate his approval of the proposed plan.

The walk around town proved to be more complicated than Lisa had anticipated. It was a pretty winter day and it seemed that most of the residents of Alpine Grove had gone outside to see the sun before it disappeared again. Lisa was stopped by almost everyone she walked by, asking how she was, where her kids were going to college, how her parents liked their new house, and how her siblings were doing.

The months after Christmas were the slow retail season, so apparently none of these people had been visiting Lowell's Hardware to get the lowdown on her family. Of course, she hadn't been to the hardware store either, but for different reasons.

No one seemed interested in adopting Harley either. It was too bad because he'd been so good about sitting next to her too. How could people not notice what a sweet dog he was?

By the time Lisa made it back to the truck, she was feeling anxious about having ditched Pete for so long at the library. It was his first trip anywhere, other than trips to physical therapy, and he had to be exhausted by now.

Lisa parked in front of the library and encouraged Harley to behave himself for five minutes while she went inside to let Pete know she had finally returned. She ran up the stairs and opened the door. People reading in a row of comfy chairs all looked up at her. Maybe she was breathing a little hard. Somehow she'd managed to forget about her exercise program. Again.

She turned her head, looking for Pete. A burst of laughter came from the direction of the librarian's desk and then a shushing noise and giggles. She started across the room, heading toward Pete, who was sitting at a table. Jan, the librarian, was leaning over him pointing at something in a book, and whispering.

Lisa stopped walking. Well gee, weren't they looking all cute and cuddly together? And Pete certainly didn't look tired at all. They probably didn't want her interrupting their little tête-à-tête.

Turning around, Lisa ducked behind a stack of books, pretending to look interested in the latest releases in the horror section. She picked one up and put it back. How disgusting. Even the cover was disturbing.

Lisa let her arms drop to her sides. How stupid was this? Was she *actually* jealous that Pete was enjoying hanging out with the pretty librarian? Pete was handsome and she enjoyed his company, but sheesh, she wasn't fourteen anymore. She was behaving like an idiot.

She straightened her shoulders and walked back out of the aisle of books and up to the table. "Hi, Pete. Sorry it took me so long."

He looked up at her, gathered up his crutches, and pointed at a bag of books. "Could you get those?"

Jan patted Pete on the shoulder. "It was great meeting you. When you're done with those, I'll show you the rest of that series. I know you'll like it."

Pete's brilliant blue eyes sparkled with mirth. "Oh, I'll definitely be back. You can count on it."

Lisa clutched her bag of books and said to Pete, "I'll take these out to the truck and drive around back again."

He nodded and Jan walked toward the back of the library to open the doors for him. Lisa tried to shove down the feeling of annoyance that seemed to bubble up out of nowhere. She had nothing to be annoyed about. The librarian was just being nice and Pete was certainly well read, so they undoubtedly had a lot to talk about.

Lisa shoved open the doors to go back outside, and the blast of cold air that hit her face was refreshing. Harley stared up at her as she descended the steps back to the truck. She got in and turned to Harley. "I think your favorite person found a new girlfriend who likes reading as much as he does."

Harley didn't seem to have any input on the topic, so Lisa started up the truck and drove around to the back. Pete was leaning on the back wall of the building, waiting. The librarian had gone back inside, which was a relief to Lisa.

As she parked the truck, she gave herself a mental shake. Pete was her roommate and being jealous of a librarian was beyond pathetic. It was so easy to imagine Bev ranting about how Lisa didn't get out enough, but the idea of having any more awful first dates made her want to crawl in a hole and hide.

Disgusted with her thoughts, Lisa smiled at Pete as she got out of the truck. She helped him in, threw the crutches in the back, and returned to the cab.

Pete put his arm around Harley and gave him a bear hug. "Did you have a fun walk?"

"He was very good and has now met most of the people who live in the greater Alpine Grove area."

"Wow, you had big day."

Lisa glanced at him as she turned down the alley. "How was the library? You looked like you were having a good time with the librarian."

Pete peered over Harley's head at her. "She's probably one of the smartest women I've ever met. I don't think she's forgotten anything she's ever read. It's wild. Apparently, she has an incredible semantic memory. I've never met anyone like that before."

"Interesting."

"Is something bothering you?"

Lisa glanced away from the road momentarily to look at him. "Not at all. I'm driving."

"You have an extremely expressive face, you know. It's obvious when you lie."

"Maybe it is to you, but you have all those interrogation skills that most people don't."

"I usually look at a person's mouth more than any other feature when I'm trying to read someone's emotions. Yours reveals a lot."

Lisa briefly glanced away from the road to look at him again. "Stop staring at me."

He leaned over and pulled a book out of the bag. "Fine. I'll be reading then."

"Fine."

~

After they returned to the house, Pete retreated to his room. Lisa was more than a little embarrassed about snapping at Pete on the drive home. She decided that since she already was in a bad mood, she'd tackle the conversation with Craig about the wallpaper-removal project. He kept whining that it wasn't going well, and she'd been avoiding the inevitable fight about it. Listening to his lectures was like enduring the sound of fingernails scraping on a chalkboard and somehow every conversation with him turned into an argument.

His latest lament was about the wallpaper in Larry's old room. It was a hideous harvest-gold pattern coated with some type of plastic that, according to Craig, was impervious to steam machines and all known chemicals typically used to remove wallpaper. Craig was worried about how this slowdown was going to affect his schedule. Lisa was more worried that the wallpaper would remain in tact and end up as an archaeological find that would mystify scientists in the year 2310.

After they discussed the project for a while, she encouraged Craig to move on to something else that wouldn't affect his precious schedule. If the wallpaper was giving him so much heartburn, she'd have to figure out something else. Maybe she'd deal with it herself. It wasn't like she wasn't capable of wielding a paint scraper. This wasn't exactly rocket science they were dealing with, after all.

She was fed up with workmen and all their whining. Half the time someone or another who was supposed to show up didn't. Then when they did show, they didn't want to work on the house. Why couldn't Craig keep these guys in line? That was supposed to be his job and was why she was paying him so much money. The endless problems and complaints made her want to scream.

Completely sick of the house and the constant noise, she stomped back down the stairs and turned down the hallway toward her father's office, almost mowing down Pete in the process. She reached out to grab his shoulders. "I'm so sorry. Are you okay?"

He leaned on the wall to steady himself and rearranged his crutches. "I'm fine."

Realizing that she was still clutching him, Lisa dropped her hands to her sides. "Do you want something to eat? I was just coming downstairs to see if you're hungry."

"It's kind of early for dinner, isn't it? I heard you and Craig yelling at each other."

"I wasn't yelling. We were having a discussion. Do you want some ice cream? I'll bring you a bowl if you let me stay in your room until everyone leaves."

He chuckled. "That bad, huh?"

"It may require chocolate sauce too. I'll be right back."

Lisa made the sundaes and even added a few candy sprinkles for color. Pete didn't need to know that the label on the container indicated they may have been purchased for a birthday party sometime in the early eighties. Sugar didn't go bad, did it?

She pushed open the door to the office. Harley was on his dog bed in the corner, snoring quietly. The fact that he didn't even stir indicated that the socializing in town had worn him out.

Pete was lying on his bed with a book. He set it aside when Lisa sat down next to him and handed him the bowl

of ice cream. Taking the dish, he said, "Impressive. You really went all out."

"It was necessary. Craig drives me nuts. He and his all-important schedule."

"So you've said. If you don't like him so much, why don't you fire him?"

"Do you know how hard it was to find a general contractor in the first place? I called everybody. No one wants to work on a remodel at this time of year. Half of the contractors in Alpine Grove don't work at all in the winter, so they don't even answer the phone. Craig was practically the only person willing to talk to me because he knew my family."

"I guess that would be a problem." Pete put a spoonful of ice cream into his mouth and smiled. "Yum. This is good."

"I also felt like I should apologize for being unpleasant to you in the truck."

"Ice cream is a great peace offering."

Lisa laughed as she licked her spoon. "It really is."

They ate silently for a few moments, and Lisa focused on her own thoughts and how much she adored ice cream. Even in February, there was nothing like frozen comfort food to improve her mood after a bad day.

Pete put down his spoon and said, "Are you going to tell me why you were upset? Did you see someone in town that you didn't like or something?"

Lisa took his empty bowl and set it with hers on the side table. She wasn't sure what to say. Was she really gutsy enough to tell the truth? "It wasn't that. I...well...I guess I spend so much time with you, it was a little funny seeing you laughing with that librarian."

"Funny?"

"Not funny, ha-ha funny. Just odd, I guess." Lisa looked into his eyes. "I feel like an idiot saying this because obviously you see people all the time."

"Like George, my sexy yet slightly sadistic physical therapist? I'll grant you that he's hot and I'm pretty sure he's gay, but I think he knows I'm not interested."

Lisa giggled. "I'm glad I'm not the only one who noticed. He *is* definitely hot! Oh well, it's another loss for the ladies of Alpine Grove."

Pete put his hand on hers. "I might be interested in someone else anyway."

"I know. That librarian Jan is really pretty. And I bet she knows as much Shakespeare as you do."

He slid his hand up her arm to the base of her neck, glanced at her mouth, and gazed into her eyes. "That's not who I was thinking of actually."

Lisa was too stunned to say anything, and he curved his hand around the back of her neck, never taking his eyes off hers. He caressed the nape of her neck gently as he pulled her head forward slowly toward him. Lisa closed her eyes and let him kiss her. His lips were warm and soft, and the feel of his fingers curling through her hair was delicious, sending little tingles galloping down her spine.

It had been more than two years since Lisa had kissed a man. Part of her was terrified, while the other part was desperate to jump on top of Pete and have her way with him. But that probably wouldn't be a good idea for many reasons, not the least of which was that she'd probably re-injure his knee.

Finally he pulled away from her and Lisa opened her eyes. "I, uh, I wasn't expecting that."

"I know, but I've wanted to kiss you for so long. It was probably a bad idea though."

After her divorce and the bad dates, Lisa was getting used to rejection. "Well, there's always the librarian."

"That's not what I meant." He took her hand in both of his. "You've told me how you're not interested in getting involved with anyone. I should respect that, and I'm not good at these things anyway."

Lisa leaned over and gave him a chaste kiss on the lips. "Don't sell yourself short. I can tell you one thing you're exceptionally good at."

"That's kind of you to say." He ran his fingertips along her jaw. "And so you know, the librarian spent quite a bit of time telling me about her trip to Russia with her boyfriend. It sounds like he's almost as pretty as my physical therapist. Apart from that, I think you are way sexier than Jan is. Seeing you every day has become more…difficult."

"I know what you mean."

"But I'm serious that I'm probably the last person you'd want to get involved with. I don't want to screw up our friendship."

Intellectually, Lisa was relieved. It was true. They'd been getting along well since Pete had moved in, his recovery was progressing, and she considered him a good friend now. She bit her lower lip and looked into his eyes, which had turned deep blue, like the color of a lake instead of the sky. "I suppose you're right. We should just be friends."

He moved his arm to pull her closer to him again and whispered, "Or maybe I'm an idiot. I could be completely wrong," before pressing his lips to hers again.

A few long and very pleasurable moments later, Lisa gasped for breath and released her hold on him. "I think there may be some issues with this whole being-friends idea."

"No kidding." Pete ran his fingers through his hair. "There is nothing either good or bad, but thinking makes it so."

"Shakespeare?"

"Hamlet. It seemed appropriate."

"I really need to borrow some of your books."

Pete gave her another kiss. "Any time."

~

By the time she'd finished dinner, Lisa's hormones had settled down enough for normal brain function to return, and she had an idea about the wallpaper problem. After Pete and Harley retired to his room for the evening, she picked up the phone to call Bev.

Bev answered and at the sound of Lisa's voice, proclaimed, "What in heaven's name have you been doing? You tell me you have some roommate moving in and then I never hear from you again. I'm hurt."

"I'm sorry, but dealing with taking care of him and managing all these awful contractors has kept me a lot more busy than I expected. The house is a complete disaster. Everything is torn up, except for my father's office, where Pete is staying."

"So am I ever going to see you again? I was hoping to get away from here for a girl's night before you leave town again."

"You don't have to worry. These contractors are so slow, it's looking like I'll be here for a while. That's why I'm calling. Are the boys still in trouble?"

"At this rate, they'll be grounded until they're thirty-five. The only good thing is that Kevin has lined up enough chores for them to do until they move out of my house."

"That bad?"

"You don't want to know, bless their sneaky little hearts. I thought I was going to kill Robby the other day. Kevin had to remove me from the room. Thank God I married such an even-tempered man."

"The teen years are rough."

"I have no sympathy for you. You had girls. Teenage boys seem to feed off each other's evil deviousness."

"I had an idea to keep them busy. But you'd have to un-ground them for the day."

"I'm listening."

"I need cheap labor and youthful energy because we have a serious wallpaper problem in Larry's old room. The stuff won't come off and the contractors are whining about how scraping it takes too long. You have to use a putty knife and it comes off in teensy-weensy quarter-inch pieces. It's as bad as scrubbing a bathroom with a toothbrush like they do in the military."

Bev chuckled. "Oh, I'm liking this idea. Meanwhile, you and I can chat while we watch them slave away."

"Watching wallpaper being scraped off the wall is about as much fun as watching grass grow. It's deadly dull. Tell them to bring whatever horrible music they want to listen to. We can lock them in Larry's room with it and go hang out in the kitchen."

"We're talking about Robby and Kenny though, so we'll have to check in regularly to make sure they are actually working and not goofing off."

Lisa laughed. "I'll leave it to you to crack the whip when necessary."

"It's a date. I'll drag my lazy offspring out of bed, and we'll see you tomorrow bright and early."

The next morning, Lisa responded to the knock on the door and found Bev and two unhappy-looking boys standing on the front steps. Kenny and Robby shared the sullen expression of teens who have been tasked with something they don't want to do. They looked as if they were being dragged into an arena to battle an ogre to the death.

Bev said, "All right, we talked about this and you know what you're supposed to do. Let's go upstairs."

They glared at her and she pointed at the steps. "Now."

Robby mumbled, "Hi, Mrs. Ryan," as he walked by Lisa.

Bev said, "It's Ms. Lowell. Move it."

Lisa followed them up the steps. "Larry's room is on the left. It's got gold-and-white wallpaper."

The boys stopped into the middle of the room and Kenny put down the portable CD player with a thump. Most of the furniture was gone, but two stepladders had been placed near the walls and a large drop cloth covered the floor. Lisa pointed at a corner near one of the ladders, where an infinitesimal strip of wallpaper had been torn off. "See that? That piece of wallpaper was removed with a scraper. The steamer and chemicals had no effect on this wallpaper because it's made of some sort of indestructible plastic."

Both boys slumped their shoulders and groaned. Lisa said, "If it helps, feel free to play the music as loud as you like. We'll be downstairs."

Bev pointed at her sons in turn. "I will be coming up here to check on your progress. And I had better see some *very good* progress."

Robby and Kenny mumbled their assent, and Lisa smiled at Bev as they walked out of the room. She leaned toward her friend and whispered. "Man, you are the meanest mom *ever*."

"You better believe it. What do you have for breakfast snackables? We have some serious catching up to do."

Lisa walked into the kitchen, grabbed a mug from a cabinet, and held it out. "Coffee?"

"Yes, please, and ASAP." Bev took the mug and examined it. "That's one classy Garfield mug you have there."

Apparently, worried that he'd missed out on the possibility for food, Harley stormed into the kitchen and started hysterically snuffling the floor.

A few seconds later, Pete thumped into the kitchen on his crutches. Bev waved her empty mug at him, "Hey there. You must be the new roomie!"

He smiled. "And you must be Bev, the best friend who knows all Lisa's deepest, darkest secrets."

"That's me. If you want the Lowell family dirt, I'm your woman."

A crash came from upstairs, and Lisa and Bev looked at each other. Bev handed her mug to Lisa and said, "Those kids are going to be the death of me. I'll be right back."

Lisa got a mug for Pete, poured some coffee into it, and handed it to him. "I know I'm counting down until tomorrow when I get to talk to Carol and Cheryl again, but there are things I don't miss about being Mom all the time."

"Now you only have to take care of one kind of gimpy guy."

Lisa took a sip of coffee and raised her eyebrows at him. "It turns out there are some extra perks I hadn't anticipated."

Pete laughed. "I suppose…"

Bev came back into the room and took her mug of coffee from the counter. She took a sip and narrowed her eyes at Lisa. "What did I miss?"

"Nothing. Have the boys destroyed Larry's room yet?"

"They're working on it. To hear Kenny tell it, Robby managed to trip over his own feet. However, Robby says that Kenny pushed him." She rolled her eyes melodramatically. "Who knows? I told them that they'd better get to jumping like hot grease on a skillet or there would be serious trouble."

"I hear music, so that's promising. Maybe they decided to get to work," Lisa said.

Bev put down her mug and looked up at the ceiling. "They're probably plotting some nefarious scheme to get out of doing anything. I swear, if they put half as much energy into working as they do trying to get out of it, my life would be a lot simpler."

"How old are they?" Pete asked.

"Kenny is fifteen and Robbie is thirteen," Bev said.

"Those are difficult ages for the male of the species." Pete took a sip of coffee. "When I fourteen, I decided to see if I could ride my bike down the slide at the playground near our house. I dragged the bike up the ladder, and I got to enjoy a massive thrill for about three seconds before the crash landing."

Lisa said, "I guess the whole Evel Knievel thing didn't work out well, huh?"

"It wasn't that different from my skiing experience, now that I think about it," he said.

"Yeah, that smash, crunch, ouch gets you every time," Lisa said.

Bev looked at Pete, then at Lisa. "Holy hogs on fire, would you look at this? You two are as thick as fleas on a farm dog. I'm thinking that you aren't just roommates, are you?"

Lisa quickly touched her hand to her cheek, even though she knew full well that it was an incriminating shade of crimson. "I have no idea what you're talking about."

"Sure, you do, although at this point, I'd say that's a gray area." Pete set down his mug, "You may as well give it up, Lisa. Bev already said she knows all your secrets."

Bev nodded. "He's right, sweetie. And I'm pleased as punch that this secret is finally a good one."

∼

After finishing his coffee, Pete went out to the back porch to throw tennis balls for Harley.

Lisa poured herself another cup and returned to the table. "Pete says that part of the reason Harley was such a problem when I got him is because he wasn't getting enough exercise. Now he's like a different dog."

"That's nice. So are you going to tell me what's going on with you and this maybe-not-only a roommate guy?"

"I'm not sure what's going on."

Bev set her mug down and leaned forward. "I think you can do better than that. What does he mean by 'gray area'? That's cryptic. I want details."

"Well, last night we were talking and then we kissed. And it was...I don't know."

"It was *what*? You're killing me here. Spill it. Was it good?"

"Very, very good. But then he said us getting involved was a bad idea."

"Yeesh, Lisa, not again! Did you tell this guy you're dying or something?" Bev shook her index finger at her. "I *told* you that's a turnoff."

"No, he knows all about the cancer, my accident, everything. We talk all the time about my past because we're going through all this stuff in the house. He doesn't have much else to do most of the time, so he's been stuck learning probably more than he ever wanted to know about me and the entire Lowell family history."

"Then what's the problem?"

"I think it's something with him, not me."

Bev made a wry face. "Okay, I'm not sure I believe that, but in any case, what do you plan to do?"

"I have no idea." Lisa sipped her coffee. "Just see what happens, I guess."

"This is you being passive and wimpy again. Are you interested in him? What do you want?"

"Mostly for this house to be finished, sold, and out of my life."

"And after that? Then what?"

Lisa shook her head. "I hate it when you hassle me like this. How many times do I have to say 'I don't know'?"

"Until you make a decision about...well...anything."

Rather than blurting out the nasty comment she desperately wanted to hurl at her friend, Lisa fell back on her mother's advice that if you couldn't say anything nice, don't say anything at all. She unloaded the dishwasher in silence. Sometimes she wished Bev didn't know her quite so well.

Bev put down her mug. "It's too quiet up there. I'm going to go upstairs and crack the whip again."

Harley bounded into the kitchen, followed by Pete a few moments later. He stopped and looked at Lisa. "What happened to you?"

"Nothing."

"Whenever you say nothing, it's usually something."

"Bev was badgering me, that's all. She says I never make decisions."

"You don't."

Lisa put the last dish into the dishwasher and slammed the door shut. "Not you too. Of course I make decisions! All the time."

"I came up with the idea for letter 'a' because you couldn't think of anything."

"So what?"

Pete set his crutches aside and leaned on the counter. "What are you so afraid of?"

"Nothing."

"That's not true. I already know you're afraid of skiing."

"Okay, I'll give you that one." Lisa gestured toward the window. "But you know why I have good reason to be afraid."

"Maybe it's time you face that fear. When you found me, you skied before you remembered you were afraid."

"That was an extreme situation and I'm a long way from 's,' anyway. And we all know how well skiing worked out for you."

"Go skiing with Bev. That's a good use of the letter 'b,' I think."

Bev walked into the kitchen. "What about Bev?"

Lisa glared at her. "Your name starts with 'b.'"

"Thanks for clearing that up, sweetie. I learned that in elementary school," Bev said with a smile.

Lisa gestured toward Pete. "He has list of things he does in alphabetic order. Skiing was 's,' although it morphed into 't' when he broke his tibia."

"For the letter 'a,' Lisa is going to buy an anklet. But we're waiting until the next time it rains, so she can hold an umbrella for me," Pete said.

"The umbrella is for his 'u.' There aren't many options for that letter, so he's going to walk in the rain with an umbrella," Lisa said. "I have to hold it though, so he doesn't fall over."

"Aww, that's adorable. I love this idea," Bev said, "They have some gorgeous anklets at Bea Haven gifts. Check out the jewelry cases in the back of the store."

"For 'b' I suggested that Lisa go skiing with you," Pete said.

Bev clapped her hands together. "Well, let's shoot out the lights, that's a fan-dam-tabulous idea! I've been trying to get her to do that for years! How'd you finally talk her into it?"

"He didn't and I don't want to. The whole idea of the list is to do things you think might be fun," Lisa said. "And that's not my idea of fun. I don't *want* to go skiing."

"No way! You're absolutely *not* wimping out on me this time," Bev said.

Lisa turned to Pete. "This isn't fair. What's your 'v' supposed to be?"

"I'll go with you and call it a vacation, since my last attempt at a vacation was a bust," Pete replied.

"I'll have to get back home and deal with the family, but y'all could stay over at the lodge." Bev wiggled her eyebrows and batted her thick lashes flirtatiously. "Kevin is too cheap to take me there, but I'm told it's really romantic."

Lisa gave Pete a questioning look, not sure how he'd react. "Well, maybe…"

"I could hang out in front of that huge fireplace and drink hot cocoa while you ski," he said evenly.

Lisa wondered if he hadn't completely thought through what going away together might mean. Did he think they would stay in separate rooms? "We'd need to board Harley."

"Aww, come on. The hero dog doesn't get to return to Snow Grove?" Pete said.

"I don't think that would be a good idea. When do you want to do this?" Lisa asked, with some trepidation. Was she really agreeing to ski and go off on romantic weekend with Pete? Talk about facing fears. She turned to him. "Are you sure you're up for this? It would involve a lot of walking around."

"I'll be okay. It would be nice to get out of the house for a couple days," he said.

"I can go next weekend," Bev said.

"Okay, I'll call Kat and see if she has room at the kennel for Harley." Lisa wasn't sure if this was a good idea, but she couldn't get the memory of last night's kiss out of her head.

It had been decades since she'd been infatuated with a man and unsure of what he was thinking. Lisa was way out of practice. If nothing else, going away for the weekend would resolve the issue one way or another.

It was a long day, and Bev and her kids finally left late in the afternoon. Bev said she had to get home, make dinner, and drag her husband away from the televised sports events he had undoubtedly been watching all day. The wallpaper was almost gone from the walls, and Bev had made the boys promise to return after church the next day to remove the last dregs of it.

Lisa had been festering about Pete's "gray area" comment all day. What was that supposed to mean? After dinner, she knocked on Pete's door.

He looked up from his book. "What's up?"

"I need to talk to you."

Patting the mattress with his palm, he said, "Have a seat."

Lisa got on the bed next to him, suddenly unsure of what to say. "I feel sort of funny asking about this."

"I'm guessing this is not ha-ha funny."

"Not really. So we decided to go away for a weekend next weekend. What does that mean?"

"It means you're going to ski."

"Not that." She turned to face him. "When I make reservations at the lodge, am I reserving one room or two? Because I don't know what you mean about a gray area."

"Well, like I said, if you're smart, you won't want to have anything to do with me. Not to mention that I'm not exactly in the greatest physical shape right now."

Lisa moved closer to him and slowly ran a fingertip down his chest. "I'd like to point out that I was injured in a similar way and managed to get pregnant while I was recovering. Let's just say that it's quite possible to work around any physical limitations you might have."

"Well, that's intriguing..." He pulled her hand from his chest, kissed her knuckles, and looked into her eyes. "If you're sure about it, I'm certainly not going to argue, so I'm thinking one room will be sufficient."

~

The next week flew by in a blur of construction annoyances. The only bright spots for Lisa were talking to her daughters on Sunday and getting out of the house to take Pete to physical therapy. He found going to the Alpine Grove Care Center significantly less enjoyable than she did, but they both had a good time on the trip to Bea Haven Gifts in the rain.

They walked through town slowly and carefully because the sidewalks were wet. Pete had become remarkably adept at using his crutches and it was only a matter of time before he'd be able to switch to using a cane. Lisa was impressed at his progress and at how little he complained. She knew how uncomfortable and unwieldy crutches were and how much your hands, shoulders, and other muscles hurt, especially in the beginning. However, most of the time he seemed to be able to manage his impatience and aggravation about the situation. Maybe there was something to be said for meditation.

Bea Sullivan was one of Lisa's favorite people in Alpine Grove. She'd owned the gift store for years and knew everyone, including Lisa's parents. Bea spent ages chatting with Lisa about everything from the current retail climate in Alpine Grove to land conservation while she helped Lisa select the perfect anklet.

The trip to town turned out to be far more fun than Lisa had expected it to be. They'd left Harley in the truck right outside the store so they could keep an eye on him.

The dog had slept most of the time and managed to refrain from chowing down on any automotive parts, so Lisa viewed the excursion a complete success. And whenever she looked down at the pretty beads encircling her ankle, she smiled. Pete was onto something with this whole alphabet-of-fun idea.

Every night after dinner when the house was quiet, Lisa stopped by Pete's room to say goodnight. She had started to look forward to her evening chats with him. Somehow it seemed like they had tacitly agreed not to do anything beyond a goodnight kiss during these rendezvous in his room. It was like they both were waiting for the trip to Snow Grove to solidify something first. Lisa wasn't sure why exactly, but it felt right.

Maybe he wanted her to get over her fear of skiing. Maybe he wanted some more time to get used to the idea of being involved with someone. Whatever it was, he didn't seem to want to elaborate, and Lisa was finding it more and more difficult to leave his room at night. It was like high school, with make-out sessions that went late into the wee hours, until one or the other of them finally pointed out that maybe they ought to get some sleep. Reluctantly, Lisa would go upstairs to her bedroom, but half the time she would lie there staring at the ceiling, wishing she were still downstairs with him.

Lisa had negotiated with Kat to drop off Harley Friday afternoon, since they were leaving for Snow Grove early Saturday to meet up with Bev. Her friend was eager to get up to the mountain when the lifts opened like they used to when they'd skied in high school. Lisa was significantly less enthusiastic, but Bev kept calling her and reciting the weather statistics, which showed that all the rain that week in Alpine Grove had been snow at the resort. The ski reports from the mountain claimed the conditions were outstanding, and Bev was raring to go.

After the contractors left on Friday afternoon, Lisa and Pete loaded Harley into the truck for the trip out to the kennel. Exhausted from a long retrieving session in the backyard with Pete, Harley was quietly snoring between them on the seat.

Pete had his hand on Harley's back. "So this place you're taking him is okay, right?"

"Harley loves it. There are lots of other dogs, and he gets to go on long walks in the forest."

Pete didn't respond and stared out the window as they passed miles of soggy evergreens that were dripping with moisture.

"You're unusually quiet over there. Are you having second thoughts about this trip?"

"You need to get past your problem with skiing, so you can move on."

"I wasn't talking about me. Are you sure you're feeling okay? Is your leg swollen again? We probably shouldn't have walked so much around town yesterday."

"It's fine. Going out makes me more impatient to get my life back. I would do almost anything to be able to get off these stupid crutches."

"I know."

"It feels like it's taking forever to walk like a normal person again." He stared out the window again. "So where *is* this place? Are you sure you know where you're going?"

"It's just a ways out of town, that's all." She took her eyes away from the road to glance at him quickly. "Are you sure you're okay?"

"I probably should have spent more time meditating this afternoon while you were at the store."

Lisa pulled into the driveway and up to the kennel. Realizing where they were, Harley stood up and began doing an excited tap dance on the Naugahyde seat.

"This won't take long." Lisa said.

"I'll hang out here and stare at the trees. They're massive."

After unloading Harley, Lisa slammed the door and smiled at Kat, who had emerged from the kennel building.

"Hi again," Kat said as Harley launched toward her. She dodged out of his way and took the leash from Lisa. "Harley, sit. Your special kennel awaits you."

Harley complied and Lisa sighed inwardly. Everyone seemed to be able to make this dog sit routinely, except for her. Pete was right. It was like Harley was laughing at her pathetic efforts at obedience training, acknowledging her commands only when the spirit moved him. She said, "I got the invitation to the party. Thank you. I noticed there was no mention of costumes, so I guess you succeeded in nixing that idea."

"Yes, thank goodness. I remain concerned, however. Maria's parties have been known to get a little bit out of hand."

"Way back in the dark ages when I got married, I didn't have a party, but that's what you're supposed to do, isn't it? A bachelorette or hen party is supposed to be one last big blast with your girlfriends and all that, right?"

"Why didn't you have a party?"

"We eloped."

"I am in awe of your brilliance. Unfortunately, I told some people we were getting married and decided I wanted a honeymoon. Things sort of escalated from there." Kat petted the smooth fur on Harley's head. "I'm wishing I could fly off to Hawaii and skip all the preamble that has to come before it."

"I think it's sweet that your friend wants to celebrate."

"I'm trying to look at it that way, but the last time Maria threw an office party, there was a "Queen" tribute band with a guy dressed up as Freddie Mercury, stage lighting, audio equipment, and a cake with a cell phone rammed into it like a wedding-cake topper."

"All that for an office party?"

"Yes, I can't even begin to imagine what she's going to come up with for a bachelorette party. I mean, those are *supposed* to be wild. Every time she starts talking about it, I cringe and want to crawl into a hole somewhere."

Lisa laughed. "I was worried that maybe I shouldn't come, but it sounds like I don't want to miss this, do I?"

"Probably not. People are likely to be talking about it for years."

Lisa put her hand on Kat's shoulder. "I'm afraid you're wrong about that. This is Alpine Grove. They'll be talking about it for *decades*."

Kat put her palms over her face. "Oh my God, you're right. I'm never going to live this down."

"We all have our crosses to bear. You may as well get used to it."

~

Kat went back into the house, where she was greeted by the unmistakable sound of feline hairball expulsion. The all-too-familiar rhythmic urka, yurka, blerk, aaaack sounds were emanating from her bedroom. Kat launched through the kitchen and dining room toward the bedroom, but not before the hairball had landed.

Quincy sat on the middle of the bed looking quite pleased with himself for creating such a fine hairy prize. Kat reached for him, but the cat leaped over her arms and shot out of the bedroom. Kat gazed at the gooey wad of gray hair and stomach contents lying on the bedspread. The cat was probably off to terrorize Tripod now. He was having quite a busy day.

Kat jumped when Joel put his hand on her shoulder. She whirled around. "I hate it when you sneak up on me like that."

"You probably couldn't hear me over the sound of barfing."

"Long-haired cats have a few disadvantages."

"I'd really, really like it if you can get Maria to take Quincy off our hands. This isn't working out. I think we've reached our critter limit."

"I know. I'll talk to Brigid too. Maybe one of her dog-foster folks would like a cat to round out their family. Anywhere would have to be better than here. I've never seen two cats hate each other like Tripod and Quincy do. It's like a war zone."

"Except with hairballs." He pointed at the bedspread. "That's quite a spectacular Technicolor one you've got right there."

Kat laughed and wrapped her arms around his waist, giving him a hug. "Extra-credit points to the guy who puts up with cat barf on his bed."

"Well, you're cleaning it up, and if that hairy creature hurls on my pillow, all bets are off."

"I know. No cats on the pillows, *ever*. That's the rule."

He bent his head to kiss her. "It is if you want to continue sleeping with me."

"I definitely do."

"I'm glad to hear it. Have you returned your mother's call yet?"

"No. Are you going to talk to your sister?"

"No."

Joel gave her another kiss and left the room. Kat got some paper towels from the kitchen and cleaned up the bed. It was not the first time Quincy had decided to lose the contents of his stomach there. Why the cat had to wait to vomit precisely in the center of the mattress was anyone's guess. Once she'd removed the mass of hair, she scooped the bedspread up into her arms and carried it to the laundry room, making sure to close the bedroom door behind her.

After starting the laundry, she went downstairs to her office. At last the nightmare book project was finally over and she was back to writing articles again. Not having book deadlines hanging over her head felt like a miracle after months of late nights. The downside was that now she needed to find more writing work. The life of a freelance writer was an endless flip-flop between being overwhelmed with deadlines and scrabbling for new projects.

Kat stared at the telephone. At some point, she was going to have to call her mother back. Kat knew it was about the wedding. Every time they spoke, her mother asked what church Kat and Joel were going to get married in. It still had not registered with her that the couple had no intention of getting married in a church.

Kat had never gotten along with her mother. They operated from completely different world views, had no shared interests, and had virtually nothing in common beyond the fact that they'd lived in the same house for eighteen tumultuous years.

Although her mother had finally conceded that Joel was in fact a decent person and not a con man trying to part Kat from her money, in subtle and not-so-subtle ways she'd made it clear that she disapproved of Joel living in the house Kat had inherited from her aunt. Since Kat's father died, her mother had rediscovered religion, so when Kat told her mother that she was getting married, the first thing she'd said was, "I need to make arrangements at the church."

Kat had repeatedly pointed out that she didn't want to get married in the city or at her mother's church and that because she and Joel lived in Alpine Grove, they planned to get married there. Then her mother started asking about ministers and churches in town. It was like talking to a wall, and Kat was tired of fighting about it. But time was running out, so she had to try again.

With a heavy sigh, she picked up the receiver and dialed the number to the house where she'd grown up. Kat's sister Kim answered and then shouted for their mother. Kim was younger than Kat and had moved back home until her fledgling acting career took off. After more than a decade, her elusive big break remained elusive.

Mary Stevens's voice came on the line. "Katherine, is everything all right? I'm vacuuming."

Kat wanted to roll her eyes. Her mother was *always* vacuuming. No stray micron of dust was permitted to get past her daily morning vacuuming ritual. Kat cleared her throat and said carefully, "I wanted to, ah, talk to you about the wedding again. It's coming up before too long."

"I got the invitation about the reception, dear, but it did not say where you plan to hold the ceremony or who will be officiating."

"I've told you before, but I'm not sure you understand. Before the reception, we're planning to get married at the courthouse with a few family members as witnesses. If you'd like to come, I'd be happy to have you there."

"You can't do that."

"I told you. It's what we've decided, Mother." Kat put her palm over her eyes. This was not going well.

"You have to get married in a church. Although you may have rejected the idea of getting married here at *our* church, I am quite sure they have churches in Alpine Grove."

"It's not my church and it's perfectly legal for us to be married in a civil ceremony."

"So you're saying that there's not going to be a priest or a minister involved at all? That's completely unacceptable."

"But that's the way it's going to be. It's our choice." Kat gripped the handset more firmly. "I know you like your pastor and your church, but it's not what I want."

"You have to get married in the church. I've talked to everyone already!"

"I'm sorry, but that's not going to happen. You can't force your religion on me."

"You will regret this, Katherine. Your marriage will fail without the blessings of the Lord!"

"I'm know you're upset, but…"

"I absolutely cannot let you do this, Katherine! You're going to burn in the flames of hell. This sin will result in eternal pain, damnation, and suffering. I simply can't allow you to do it."

Kat said through a clenched jaw. "Mother, you're really…"

"I want to talk to…what's his name?"

"Joel."

"Put him on the line."

Kat paused for a moment. "I don't think…"

"I demand that you put him on the phone right this instant!"

"All right…fine." Kat set the receiver on the desk, stepped over Linus, and walked across the hall to Joel's office.

He looked away from his monitor at her. "What happened to you?"

"My mother wants to talk to you." She pointed at the phone. "She's all yours."

"I'm not going to like this, am I?"

Kat shook her head. "I seriously doubt it."

Joel picked up the line and greeted Kat's mother. He raised a single eyebrow at Kat in response to whatever her mother was saying. Fortunately, Kat couldn't hear the specific words, but the timbre of the rant was familiar. Mom had moved into power-lecture mode.

Joel sat silently, periodically glancing at Kat, who leaned in the doorway watching a variety of emotions reflect in his eyes as he patiently waited for a pause in the diatribe. Finally, he said, "I'm sorry you don't approve, but Kat and I have decided on these plans together, and that is what are going to do."

There was more ranting and Joel made a face at Kat, who grinned at him in sympathy. He said, "Well, I hope you decide to come to the reception."

There was final outburst from the other end of the line and then Joel held the receiver out toward Kat. "Your mother hung up on me."

Kat walked to the chair, took the receiver from his hand, and put it back on the cradle. She sat in his lap and put her arms around his neck. "You were remarkably polite. I'm impressed."

"I couldn't get a word in edgewise." He gave her a kiss. "By the way, we're going to hell."

"So I was told. At least we'll be all toasty warm together. Did you talk to Cindy?"

"No, and I don't want to."

Kat sighed. "After this, talking to your sister doesn't have appeal for me either. New plan. Forget family. Let's elope the day before everyone *thinks* we're getting married. The first day of spring is on a Thursday this year."

"So sneak off to the courthouse, get married, then deal with the fallout at the reception on Friday?"

"I'd prefer not to deal with tons of people on the same day we get married because I'll probably cry at the ceremony.

I'll ask Maria to be a witness. We worked together, so she's already seen me cry a lot."

Joel smiled. "Only if she takes the cat."

"All right. I'll try to negotiate that as part of the deal. Jack isn't religious. Do you think he'd be willing to be a witness?"

"I'll ask him. He and Becca would probably get a kick out of it."

"I can't believe how complicated family stuff always ends up being." Kat leaned her head on his shoulder. "I'm glad you're my family now."

"Me too."

Chapter 10

Excursions

Early Saturday morning, Lisa was rushing to get ready to go up to Snow Grove with Pete. At least she didn't have to drag around ski gear. Pete obviously wasn't skiing and she was going to rent equipment. The phone rang and even before she picked it up, she knew it was Bev.

"You're going, right?" Bev said.

"Why are you calling? I said I would. I'm almost ready. I'll meet you at the rental shop in the village like I said."

"Okay, I was checking in to make sure you're not going to flake, and now I'm outta here. See you there. We're going to have a great time!"

Yeah, right. Lisa hung up the phone and scowled at it. Everyone was a critic. To be fair, it was a reasonable concern on Bev's part, given that Lisa had been avoiding this day for so many years. So far, not thinking about what she was about to do and going through the motions of packing on autopilot was helping. If she didn't think about the reality of getting on a ski lift and ascending the mountain again, everything was fine.

Pete came into the kitchen and sat down. "Was that Bev?"

"Yes, and it annoys me that she thinks I'm going to stand her up."

"Well, you want to, don't you?"

"That's not the point."

He smiled as he stood up again. "I see your mood hasn't improved. I'll limp my way out to the truck. Could you get my stuff for me? It's on the bed."

"Yes, I'll get it in a minute." Lisa threw their coffee mugs and cereal bowls into the dishwasher. "I just need to get my suitcase."

She turned around and realized Pete was still in the kitchen leaning in the doorway. He put his crutches aside and opened his arms toward her. "It's going to be okay."

Lisa walked into his embrace and hugged him hard, resting her cheek on his shoulder. "I'm really scared."

"You skied the last time you went up to Snow Grove. On only one ski with a boot that didn't fit."

"I know. But I wasn't thinking. All I was worried about was you dying before I could get help."

"I'm glad you didn't want me to die." He gave her a final squeeze, released her, and looked into her eyes. "This time it will be a lot more fun. I promise."

"Well, for you anyway."

He laughed. "I sure hope so."

They loaded everything into the truck and headed south. The weather steadily improved as they got closer to the turnoff to the resort and it looked like Bev's enthusiasm about the fantastic ski weather was warranted. Although it had been gray in Alpine Grove, it was going to be a beautiful sunny day at Snow Grove.

Lisa turned on the road to go up the mountain and was again flooded with memories as the walls of snow alongside the road grew higher. She clutched the steering wheel to try to still her shaking hands. Fortunately, the old truck had so much play in the steering that her movements had little impact.

Pete put his hand on her leg. "You were here a few weeks ago. It's no big deal."

"I came to drop off papers, not ski. That was it."

He didn't say anything, but left his hand resting on her leg. Maybe he knew the contact was soothing. Lisa took a deep breath. She was being such a baby about this whole thing. It was only one day and she'd get through it.

Lisa had called to find out about access and parking and learned that there was an elevator at the bottom of the lodge near handicap parking spaces, so Pete wouldn't have to go up the thousands of stairs she and Harley had ascended to get to the village.

Although they'd rarely used it in Alpine Grove, Pete had gotten a handicapped placard for the truck and she hung it off the mirror. She carried the suitcases, they checked into the lodge, and went up to the room.

She dropped the luggage on the bed and walked to the windows that overlooked the view down over the valley and the lake. "Wow."

Pete came up alongside her, moved his crutches, and rested his hands on the windowsill. "This is almost as cool as the view from the ski lift. Which is where you need to be. It's getting late. You need to go and meet Bev."

She turned to him. "I don't want to."

"You'll be glad you did."

"Why are you so sure of that? I don't understand why you think putting me on skis is so important."

He smiled. "I'll tell you when you get back."

"You promise?"

"Promise." He leaned to kiss her. "Have fun. I'm going to hobble down to the spa and get a massage."

"This isn't fair."

"Have fun."

Resigned to her fate, Lisa gathered her gloves, goggles, and other ski accoutrements and left the room. She went downstairs out to the village and crossed the courtyard to the rental shop. As she entered the building, Bev jumped up from her chair waving at her. "You made it!"

"I'm here." She'd far rather be getting a massage with Pete, but she was there.

Bev pointed at a rack of skis. "You have to check these out. They're the new ones that are shaped so it's easier to turn. I'm telling you, they're the best thing to happen to my old flabby leg muscles in years."

"I'll take your word for it."

A young man came over to take her information. "We've got a special on them to encourage people to try them out."

"Fine, whatever you think is best." Lisa filled in her height, weight, and shoe size on a note card. Why did they have to ask about weight? That was more than she wanted to share, even though it had to do with binding release during a crash. Lisa gave herself a mental slap across the face. Don't think about crashing. Do *not*.

Finally, Lisa was fitted with her skis and she and Bev went outside. Bev collected her skis from the rack and put them on. Lisa dropped the skis onto the ground with a thump and snapped her boots into the bindings.

Bev patted her on the back with her gloved hand. "See! It's just like old times. We're going to have the best bluebird day. It's absolutely perfect. Look at that sky!"

Lisa nodded and carefully moved her skis forward, pushing herself with the poles as she followed Bev over to the line for the quad chair lift that would take them up the mountain. She felt old, out of shape, and awkward. Why was she doing this? Bev had been right when she'd pointed out that if Lisa never stood up for herself, she'd end up being roped into doing things she didn't want to do. Remodeling a house, skiing, fostering a dog, taking on an injured roommate. Well, okay, to be fair, not all of it had been completely terrible.

Lisa ruminated and worried as Bev chattered on about the weather while they stood in line. Suddenly it was their turn and they hustled to move into place in front of the chair. Then Lisa was whisked up off the snow. She clutched at her ski poles, worried she'd drop them on the liftie's head. It was undoubtedly not the most graceful chair access he'd ever witnessed. How humiliating.

Bev turned to Lisa and pointed behind them. "Look! How could you forget that view? I love this so much."

Lisa nodded at her friend, worried that if she spoke she might burst into tears. There was no turning back now. When they reached the top, she managed to get off the lift without causing an incident and slid to the bottom of the little hill that led down from the lift to the ski run. Bev waved, indicating they should go down Midway.

Lisa moved over next to Bev, who grinned at her and pulled her goggles down over her eyes. "You ready?"

Lisa shook her head. "I don't want to."

"You can do this, Lisa. I know you can. Relax! You've skied Midway a million times and your muscles know what to do. Just follow me." Bev pushed off and Lisa wished she could reach out and pull her friend back.

It was now or never. She put her ski goggles over her eyes, then closed her eyes and took a long, deep breath, letting the cold air fill her lungs. When she opened her eyes, she pushed off and the wind hit her face. A moment of complete terror was replaced with a thrilling rush of adrenaline as she leaned into her first turn.

By the next turn, she was grinning like an idiot and catching up to Bev. As she whooshed by her friend, she raised her ski pole and yelled, "Hey slow poke, I'll race ya!"

~

By the time Lisa and Bev stopped skiing for the day, Lisa was tired but exultant. After their last run, they took off their skis and Lisa returned her equipment to the rental shop. When they hugged goodbye in the courtyard, Lisa felt like crying because she was so happy. "I don't know how to thank you. This was the best ski day ever."

"I think you just did, sweetie." Bev smiled weakly and wiped a tear away with her glove. "I've been waiting for this day for so long. I wish I didn't have to go, but I need to get home to the family. You go thank Pete. I never would have convinced you if it weren't for him."

Lisa gave her another hug. "Yeah, we'll see how that goes. I can't figure him out."

Bev gave her a lascivious grin. "Well, you have all night all by yourselves to work on that. And I can't say I'm not jealous, because in case I haven't mentioned it, he's cute. Those blue eyes slay me."

"I know what you mean. I'm trying not to fall all over him like I did with Mike, but I'm not being completely successful."

"Let me know what happens. I want all the dirt. The most romantic moment I've had lately was Kevin saying, 'I'll throw that into the laundry for you.' I swear I just about swooned."

Lisa laughed. "Be still my heart."

The two women shared a long, last hug goodbye and Lisa walked across the courtyard to the lodge. She was looking forward to taking a hot shower and having dinner with Pete. Skiing had a way of making you ravenous like almost no other activity.

She walked into the room and found Pete sprawled out on the bed, fast asleep. Apparently the massage had worked. He was passed out cold. She gathered her things and took a very hot, very long shower. By the time she turned off the water, her skin was pink, but her muscles had relaxed enough that she might be able to make it through dinner without them seizing up. She'd never had to worry or even think about that kind of thing twenty-five years ago. Getting older happened to everyone, but she didn't have to enjoy the signs of impending decrepitude.

She emerged from the steamy bathroom clad in a thick, snuggly white robe. Pete had awakened and was sitting upright on the bed, reading. He looked up and threw the book aside. "You look happy."

She capered over to the bed, crawled over next to him, and gave him a kiss. "It was a fantastic day. You were right. I can't believe it, but we had so much fun!"

"I knew you would. It sounds like the letter 'b' was a success."

"How did you know? You promised you'd tell me."

"After I was stabbed, I had to go back to work and face what I was afraid of in order to move forward."

"That sure wasn't the answer I was expecting." Lisa sat up straight, looking down at his face. "I thought you were shot and then retired. You were shot *and* stabbed?"

"The guy with the knife was first. It was when I was with the K9 unit. I'd only been on the force for a few years and I made a stupid mistake." He pulled up his shirt and pointed at the long scar on his abdomen. "Fortunately, he missed anything important. But the knife made a mess."

"I wondered about that, but I didn't want to ask."

Pete closed his eyes briefly, then sighed. "The whole thing was a massive screw up on my part. I told you about Lakota. He was what they call a dual-purpose police dog. He was trained to sniff drugs, but also to attack to protect his handler; i.e., me."

"What happened?"

"We had staked out the dealer because Lakota had already let us know that drugs were on the premises. My partner Tom and I had agreed that we'd surprise the guy. So we waited two hours for the right moment, lying in wet grass near an old warehouse. We had it all planned out."

"Did you get him?"

"We did apprehend him, but it was sloppy, and everyone got hurt because of me. I was tired of sitting there doing nothing. Then the guy walked so close to us that I took the opportunity to jump him. It was a big mistake."

"Is that when you got stabbed?"

He nodded. "It was like the whole thing happened in slow motion. I didn't know he had a knife. So he jabbed me, I went down, and he ran. I saw Lakota run after him, followed by Tom. Turned out the guy also had a gun. He hit Lakota in the paw, and grazed Tom's chest, but Tom was wearing a vest and was able to tackle the guy and take him down."

"So you got your man."

"Tom got his man, in spite of me. He's six four and probably weighs three hundred pounds, so when he tackles someone, they're done." Pete shook his head. "Lakota had to have surgery on his paw and then retired. Tom transferred to a different division to get away from me. I can't say I blame him."

"What happened to you?"

"I was on medical leave for a while. There was an investigation because Tom was shot, but he refused to say I was at fault, so all I got was a reprimand."

Lisa touched his hand. "It sounds like you think you were at fault."

"I did and I do."

"I'm not sure why you're telling me all this."

"You and I both know that everything can change in an instant. One tiny mistake and everything is different. It's easy to let that define the rest of your life. Sometimes going back and facing it can be a good thing."

"But you retired."

"I retired two years ago. I was only twenty-six when everything went down with Tom and Lakota. At the time, I didn't know what to do. Being a cop was who I was and all I knew. After a lot of counseling sessions, I decided I needed to go back to it. At the time, it was the right thing to do."

"So why *did* you finally retire?"

"By that time I had my twenty years in and I'd seen way too much. While I was lying in the hospital after being shot, I knew I was done being a cop. My heart wasn't in it anymore." He smiled, "To throw a little more Shakespeare at you: 'One man in his time plays many parts.' I decided it was time for me to find a different role to play."

"It sounds like you were ready."

"I thought I was, but like I told you, I didn't go gently into that good night. Adapting to retirement was more difficult than I'd expected, and it didn't go quite as well as I thought I would."

"You certainly tried. The alphabet of fun is very creative."

"It worked okay up until 's,' I suppose."

"Well, I'm glad I met you." She put both hands under his shirt, running her fingertips along the contours of the long scar. "If you live long enough, you're bound to end up with a few extra lumps, bumps, and imperfections. Or stretch marks, in my case."

He pulled her hands out from under his shirt and wrapped his arms around her, dragging her down to him as he nuzzled her neck. "You always smell like roses."

She tilted her head back. "It's tea rose."

"It reminds me of when I was little. There was this long rose hedge that ran down one side of our yard and I used to lie down next to it because it smelled so good." He moved his lips over her collarbone. "This is such a bad idea. I'm sorry."

She moved to look at him. "You said that before. I'm here because I want to be here."

"You're going to regret it. I'm a mess." He raised his eyebrows. "Every relationship I've ever had ended in disaster. Women have told me there's something fundamentally wrong with me."

"Well, if you're a mess, then I must be too. If this is some type of contest, I think my divorce after more than twenty years of marriage probably trumps your romantic failures."

He ran his fingertip along her collarbone. "You have to be one of the kindest people I've ever met. I thought, hey, maybe we could have a fling and it would be fun. No harm, no foul. But you're not built that way. If we do this, you're going to end up hating me."

Lisa leaned over and kissed him forcefully and passionately. "I'm a big girl."

"I'm not sure you know what you're dealing with. I feel like you haven't seen the real me because I've been immobilized. I'm impatient. I rush everything. Being on crutches has been an extreme exercise in patience. I'm afraid that when I'm back to normal, you'll realize what a selfish troglodyte I really am."

"Troglodyte?" Lisa giggled. "Is that like a hobbit?"

"But a lot less cute." He put his palms on both sides of her face and gazed into her eyes intently. "I'm serious here. I've seen things no one should see. I've seen women who were raped and beaten. Told mothers their sons were killed in some senseless drive-by shooting. Heard too many people scream in terror and watched them die. It changes you."

Lisa pulled his hands away from her face and clasped them in front of her. "I understand, but I've spent a lot of time with you. Nothing you've said makes a difference in how I feel."

"All right, but don't say I didn't warn you." He gave her a sly smile. "And I have to say I'm more than a little curious about the creative work-arounds to my physical limitations that you mentioned."

Lisa returned his smile. "It's been a long time, so I hope you'll forgive me if I'm a little rusty. But it could be fun."

"Fun is good. I like fun."

~

The next morning Lisa opened her eyes and gazed at a pretty wooden Shaker-style dresser. Wait a minute. Where was the French Provincial gilt horror she knew so well? She rolled over and saw that Pete was lying next to her, reading. Oh, yeah. The Snow Grove Lodge. With Pete, who looked, if possible, sexier than he had last night. The whole slightly rumpled and mussed hair thing definitely worked. She nudged herself closer to curl up next to him.

He looked up from his book. "Good morning. Do you want to order room service again, or consider getting out of bed?"

"I'm not sure I ever want to leave this bed." She sat up and put her arms around his neck. "Returning to a torn-up house isn't enticing."

"Well, check-out time isn't until eleven." He smiled as he ran his fingers down her arms and across her hip. "I vote for room service."

Lisa kissed him and put the book on the nightstand. "And checking out at ten fifty-nine."

On the way home, they chatted about the various ski runs Lisa had traversed with Bev the day before. She shook her head. "I feel sort of silly now about the whole thing. For years, I didn't want to visit my parents in the wintertime to avoid driving past the ski resort and seeing the snow. I'm not sure what I was so afraid of exactly."

"Being afraid can be good if it keeps you breathing. For example, I can tell you that if you're being chased by a drug dealer with a gun, fear is a rational emotion to have. Fear is good for self-preservation." Pete looked out the window at the scenery whizzing by as they drove. "Obviously, almost dying in a skiing accident would give you a reason to be afraid of skiing again."

"But for years? It doesn't make sense. I think my fear of skiing got worse instead of better over time. I felt like I let everyone down by not going to the Olympics. Like I was a huge failure. Everything got all twisted up in my mind." Lisa glanced at him. "That probably doesn't make any sense at all."

"Maybe it's related to why you have so much trouble making decisions.

"I make decisions. I'm on 'b' remember?"

"I suggested that, along with 'a,' because you couldn't think of anything. And then Bev encouraged me. You haven't even selected the paint colors for the house. I think Craig is going to start stalking you with those paint chips."

"I suppose I have been avoiding that a little."

"The next time you talk to him, say to yourself, 'no one will die if I pick the wrong paint color.'"

Lisa laughed. "Now you're just being obnoxious."

"You get my point though, right?"

"I never really thought about it before. In a strange way, when I got cancer and thought I was going to die again, I think that made the skiing fears worse. It was all intertwined in my mind. Part of me is still afraid the cancer is going to come back. Then right before I moved here, I started not to care if it did."

Pete put his hand on her leg. "You really felt that way?"

"Maybe it was more like I was afraid no one would care. Like I'd raised my kids, and no one needed me anymore. I was done. So if I died, no one would notice I was gone."

"I seriously doubt that. You have a family that loves you, for one thing."

Lisa's eyes widened. "Oh, no! I forgot to call Carol and Cheryl. I always call them on Sunday mornings."

"You were busy."

"But they don't know that. I *always* call. Cheryl says she can set her watch by my Sunday phone call. They probably think something is horribly wrong." Lisa tried to stifle a giggle. "If they only knew."

"Your secret is safe with me. Just tell them you're trying out the alphabet of fun."

"So what are you up to? 'V'? No wait, vacation was 'v.' You're on 'w' now."

"I guess so. Maybe I'll whittle a walking stick while I'm sitting around watching you choose paint colors. Next week, the doctor claims we can talk about switching to partial weight-bearing status with a cane or something. I've got to get off these crutches someday."

"I already did 'c' for cooking. So what can I do for 'd'?"

"You're supposed to decide, remember? What do you *want* to do?"

"I don't know."

"You must have some ideas. Hopes, daydreams, fantasies, aspirations? What?"

Lisa paused and tried to think of something—anything—that would be fun. "Well, if you're whittling, maybe I can do some type of craft too."

"Forget about me and what I'm doing. What do *you* want?"

"I have an idea." She glanced at him. "But you'll think it's stupid. It does start with the letter 'd' though."

"I won't think it's stupid. What?"

"Remember how I found that pile of magazines?"

"You called it the leaning tower of *Cosmo*, as I recall."

"Who knew Mom had a secret stash back there in that closet? I've always wanted to try decoupage."

Pete glanced at her. "I have absolutely no idea what that is."

"Finally!" Lisa smacked her hand on the steering wheel. "I finally found something you haven't run across in your reading. Now, I *have* to do it. I'll need to get some Mod Podge though. Maybe I'll try it on that awful end table in the office."

"And still, I have no idea what you're talking about."

"Decoupage involves pasting paper onto a surface. You cut up magazines into pieces, then glue the paper onto a surface like the ugly end table. Then you seal it, so it's permanent."

"That could be fun, I guess. Certainly messy, anyway. Messy can be fun."

"The wood chips from your whittling might mingle with my tiny pieces of paper. Who knows what might happen when all that wood pulp gets together?"

Pete laughed. "Oooh, that sounds dirty. I'm in."

They picked up Harley and Lisa met Kat's kennel assistant, Mia, who seemed nice enough, although not very talkative. Harley leaped into the pickup, excited to see his favorite human again.

Lisa got in and gave Harley's rear end a pat. "Yes, I'm here too. That's not your good side. Why don't you sit down?"

Pete said, "Harley, sit," and it was like the dog suddenly had a brain. As far as career options went, Lisa clearly had no future as a dog trainer.

After they arrived home and ate a late lunch or early dinner, Pete set his crutches aside and gave her a hug. "I hate to say this, but I'm completely exhausted. I'm going to hobble off to my room and take a nap. But I had a really good time this weekend."

Lisa kissed him. "Me too. I'm not sure how to thank you for all your encouragement."

"You thought up a few ways last night." He gathered up his crutches again and left, followed by Harley.

Once she was alone, Lisa suddenly remembered again that she still hadn't called her kids. On the East Coast it was late and they were probably out. Oh well, it was worth a shot. She ran upstairs to the phone in her parents' old bedroom and had unsatisfying chats with her daughters' answering machines. She set down the receiver and stared at it. With a pent-up need to talk to somebody, she picked up the handset again and dialed Bev's number.

At Lisa's greeting, Bev said, "Hey, I've been thinking about you all day! How was the lodge? Tell me everything."

"We talked about all kinds of stuff, and ordered room service, and…"

"And? And *what*? You're killing me here."

"You can figure out the rest."

Bev shrieked in her ear. "It's about time!"

"Ouch. Settle down. There's no need to yell."

"So how was it?"

Lisa twisted the phone cord around her finger. "Amazing, but…"

"But nothing. Why is there always a 'but'? Can't you just enjoy something for once? I swear, you could start a fight in an empty house."

"He keeps saying that this is all a mistake and I'm going hate him."

"It sure doesn't sound like you hate him."

"No, and that's the problem. I'm falling in love with him. I'm afraid it's going to be like Mike all over again. I fall head over heels like some overgrown teenager, because that's exactly the type of thing I do. And then what happens? I end up with my heart broken into teeny-tiny pieces. *Again.*"

"You don't know that, sweetie."

"I'm not sure I can stand going through that again. It's too painful."

"So what are you doing to do?"

Lisa looked down at the phone cord that she'd twisted into a knot. "Shut up, stop over-analyzing everything, go back downstairs, and crawl into bed with him."

"That's my girl."

Chapter 11

X-rays & Walls

The next morning, Lisa woke up next to Pete. The hospital bed wasn't completely comfortable, since it was designed for only one person. She was curled up behind him, snuggled up with her cheek resting on his back. His dark brown hair was streaked with silver and had gotten longer since she'd known him. She wanted to reach up and thread her fingers through the soft curls at the back of his neck. Trying not to wake him up, she moved her head slightly so she could see the clock. She jolted up on her elbow.

Pete started awake. "What's going on? Are you okay?"

"It's really late." She looked down at the floor, where Harley was passed out on his side, looking like a furry yellow rug. "Apparently, our canine alarm clock wore himself out over the weekend too."

Pete moved to get up and whacked his elbow on one of the bed rails. "Ow. The construction crew is going to be here in fifteen minutes and you have to take me to physical therapy. I need to take a shower."

While Pete stumbled around gathering his clothes and crutches, Lisa clambered out of bed. She left his room and let Harley out for a brief excursion into the backyard. Once Harley returned, she ran upstairs to take her shower. Good thing she'd had such a great weekend, because this was obviously destined to be a rushed and annoying Monday.

By the time she got out of the shower, the workmen had arrived. She dressed and ran downstairs to grab a bowl of cereal before she and Pete had to leave for Alpine Grove Care Center. Pete was going to be so incredibly late for his appointment.

As she splashed some milk into her bowl of cornflakes, Craig came into the kitchen followed by Pete, who still looked disheveled and irritated, but cleaner. He crossed his arms and leaned on the wall, impatiently waiting for her to finish.

Lisa was not in the mood to deal with Craig. He was the last person she wanted to see. "Hi, Craig. I can't really talk right now. We're really late."

"I just wanted to let you know that we need to order the paint, so we need your color choices. Also I wanted to alert you to the fact that we found some indication of water damage."

Lisa gulped down a mouthful of cereal. "Where? From what? My parents put a new roof on this place a couple of years ago. And my father is hysterical about pipes because of his early years as a plumber. Nothing ever leaks. Or it never has before."

"I'm not sure, but we'll need to investigate. There could be dry rot, too."

"I don't know what that is."

Craig settled into what Lisa thought of as his lecture stance. "Well, dry rot happens when…"

"I'm sorry, but right now, I have to go. Do what you need to do." Lisa put down her spoon, got up, and put her bowl in the sink. "We'll be back in a couple of hours and you can explain it to me then."

"Sure thing, ma'am. See you later."

Lisa rounded up Harley and went with Pete out to the truck. His hair was wet, so it was going to be a cold ride for him this morning. Unlike Pete, Harley was enthusiastic about heading out.

Once they were on the road, Lisa turned to Pete. "Are you all right? You look awfully pale."

"I'm angry at myself. I was in a hurry and I lost my balance. I whacked my bad leg, and probably put more weight on it than I should have. Tile is unforgiving. Gorgeous George, the physical terrorist, is going to have a fit. But I didn't hit that hard and I had my brace on."

"Well, you're obviously in pain."

"Maybe they'll give me some extra-cool drugs. Don't worry about it."

"Sorry, but I'm going to worry. I'll drive faster."

When they got to the care center, Pete went on ahead while Lisa signed in. They were really late and George was probably not going to be happy. Lisa sat with Harley in the lobby and talked to some of the residents.

Because she'd been to the facility so often, more and more people were starting to know Lisa and her exuberant yellow lab. She'd told and re-told Harley's big rescue story countless times. Sometimes she told it to the same people, but that was okay, because even if they remembered hearing it before, they still loved it. Harley the hero dog ate up all the attention and praise for his exploits at Snow Grove.

After she'd told Harley's story yet again and the group of people had dispersed, Lisa decided it was time to visit Betty.

Every time she came, she stopped by and tried to see if her aunt was going to give any clues to the whereabouts of the ever-so-elusive "stuff" that was supposedly somewhere in the house. Many bad jokes and random comments later, Lisa usually ended up annoyed and uninformed. The only good aspect of her visits was that like everyone else, Betty was a Harley fan. She said he was the "best dog in the whole wide world." Thankfully, Harley didn't seem to be letting all the accolades go to his head.

Lisa walked down the long hallway and tapped on the door of her aunt's room. Betty was sitting up in bed, holding what looked like an amorphous blob of yarn. Maybe she was crocheting.

Lisa smiled. "Hi Betty. It's me and Harley again."

"Linda! Where have you been?"

"Still in Alpine Grove. I'm staying at my parents' house, remember?"

"Where's my stuff?"

"You haven't told me where the stuff is, Betty." Lisa watched as Harley put his head on the bed and Betty ran her fingers along his soft ears.

Betty was silent, seeming to ponder the velvety smooth fur of the dog's floppy ears. Lisa leaned closer. "Betty, where is the stuff? I've already sold a lot of the furniture. I've thrown away a lot of junk and donated some old toys. Once the weather is better, I'll probably have to do a big garage sale."

"You're selling the garage? It's not that big."

"No, Betty, I'm clearing out all the old stuff from the house, so Mom and Dad can put the house back on the market this spring. They're selling it, remember?"

"They can't sell my stuff!"

"I won't knowingly sell anything you want, but you have to tell me what the stuff is and where I can find it in the house."

Betty looked down at the yarn in her lap. "So I have a question for you. Why are men like diapers?"

"No jokes, Betty. I mean it." Lisa clutched Harley's leash. She was getting nowhere with this conversation *again.*

"Then give me my stuff."

Lisa wanted to scream. Saying the same thing repeatedly was making her insane and her patience had finally run out. She was already in a really bad mood, worrying about Pete. What if he had really hurt himself? No one should have to put up with this level of aggravation from their relatives, no matter how nutty they might be. "Listen Betty, I'm going to ask you one last time and then I'm not asking again. What is the stuff you want? Where is it?"

Betty sat up straight and threw her yarn aside. "Don't you talk to me in that tone of voice, young lady. I've probably told you fifty times now. It's *in the house.*"

Lisa practically shouted, "*Where?*"

Harley sat down and looked up at Lisa.

Betty shook her finger and pointed at the door. "Get out of my room, Linda. If you're going to be rude and won't listen to me, then get out."

Lisa gathered up Harley's leash and stormed out without another word. She was so tired of this whole situation. Maybe Pete was finally done with physical therapy and they could get out of here. She stomped down the hall and peered into the therapy room, which was empty. The scary-looking stainless-steel equipment sat in metallic silence. Where had everybody gone? It wasn't like Pete could run away. Or at least, not very quickly.

Lisa walked around until she found a nurse, who told her that George and Pete had gone to get x-rays, but that they'd be back soon. And unwelcome barrage of possible medical complications marched into Lisa's mind. What if Pete had hit his head on the tile in addition to his knee? He could have a brain hemorrhage and die. Lisa took a deep breath to will her brain to shut up. She slowly walked to a row of chairs outside of the physical therapy room and sat down to wait. Harley settled into a spot on the floor near her feet, looking sad. He occasionally lifted his head when she flipped a page of the ancient *House and Garden* magazine.

By the time Pete returned, Lisa had exhausted her supply of antique periodicals and had made up several-hundred possible scenarios about Pete's current physical condition and potential demise. She was staring into space, fretting and reliving the fight with her aunt, when Harley jumped up at the sight of his favorite human. Startled into action, Lisa readjusted her hold on the leash and let Harley drag her down the hall.

Pete told Harley to sit and leaned over to pet him. "Hey, what's the big deal?"

"Are you okay? I've been so worried."

"I think I'll live, although the dream of partial weight-bearing activities has been pushed back another week. I think I need your ice-cream therapy, because I'm so incredibly frustrated right now I feel like throwing something or punching a hole in a wall. Since neither of those options will make me any friends around here, it's probably better if you take me back to my man cave, so I can sulk for a while."

Lisa gave him a hug. "I'm so glad you're okay. Let's go home."

～

Lisa pulled into the driveway and was pleased to note that the workers' trucks had left the premises. It had been a long day and she wasn't in the mood to get yet another lecture from Craig.

She let Harley out, got Pete's crutches from the back, and they all trooped into the house.

Pete started off toward the office, then stopped and pointed the end of a crutch toward the wall. "What happened there?"

Lisa moved to stand next to him. "There's no wall in my wall."

"Why'd they tear off all the drywall there?"

"This morning, Craig said there might be water damage."

"Yeah, I heard him say that, but I'm not sure I buy it." Pete looked up at the ceiling. "Water damage from what?"

"I have no idea. And I don't understand why they had to take apart the entire wall."

"You've got a nice view of the dining room now."

Lisa put her face in her palms. "I don't want a view of the dining room."

"Maybe you can go for an open floor plan."

She dropped her hands. "You're hilarious."

"They pulled out all the insulation too. I'm certainly not an expert, but I think there'd be stains on the wood if there were water damage."

"I don't know. Craig said something about dry rot. I don't know what that is. How can something rot if it's dry? I didn't want to deal with it this morning."

Pete held onto the wood and leaned over to examine it. "The framing looks fine."

"How can you tell?"

"I think it would have cracks or look damaged in some way." He whacked the board with his hand and the thump sounded satisfyingly solid. "This house wasn't exactly built yesterday, but this wood doesn't look much different than the brand-new lumber you'd see at a building supply store, as far as I can tell."

"Well, I guess I'll find out more than I ever wanted to know about it tomorrow." Lisa peered at the wood. She wouldn't know dry rot if it bit her in the butt.

"You really don't like that guy Craig, do you?"

"There's something about him that makes my skin crawl. It's completely irrational and I feel like a rotten human being for even saying that to you. Never mind. Forget I said anything."

He put an arm around her and pulled her close to him. "You look like a woman who needs some ice-cream therapy."

"I think you have an ulterior motive here, but I don't care." Lisa gave him a kiss. "Go elevate your leg and I'll be right back."

Lisa turned and walked to the kitchen, noticing that holes had been cut in the drywall in the living room too. What was going on? Was the entire house about to fall down from this dry rot stuff? That would be a difficult conversation to have with her parents. She imagined Mom's incredulous face as Lisa said, "Well, everyone told me not to tell you that

I was remodeling the house, and oh, by the way, it needs to be demolished because all the wood is rotting away. Sorry!"

She scooped the ice cream into bowls while Harley supervised. Pete didn't seem to think the whole place was about to fall down, but did he know any more about construction than she did? She carried the bowls back into his room, where he was lying on his back with his arm over his eyes.

"Hey, wake up. Your frozen goodies have arrived."

He moved his arm and took the bowl from her. "Thanks. I wasn't asleep. Just thinking."

"About what?"

"Mostly feeling sorry for myself." He took a bite of ice cream. "I'll stop now."

"Here's some good news: you've got the letter 'x' covered now. What did the x-rays show?" She held up her spoon. "Can you tell me something beyond the fact that you're going to live?"

"My klutzy tile incident didn't manage to trash my knee. Everything is progressing, as they like to say. But they still want me to stick with the crutches for a few more days, just in case."

"That sounds good."

"Except for the crutches. I want to get rid of them more than you can imagine. I'm so sick of thinking about it. Did you visit Betty?"

"Briefly." Lisa set down her spoon. "I yelled at her and stormed out. Now I feel terrible."

"That doesn't sound like you."

"I guess I was in a bad mood because I was worried about you and the house." Lisa jabbed her spoon into the bowl and hacked off a big chunk of ice cream. "I know I was mean to her, but I was so frustrated I couldn't stand it anymore."

"So she still didn't tell you where the stuff is, I suppose?"

"No, she yelled at me again that it's in the house and then I…" Lisa looked at him incredulously. "Wait a second. What if that's literally what she's talking about?"

"What do you mean?"

"Did you see all the holes in the walls? What if it's not water damage? What if Craig was looking for something? Maybe Craig thinks something is *in* the house? Suppose Betty told him about it or he found out somehow."

"That's bizarre, but it would explain why he was lying about the water damage."

Lisa set down her spoon. "Why didn't you say something?"

"I did say I didn't think there was water damage."

"You didn't say he was *lying*. You said the wood looked okay."

He pointed his spoon at her. "You tend to not believe me when I suggest you might be lying about what you're feeling."

"I guess that's true. I hate to admit it, but you've never been wrong. Never! Even when I'm lying to myself. I suppose you did say you look at my mouth, but how does that work? You must have been one heck of a police officer."

"I had my moments, but I'll let you in on a little secret. It's partly because my brain isn't wired like other people's. Have you ever heard of *synesthesia?*"

Lisa shook her head and took another bite of ice cream. What on earth was he talking about? Did he have some type of disease?

"Don't look at me like that. It's not contagious. Synesthesia is a term for when your senses are mixed up. Some people hear sounds in response to a particular scent or feel something in response to what they see."

"How can you hear a smell? You smell a smell."

"Not necessarily. A person might see something a specific way, like numbers always appear in a certain color, so the number two is always green or threes are always blue."

"Do you see colored numbers?"

"No. In my case, I see when someone is lying. There's no way to really explain it, except that I know, the same way someone sees a number a certain color. It's how it appears for me. When I was a little kid, I thought everyone could tell when people weren't telling the truth." He licked the spoon. "Needless to say, that caused some problems in school."

"The other kids must have hated you."

"I got beat up all the time until I learned to shut up. No one likes a tattletale."

"I had to have a long conversation with Cheryl's second-grade teacher because Cheryl couldn't keep a secret about anything. The whole class started calling her Stinky Finky. I felt bad for her and I love her, but honestly, she really was a blabbermouth."

"Well, you wanted to know how I knew Craig was lying. Now you do." He set the empty bowl down in his lap. "I don't usually tell people about this because it's hard to explain and then they think I'm some kind of freak."

"I suppose, but the people you worked with must have loved it."

"Not as much as you might think. Criminals aren't the only ones who lie."

"I guess not."

"It's always been a mixed blessing. Knowing people aren't speaking the truth isn't necessarily pleasant. And I can tell you that some people lie as easily as they breathe." He put his hand on hers. "I don't think you've ever lied to me though, which is remarkable."

"I'll stick to lying to myself. It's a lot easier." She interlaced her fingers with his. "As Aunt Betty would say, 'Denial: it's not just a river in Egypt.'"

~

The next morning, Lisa extracted herself from Pete's bed. Once he moved to using a cane, he would be able to more easily navigate stairs and they could sleep somewhere else. With a smile, she thought about the king-sized bed in the master bedroom. Pete was going to have to move out of the office eventually so the construction crew could begin work on it. She and Pete might as well be comfortable and switch to a larger bed.

She let Harley out the kitchen door into the backyard and watched as he did his typical circuit, patrolling the area along the fence line. He picked up a stick that had been buried in the sloppy muddy snow and ran toward her, proud of his exciting new find. She threw the stick a few times for him and thought about Pete's idea for the letter 'w.'

Mom had told her a story about how after one Christmas, Lisa's nephew Leon had been so upset about taking down the Christmas tree and throwing it out that he launched into a tantrum, complete with lying on the floor, kicking and screaming. To hear Mom tell it, Leon put on quite a performance.

In an effort to quiet the screaming child, Lisa's dad had made a deal with Leon. If Leon let his grandpa remove the branches from the tree, the trunk would fit in the corner of the garage. The tree would be saved for posterity and Leon could visit it whenever he liked. Dad chopped up the tree per Leon's instructions and peace was restored. The trunk was probably still sitting there in its corner, as it had been for years. Leon was now married and living in Hawaii, so he probably wouldn't mind if Lisa appropriated part of his tree trunk for a good cause.

After feeding Harley and checking the garage, she returned to Pete's room. He looked up from his book. "You look pleased with yourself."

"I found something that will work for your walking stick. Are you up for a day of whittling?"

He set the book aside. "You didn't steal one of the legs off the dining room table, did you?"

"Nope, this is way better!"

While Lisa was gathering supplies from dark, spider-infested corners of the garage, the front door slammed, indicating the workmen had arrived for the day. If Pete was going to make a big mess whittling, they were already in a construction zone and a few more wood chips wouldn't make a difference.

When she went back into the kitchen, Pete was chatting with Luke. The workman was laughing, but stopped abruptly when he saw Lisa.

Lisa said, "I need to talk to Craig. Is he here yet?"

Luke shook his head. "No, ma'am. I'm not sure what we're supposed to be doing today."

"He didn't tell you yesterday?" Lisa pulled a bowl down from the cabinet and turned around. "I was hoping you'd do something about the wall."

"Well, we need you to pick out some paint colors. I do know that," Luke said. "Then we can get started on painting some of the rooms."

Lisa slammed the silverware drawer. "Yes, I know. But it would be nice to have a wall to put the paint on first. Why did you rip it out that wall between the living room and dining room?"

"I didn't take out no wall." Luke said.

Lisa turned and pointed a fork at him. "What do you mean, you didn't? I'm missing a wall in my house."

Luke's eyes widened in innocence. "I was working upstairs yesterday, steaming that hall wallpaper. Or trying. It wasn't working too good. Rod was with me, scraping wallpaper and sanding some of the trim."

Pete said, "What was Craig doing?"

Luke moved his shoulders in a halfhearted shrug. "I dunno. Rod and me were busy. I guess Craig was downstairs the whole time."

Lisa sat down at the table. "Could you call Craig and find out what you're supposed to do?"

"I already tried this morning and left a message. He gets really pissed if we do stuff outta order or not on the schedule. I learned that the hard way." He frowned. "Man, I don't need that kinda lecture, you know."

"Unfortunately I do," Lisa said. "Why don't you and Rod take the day off? If Craig shows up, I'll have him call you. Honestly, I don't understand why this incredibly special schedule isn't kept here, so you know what to do every day."

"Craig says we need to remain flexible and the schedule is fluid, like an ocean with currents. Or something like that." Luke shrugged again. "Heck, I don't know. It's a job, you know what I mean? There's not a lotta work here in the wintertime."

Lisa said, "I know how that can be. Have a good day."

After Luke left, Lisa turned to Pete. "So, Mr. Synesth-whatever-you-said, was he lying?"

"Nope. He has no idea what happened to your wall."

"Well, then let's enjoy the quiet day and make a huge mess."

He laughed. "That sounds like more fun."

They settled into Pete's room with lots of tools. Pete used a hand-saw to cut down the old Christmas tree trunk to a manageable size and began peeling off the old, dried-out bark. Underneath, the wood was a warm yellow-gold color.

Lisa busied herself flipping through the huge stack of *Cosmo* magazines. She held up an image of a woman with a bouquet of flowers. "What do you think of this?"

Pete looked up from his wood. "It's not my table. It's yours. What do you think?"

"I don't know. This is harder than I thought it would be."

"No one is going to die if you cut out the wrong picture from a ten-year-old magazine."

"Thanks for your input." Lisa picked up the scissors and began cutting. She held up the bouquet. "I like these colors."

"Find more things you like. You're on a roll." He pulled off a long strip of bark and held it up. "Check it out! A new record. I'm getting good at peeling."

She smiled at him. "You seem to be having fun over there."

"That's the goal."

Once she started cutting, Lisa enjoyed the shredding process. The more magazines she looked at, the more colors and patterns she found that intrigued her. She started laying out her selections on the top of the old nightstand, trying to envision what it might look like once it was decoupaged.

She was so absorbed in her work that she was startled when Pete broke the silence by saying, "So I've been wondering what you plan to do after the work on the house is finished."

"My parents will list it for sale again."

"I know that, but what are *you* going to do?"

Lisa put down the scissors and smoothed her pieces of paper on the nightstand, trying to think of something to say. She had no good response to that question. "I'm not sure. Before I came up here to Alpine Grove, I took a couple of classes at the community college."

"In what?"

"I took English 101 and a U.S. history course because they were requirements. You know why I never went to college. While Bev was busy selecting her major, I was changing diapers. When I signed up for classes, I wasn't sure what to take, but I had to start somewhere."

"Aren't you missing classes now?"

"The deadline to sign up was ages ago. I didn't know what I wanted to take and my car died. I also was worried I was sick, so I didn't want to commit to another semester of classes. It turned out I wasn't sick, but then I ended up here, so it's just as well."

Pete didn't say anything for a few moments and continued chipping away at his wanna-be walking stick.

Lisa looked down at her magazine. "At the rate this remodel is going, it could be quite a while before the house can be listed for sale. It's not like I'm going to throw you out tomorrow or something."

He looked up. "That's not what I was asking. I am wondering what you want to do next. What's the next thing you plan to do with your life? Are you going to return to Gleasonville and go back to school?"

"Maybe. I'm not sure. I guess so. Are you going back to Phoenix?"

"It's where I live. Right now, I'm paying rent on two places, which isn't the smartest financial decision I've ever made."

"I suppose not." Lisa looked down at her magazine and closed it. She glanced at Pete, who had returned to silence, engrossed in his wood peeling. Why was he asking her these questions? Was something wrong? With a sigh, Lisa opened the magazine again, trying to distract herself from questions that she didn't know how to answer.

～

Lisa continued cutting up magazines, but she remained disturbed by Pete's comments. She had no idea what was behind his concern about her future. Maybe she wasn't the only one who was wondering if they had a future together. Her ruminations were interrupted by the jarring sound of the phone ringing.

Jumping over the scraps of paper and magazines, she ran to the bar and picked up the phone.

Craig said, "I'm returning your messages."

"I've been calling all day. Thank you for getting back to me. Is something wrong?"

"I had to go out of town."

"When are you coming back?"

There was a pause. "Well, I've got to take care of some business, so it might be a while."

"How long is a while?"

"I'm not sure."

Lisa's angry reflection stared back at her from the mirror behind the bar. "So when do you plan to put my wall back together?"

"Well, it could be a while."

"Why did you rip it out in the first place?"

"I told you there was water damage."

"Do you think I'm blind? There's no damage there. Were you looking for something inside the wall?"

There was a suspiciously long pause before Craig replied. "We were looking for dry rot, like I said."

"Did you find it?"

"Well, there might be some rot. I think there is, so we were checking."

"No, I mean whatever it was you were looking for in the wall. I know you weren't looking for damage and that there wasn't any dry rot. What did you take from this house?"

"I don't think I appreciate your tone, Ms. Lowell."

"Did you steal from me?" Lisa knew her voice was shrill, but she didn't care. "Did you? Tell me!"

"I'm not sure what you're insinuating, but I think you need to find someone else to finish your remodel."

"Answer me! What did you steal? I know you found something in this house." Lisa heard the sound of Pete's crutches on the floor as he came up beside her. The line went dead and she turned her head to look at Pete. "He hung up on me."

Pete put his arm around her. "Did he really take something?"

"He won't admit it, but I know he did. I could tell from his voice. He knew I was on to him." Lisa leaned her head against Pete's shoulder and closed her eyes. "Even worse, I think I just lost the only general contractor in Alpine Grove. What am I going to do?"

The front door opened and Harley shot out of the room, barking furiously. Lisa looked at Pete. "I doubt that's a contractor."

Harley ran back into the room, followed by Lisa's mother, who stopped in the doorway of Pete's room, taking in the scene. Pete dropped his arm and Lisa took a step away from him, smiling meekly. "Hi, Mom."

Natalie Lowell opened her arms toward the room. "Lisa, what in heaven's name have you done to my house?"

"Um, well, Dad was supposed to talk to you about that," Lisa said.

Pete looked at Lisa and raised his eyebrows. Lisa closed her eyes in silent affirmation that yes, she was in fact lying to her own mother.

Natalie put her hands on her hips. "Where is the dining room wall? And the carpet, and the furniture and the wallpaper? Lisa Marie Lowell, you need to tell me exactly what is going on, right this second."

"All right. The truth is that Dad and Larry asked me to remodel the house, so it will sell. That's why I'm here. But they didn't want me to tell you," Lisa said.

"But it was professionally decorated! It doesn't need to be remodeled. Before you tore it apart, it was beautiful!" Natalie pointed at the bar. "I mean, look at that fine leather. It's gorgeous. You can't get that type of thing anymore."

Lisa stepped farther away from Pete. "I know, but it's really old now, Mom. Styles change."

"Why is there a hospital bed in here? Where is the desk?" Natalie's eyes widened and she moved toward Lisa with her arms outstretched. "Oh honey, are you sick again? The cancer didn't come back, did it?"

Lisa hugged her mother. "No, I'm fine, Mom. The bed isn't for me."

"You're sure you're okay?"

"When I got here, I had a little cold, but it's gone. I've been feeling great lately."

Natalie stepped back shook her head and seemed to realize that Pete was standing in the room. She pointed at him. "Excuse me, but who are you? I hate to be rude, but this is my house and I have no idea who you are."

Pete lifted his hand off his crutch and extended it to Natalie. "Pete Harmon. I'm, uh, staying here."

"You're the fellow Lisa and the dog saved at Snow Grove," Natalie said.

Pete nodded. "After my accident, I was going stir crazy in the nursing home and Lisa was kind enough to rent me this room, drive me around, and feed me."

Natalie glared at Lisa. "Well, now I know why your father kept suggesting that we meet you in town. It wasn't because it was more convenient for me. You two didn't want me to find out what was going on here. I'm going to have *such* a conversation with your father. How could he not tell me about any of this?"

Lisa made a face. "Well, he does know about the remodeling work, but I might not have mentioned the fact that Pete is staying here."

Natalie narrowed her eyes. "What type of arrangement do you have?"

"Arrangement?" Lisa said.

"Oh please, Lisa. I know that look. It's the same one you had when you slithered out of your room to meet that grotesque boy, Jared Oldman," Natalie said.

Pete chuckled and Lisa glared at him. "Don't you dare say anything."

Pete raised a palm in a gesture of surrender. "There's no way I'm touching that."

Natalie looked at Lisa, then at Pete. "I see. Fine. It's long past time when I have any say in what you do, but really Lisa, couldn't anyone have told me what was going on in my own home? When is all this construction going to be finished? It's a mess. We can't list the house like this. It's a disaster."

Lisa grimaced slightly. "Well, I might have just had a big fight with the contractor, and I'm not sure he's coming back. He tore out that wall for no reason. I think he's looking for something."

"He's looking for something in the wall? You can't be serious," Natalie said.

Pete pointed toward the doorway. "I think she might be right. It makes sense in a strange way. Craig said there was water damage, but there's not. And Betty has been looking for something in the house."

Lisa nodded. "It's true. Betty keeps saying that whatever she's looking for is in the house. I've brought her everything I can think of to her to look at, but now I think she means something is actually *inside* the house. And now I think the contractor took it."

Natalie's shoulders slumped. "Oh Lisa, you've always had an overactive imagination. This sounds completely far-fetched."

"It's Betty we're talking about, Mom. Think about it. This is exactly the type of weird thing she could have done," Lisa said. "I need to talk to her and find out if I'm right."

"But why would it be in the walls?" Natalie said. "And how would I not know about it?"

"Who knows? I'll let you know if I learn anything. Why did you decide to stop by today?" Lisa said.

"Well, you know your father's birthday is coming up, and I wanted to talk to you about it." Natalie pinched the bridge of her nose. "I swear I can't get two minutes away from that man, so I lied and told him I was going to the bank. I'd like to have a get-together, but our little cottage in town is too small. I thought since you weren't busy you could make arrangements to have it here."

"Having it here obviously isn't an option, and I might be busier than you thought," Lisa said. "I need to find a new contractor."

"Yes, you do. This is quite a mess you've made," Natalie said.

Lisa tugged at her earring. "Maybe Larry could take care of the arrangements. I bet he could make a deal with the guy who owns the Italian restaurant, and you could have Dad's party there. I'm pretty sure Larry keeps that place in business, so they owe him."

"I suppose you're right. It's only a few phone calls. I didn't want to ask because he's been so snippy since he started working on that Snow Grove project," Natalie said.

"Tell me about it," Lisa hugged her mother again. "I'm sorry Mom. I promise I'll fix everything."

Natalie held onto Lisa's shoulders and looked into her eyes. "Please keep me updated. I mean it."

After Natalie left, Lisa collapsed on the bed and threw her arm over her eyes. What a mess. She felt Pete crawl in beside her and move her arm. Lisa sat up and gazed down at him. "I'm sorry. That was not how I envisioned you might meet my mother."

"It's okay. She seems nice and she reminds me of you in some ways. I don't blame her for being a little...well... startled by the state of her house."

"What am I going to do? I've already talked to every general contractor in Alpine Grove."

"You could manage the project yourself. It's fairly obvious what needs to be done to at least get the house put back together."

"A new wall in the dining room, for example." Lisa leaned to kiss him. "Thanks for backing me up and not saying I'm crazy for thinking Craig stole something."

"I don't think you're crazy. After all, he did lie about something." Pete put his arm around her and she snuggled into his embrace. He ran his palm over her hair, stroking it gently.

Lisa hugged him. "I'm so glad you're here. I love you."

Pete's hand paused on her temple. He didn't say anything, but she could feel his body tense. Oops. She probably shouldn't have said that. Closing her eyes, she pretended not to notice the silence that felt like it went on for hours.

Chapter 12

Barnacles & Bean Dip

The next morning, Pete had another physical-therapy appointment, and Lisa went through the morning routine of letting Harley out and feeding everyone before the appointment. Fortunately, getting ready to go managed to be uneventful and accident-free this time. Not worrying about being invaded by workmen made the experience quite a bit more relaxing. Of course the house was also in shambles and her mother was furious, but Lisa was trying to find bright spots anywhere she could.

After Lisa had blurted out her feelings to Pete, the awkwardness had slowly dissipated. It was like they had an unspoken agreement to ignore that she'd said anything and pretend it never happened. A little corner of Lisa's heart was devastated that Pete obviously didn't feel the same way she did. But she didn't want to make a big deal about it because he'd be more likely to leave sooner rather than later.

Inevitably, Pete had to return to Arizona, but Lisa was trying not to think about his departure from her life. Then what? Pete had asked her what was next after the house was finished, and she had no idea. Maybe it was time to start putting some real thought into those questions, instead of avoiding ugly, complicated issues and hoping they'd go away. The future was going to arrive whether she wanted it to or not. She could go back to school, but to study what?

At the Alpine Grove Care Center, Pete went to his appointment and Lisa was again crowded with people who wanted to talk to her or pet Harley. It was nice to receive such a warm welcome every time she came to the nursing home. Residents told her interesting stories about the dogs they had owned and shared other experiences about life in Alpine Grove years ago. The only person who didn't seem to enjoy her company was Aunt Betty, but Lisa was hoping that would change after she talked to her aunt about the house.

She walked down the hall with Harley and peered into Betty's room, but her aunt appeared to be taking a nap. Not wanting to wake her up, Lisa sat down in a chair near the nurses' station at the end of the hallway. Orderlies, nurses, nursing assistants, therapists, administrators, and other people milled around like bees flying through a hive, landing briefly and moving on to their next task.

Maybe because she'd spent so much time in rehabilitation centers, she didn't find the environment depressing like many people did. She watched an assistant push a wheelchair with an elderly woman in a pink robe down the hallway. It was Mrs. Gibson, who had worked at the long-gone roller rink that used to be south of town. Lisa waved as she went by, and the older woman and the assistant smiled in response.

When Lisa was young, she'd earned good grades in school and had considered the idea of becoming a doctor, but her fear of blood had nixed the idea. Her accident and then years of being a parent had caused any lingering squeamishness to fall by the wayside long ago. Although Lisa couldn't quite envision herself dealing with eight years of college and a residency, maybe she could work in the medical field some other way.

A nurse named Deanna approached her and Lisa waved. "Do you have a second?"

The woman smiled at the sight of the dog and sat down in the chair next to Lisa. "Only if you let me pet Harley."

Harley thumped his tail enthusiastically and put his head on Deanna's thigh, soaking up the affection.

Lisa said, "I think Harley is A-okay with petting. The other day, you mentioned that you've worked here forever. I was wondering how you started in health care."

"When I graduated from high school I needed a job, so I started working here as an orderly. I liked the people and there were a lot of openings for nursing assistants, so I took a training program and was an assistant for a while. I enjoyed the work and spending time with the care-center residents, but wanted to move up, so I went back to school and got a nursing degree." She gave Harley a final pat and stood up. "That was probably more than you wanted to know, huh? I told you I'd been here forever."

"No, that's helpful. I appreciate it." Lisa leaned back in the chair and watched the activity around her. What would it be like to work in a place like this? Would it be too sad to be around people who were sick or even close to death? She wasn't sure, but it was worth thinking about, and she'd read about nursing shortages for years. If she went to school, she could probably get a job fairly easily. A million years ago, she'd done well in biology class. Maybe she could read more about physical therapy too. She'd experienced it from the patient side. What was involved in becoming a physical therapist? Probably more school and definitely a lot of anatomy classes.

She looked down the hallway again and was startled to spot Pete limping toward her without his crutches, leaning heavily on a cane. Although his gait was halting, lopsided, and slow, he had both feet on the ground. Jumping up, she clapped her hands and grinned at him as Harley woofed his congratulations.

George, the physical therapist, was walking alongside Pete. Given the expression on Pete's face, George was probably nagging him about something.

Lisa walked up as Pete said somewhat irritably to George, "I got it, okay? Jeez, lighten up."

"Hey, man, I'm just sayin' take it easy," George replied as he handed Lisa the crutches. "He doesn't get to return these yet. If he gets tired, make him use them."

Lisa nodded. Yeah, right. As if she could make Pete do anything. "Thanks. We'll see you on Friday."

George said goodbye and reiterated that Pete shouldn't start going on any major hikes just because he was cleared to use a cane.

Lisa walked Harley alongside Pete out to the truck. She readjusted the leash in her hand and encouraged the dog to slow down. "I can't believe you convinced George to let you ditch the crutches. You must be thrilled."

"He thinks I'm rushing things, but I'm now that much closer to being a self-sufficient adult again. Better three hours too soon than a minute too late."

"What?"

"More Shakespeare. 'The Merry Wives of Windsor.'"

"Okay, well, I had an idea. It's so beautiful outside today and you already had x-rays for the letter 'x,' but I need to do something for 'e.' Have you ever seen a bald eagle?"

"Are you going to give me a quarter or something?"

"No, I mean a real one. I don't feel like facing the mess at the house, so I was thinking we could go see the eagles on the lake. They come to the same spot every year during the winter. I've never seen them before, which is pretty sad for someone who grew up in Alpine Grove."

He stopped to rest and turned to smile at her. "Let me guess. You were too busy skiing?"

"Yeah, I know. I was focused on one thing back then. It's getting ridiculous how well you know me. At this rate you could write a biography of me and my entire family."

"I'm not much of a writer."

"Thank heavens."

~

Lisa drove south out of Alpine Grove and turned off the highway onto a road that wound down toward the lake. They passed by snow-covered fields and densely forested areas until the road curved along a hillside perched high above the deep blue water. They passed a few houses, but most of them were summer homes. Even though they had gorgeous lake views, the steep driveways would be harrowing to navigate in the icy depths of winter, so the dwellings sat dark and quiet behind locked gates.

Lisa pointed at the stunning lake view out the driver's-side window. "The cove where the eagles supposedly hang out is up ahead down there."

"This is a beautiful area. Even better is that you chose it."

"I think the eagles chose it first."

"No, I mean you selected what you wanted to do for the letter 'e' without any input from me, your family, your friends, or anyone else."

Lisa glanced at him before slowing the truck to turn down the narrow road that led to the cove. "So what?"

"Never mind. Thanks for bringing me out here."

At the bottom of the hill, the road flattened and led to a small parking area. Lisa parked the truck alongside the fence and let Harley out. Pete grabbed his cane and limped around next to Lisa, so they could lean on the front bumper of the old truck. Harley wanted to run around, but Pete suggested that the dog sit and behave himself so they could quietly watch the birds. Harley complied, settling in at their feet with his muzzle between his paws, looking dejected.

Lisa pointed at the sky, where an eagle soared overhead. "Look! There's one circling over the water."

Pete turned his head. "There are four sitting up on that tree, just hanging out. I can't believe I'm seeing bald eagles in the wild. They're huge."

"The eagles are a big deal around here. I learned about them in school. They come down from Canada in late fall or early winter because the weather is milder here. This is part of their annual migration route, and they stop here because they feed on the salmon in the lake."

"They probably like the lack of people too. I don't think anyone is going to be building a house on that hillside with all those rocks."

Lisa smiled. "One of the great things about this lake is all the rocky outcroppings. There's an overlook I love that's amazing, but you can't really get there in the wintertime."

"Well, I'm sure I couldn't."

"It's a bit of a hike, but I bet you could do it by next summer. You're doing so well with your physical therapy."

"George says that the fact that you help me with the exercises every day makes a big difference." Pete pointed at a large conifer with branches stretching out over the lake. "Check out that eagle perched over there near the water. He's impressive. I wish I had binoculars."

"I think that one on that branch over there might be his mate. Did you know that bald eagles pair for life?"

"Unlike humans, who seem to have trouble with that concept."

Lisa turned to look at him. "Every time I think I might be mating for life or even for the time being, the mate has other ideas."

"The course of true love never did run smooth."

Lisa nudged his arm playfully. "Hey, even *I* know that's Shakespeare."

"A Midsummer Night's Dream." He pointed at the sky. "Look at that one! He's got a fish!"

Lisa sat in silence for a few moments, watching the eagles soar overhead. Pete was in an odd mood. He kept changing the subject, but she felt like there was something he wasn't saying.

She put her hand on his. "Did something happen at physical therapy? I thought everything went well, but you seem distracted."

"I got my cane, so I'll finally be able to do things like carry a cup of coffee all by myself, maybe even without spilling it."

"I'd be happy to get you a cup of coffee. I've had lots of practice."

"I know and I appreciate it." He pulled his hand out from under hers. "This whole arrangement has been great, but I think it's time for me to move on."

"What?" Lisa stood up to face him. Was he already moving out? She wasn't ready for that to happen yet. "Why now? Staying at the house has been great, hasn't it? Well, except for the contractors. But I thought you were happy with…everything."

"Happy is relative."

"What exactly are you saying? You aren't happy? What's wrong?"

"I think it's time for me to go back home."

"But why now? You still can barely walk. And what about your physical therapy? Don't you want to continue that?"

"They have medical facilities in Phoenix. I've been to a bunch of them, remember?"

"I know, but you're doing so well." Lisa threw up her hands in exasperation. "And, okay, I know you obviously don't feel the same way I do, but are you really that desperate to get away from me?"

Pete's expression softened and he gathered her hands in his, pulling her back down to sit next to him. "I don't want to get away from you, but I have things I need to deal with back home. I don't think being with me is good for you. It's time for you to figure out what you want, and I don't think you're going to do that if I keep hanging around here."

"You just pointed out that I wanted to come here and see eagles. See! That was something I wanted. You make it sound like I'm some kind of naive child who is incapable of handling the hardship of putting up with you. But I've loved the time we've spent together. I don't understand why you want to leave already."

"Staying here isn't a good idea. I told you that."

"But your reasons don't make any sense and I don't agree with them. I don't care if you've seen awful things. It doesn't make any difference to me."

"But it does to me. I don't live in Alpine Grove, so I have to leave eventually. I think it's better if I leave sooner rather than later."

Lisa pulled her hands away. "That's because you know I'll get more attached. I'm like a hideous barnacle you can't shake."

"You're a kind, caring person and you deserve to be with someone a lot less cynical and jaded than I am."

"I don't agree with you, but obviously I'm not going to change your mind." Lisa crossed her arms across her chest. "So when are you packing up your things and moving out?"

"George wants to see me one last time on Friday, so I was thinking I could get a flight out from LA on Saturday."

"You told George you're leaving Alpine Grove before you told me?"

"It sort of came up in conversation."

"Why? What were you talking about?"

"You."

∼

After they got back to the house, Lisa let Harley out into the backyard and followed Pete into the office. "I'm sorry to bother you, but I need to clean up my decoupage disaster in the corner."

"Aren't you going to finish the table? You've got half of it glued already."

"I'm done with the alphabet." She pointed at the table. "This was silly anyway."

He limped over to look at it. "Why? You were having fun with it and you said you liked how the flowers worked out on that corner."

"Yeah, but who cares? It's a crummy old table. I should sell it with the rest of the junk here."

"It's up to you. I like how my walking stick has come out so far. Using a hiking stick instead of a cane makes me feel more like an intrepid hiker and less like a decrepit old dude."

Lisa put the pile of magazines she was holding on the table. "You're not old."

"Just falling apart."

She stopped gathering pieces of paper and stood up to look at him. After their conversation earlier, neither of them were in a good frame of mind. "Maybe I'll deal with this later. Do you have any ideas for dinner?"

"It's up to you. But with any luck, I can help you now without tipping over."

"Why does it have to be up to me?" Lisa put her hands on her hips. "This is your passive-aggressive way of silently nagging me about not making decisions, isn't it?"

"Ouch. No, it's because you've been doing the shopping and it's your kitchen, so you have a much better idea of the food that's in it."

"Let me show you the refrigerator." Lisa turned and stomped toward the kitchen. She didn't look, but she could hear Pete following behind her.

She opened the refrigerator door and waved her hand in front of it like a game-show hostess. "Behold! Your options for dinner await."

Pete set his cane aside, reached into the refrigerator and pulled out a loaf of bread. "The staff of life."

Lisa grabbed the bag, opened it and pulled out two slices of bread, which she threw at Pete.

Startled, he managed to catch the bread before it landed on the floor. He held them up in his hands and raised his eyebrows in silent query.

"Nice reflexes. You might not be falling apart as much as you think."

"Oh, really?" He turned and reached into the refrigerator and pulled out a plastic container of mustard and lobbed it at her. "Catch."

Lisa grabbed it and immediately threw it back far to the left of him. Pete reached out but missed, so the container bounced across the floor.

"Oopsie, guess you're right. You are falling apart." She moved next to him, reached into the refrigerator, and pulled out a plastic storage container. "Hmm, I liked that bean dip I made yesterday. Maybe we can have some chips with the sandwich."

"Don't."

Lisa opened the container, peered inside, and then glanced at him. "It still looks good, although I might need to stir it a little."

Pete walked to a cabinet, pulled down a bag of corn chips, and put them on the counter warily, not taking his eyes off her.

Lisa ran her index finger along the edge of the container, swirled it through the middle of the dip a few times, then scooped up a glob and licked it off. "Yummy."

Pete limped toward her with his hand outstretched. "Maybe you could give that to me."

Lisa scooped up some more dip on her finger and whipped it forward, flinging a blob of brown gooey dip across his face. "Oops."

Some of the dip dripped down toward his lips and he stuck out his tongue to lick it off. "I know you're angry at me, but are you really angling for a food fight here? Seriously?"

"I changed my mind about the alphabet." She smiled and scooped up some more dip and whipped it at him. "I'm thinking food fight works for the letter 'f.' Since my plans for letter 'e' didn't work out well, I'm trying something a little different."

"'F' is also for friends, and friends don't let friends throw bean dip."

"Okay, I won't throw it." Lisa laughed as she dragged a glob of dip across his cheek with her palm. "Have you ever noticed how refried beans look kind of like dog doo?"

"No, I haven't, but thanks for that visual." Pete wiped the dip off his face and smeared it on Lisa's forehead. "Have you ever wondered what a bunch of bored cops waiting around in a police station do in the middle of the night? If you guessed food fight, you'd be right."

"Have you ever seen what nine-month-old twins can do to each other armed with only a single jar of baby food?" She smeared bean dip on his lips. "I promise you will never think about pureed peas in the same way ever again."

Pete snatched the plastic container from her, scooped out a fistful of dip, sloshed it on her neck, and pulled her to him so he could lick it off. "Yummy."

"No fair! You're cheating." When he didn't stop, Lisa moved her head to give him more access to her throat.

"Well…okay…if you don't want to fight fair, I'm going to have to do something drastic."

He straightened so he could look into her eyes. "Oh, really? And what's that?"

Taking the bean dip container from him, she carefully replaced the lid. She picked up the mustard, put the bread back in the bag, and placed everything back in the refrigerator where it belonged.

She turned back to him holding a squeeze bottle of chocolate syrup. "I like chocolate a lot better than bean dip and you've never seen the upstairs of this house. I think I should show you all of the bedrooms before you leave here."

A slow smile crossed his face. "I think you're right."

Much later, Lisa and Pete were sprawled out on the king-sized bed in the master bedroom. Lisa rolled over onto her side to face him. "I can't believe you're insisting on leaving in two days."

"I should probably pack and help you clean up the office."

"Do I need to drive you to LAX? I'm going to cry the whole way, you know, and it's a long drive."

"George knows a private pilot who owns a plane and flies from the Alpine Grove airport to LAX regularly. He flies some rich business consultant to LA a lot because the guy has to meet clients in the city all the time. I'm going to hitch a ride."

"Wow, you've really got this all figured out," Lisa said as she rolled onto her back. "I'm still going to cry."

Pete sat up and reached down to wipe a tear off her cheek. "Please don't."

Pulling the sheet up over her, Lisa sat up and wrapped her arms around her knees. "I know you don't want to hear it, but I love you, so don't you think it's natural that I'm going to miss you?"

He pulled her back into his embrace and rested his chin on her hair. "I love you too."

Lisa turned around, stunned at this revelation. "You *do*? Then why are you leaving? It doesn't make any sense."

"Just because I love you doesn't mean I should stay. For one thing, like I said, I need to get home. For another, I made my ex-wife miserable and I don't want to put you through that."

"I already told you, I don't care about what happened before. You're not a cop anymore, so really that's all old news."

"You need to figure out what you want to do with your life, or you'll resent me the same way you resent your ex-husband."

"That's not true. Even though we're not married anymore, I certainly don't *resent* him. Without him, I wouldn't have my girls. There's no way I'd have traded being their mother for anything."

"Maybe that's the wrong word then. But you're still not completely okay with how your life changed after you had your accident, and you've told me many times you have no skills. You need to discover for yourself what you're good at and things you like to do."

Lisa wanted to roll her eyes, but refrained. "Oh, please. Is this the alphabet thing again?"

"Living with me is not a career or even a hobby, once you don't have to deal with being my caregiver anymore. You'll get bored or feel like an under-paid maid and start to hate me. Like I said, I'm not easy to live with when I'm more like, well, myself."

"You keep saying that you're different than I think you are. That being a cop changed you. Maybe it did, but I've spent a lot of time with you now. What if getting shot, having a ski accident, living here, and even staying with me changed you too? Did you ever think of that?"

"I don't feel different, but I suppose all those years of counseling and PTSD support groups might have done something. Who knows? Maybe the meditation helps too. I don't know. But let's face it, I'm still pretty messed up."

Lisa rested her head on his chest. "I used to think that by this point in my life I'd have everything figured out. But I think everyone's a work in progress, making it up as we go along."

~

After their adventures in food fighting, chocolate escapades, and subsequent conversation, Lisa resolved to try not to ruin her last couple of days with Pete. He was leaving and she needed to accept it and try her best to behave like an adult.

It wasn't easy, so she decided to put off dealing with the unpleasant quest to find a new contractor until the following week, after Pete was in Arizona. She couldn't face dealing with that mess while Pete was still in residence. They had so little time left, she wanted to enjoy their last hours together in peace. Lisa resolved to finish gluing the last of the magazine pieces onto the decoupage table and clean up the mess she'd made in the office. Since Pete was definitely able to handle getting upstairs without any trouble, she had the medical supply company pick up the bed. The office seemed gigantic without the bed or desk in there.

Friday morning, Lisa took Pete to his last physical-therapy appointment. As usual, Harley had a fine time being fawned over by the residents of the facility, but today Lisa was on a mission to talk to her aunt Betty, so she dragged the dog away from his fans and down the hallway to Betty's room.

Betty was holding court with her four girlfriends again. The women were also pet lovers, so there was a lot of cooing and cuddling of the dog before Betty finally shooed them out. She leaned to pet the smooth fur on Harley's head while Lisa sat down in the chair next to the bed.

Lisa leaned forward in the chair toward her aunt. "I need to apologize to you, Betty. The last time I was here I was unkind and I'm sorry."

"It's okay, Linda. Sometimes I think you need a bit more backbone."

"There's also something I want to ask you about. It's about the stuff in the house that you want."

"That you never gave to me."

Lisa put her palms together, trying to shove down her irritation. "I haven't been able to find it, but I want to know if when you say your stuff is *in* the house, you mean it might be inside one of the walls."

"Well, I told you it was in the house, didn't I?"

"So you mean literally inside it, right? That what you want was built into the walls. Is that what you're saying?

"Of course. Weren't you listening? I put it there so it would be safe. It might be in that room that your mother turned into the dining room, now that I think about it."

"That's wonderful!" Lisa paused. "Or well, it would be, except we might have a little problem. It would be really great if you could tell me what the thing in the dining room wall actually is."

Betty's eyes clouded and she shook her head. "I'm not sure."

Lisa stood up and moved to sit on the bed, taking her aunt's hands in hers. "I have some bad news. If your stuff was located in the wall, I think it may have been stolen."

"Stolen! The whole point of putting it there was so no one would find it. You need to call the police! Call nine one one!"

"It would be really helpful if you remembered what it is because that would be the first question the police will ask. I think I know who took it, but there's no way to get it back if I don't know what I'm asking for in the first place."

"All right, I'll try." Betty looked thoughtful for a moment. "Who do you think stole it?"

"The contractor who was working on the house, Craig Maddox. I think he's originally from Los Angeles."

"That name sounds familiar." Betty shook her head. "But I don't know why. I can't remember."

"All right. If you think of anything, please let me know. I'm still at the house. Craig has disappeared and I have to figure out how I'm going to get the rest of the work done."

Betty patted her hand. "If you find that snake, I want to talk to him too."

Lisa mustered a wry smile. "Don't count on it. When I confronted him, he didn't take it well. He made it sound like he has left town."

Betty looked concerned. "I'm going to think on this, Linda. I promise I will."

Lisa said goodbye to her aunt and she and Harley walked down the hall to wait for Pete. She settled into the chairs outside the physical-therapy room and listlessly thumbed through an ancient magazine she'd already perused.

Lisa looked up when the door opened. Pete limped out, followed by George. The physical therapist really was gorgeous. Now that her sex life was about to return to a bleak, lonely wasteland, maybe she should continue to stop by here. When she visited Betty, she could wander down to the physical-therapy area and casually say hi to George so she could at least get a little eye candy.

Pete thanked George and said goodbye. Lisa and Harley accompanied Pete to the truck, and on the drive back to the house, he asked, "So did you learn anything from Betty?"

Lisa shook her head. "Whatever the mysterious stuff is, she doesn't know. She is definitely mad at Craig and demanded that I call the police. She did seem to realize that I can't report a theft if I don't know what was stolen."

"Yeah, it doesn't even count as vandalism, since the guy was working on the house. Does she know Craig?"

"I don't think so. Or maybe she did, but she can't remember." Lisa shrugged. "Conversations with Betty are confusing, but I apologized to her, so I feel better. We've mended fences and I think she understands why I can't give her the thing she wants."

Pete crossed his arms across his chest. "The fact that Craig stole something out of the house bothers me."

"That's your latent crime-fighting skills talking. There's nothing I can do about it, so it's not worth thinking about anymore. Did George give you a referral to a physical therapist?"

"Yes, although he thinks I should stay here longer for continuity and all that."

"At least I'm not the only one who thinks you should stay." Lisa's stomach was a little queasy at the thought that the next day she'd have to say goodbye and watch Pete get on a plane.

"Hey, we talked about this. It's not like we'll never talk to each other again. We agreed that I'll call you on Saturdays or you'll call me."

"Once a week isn't enough."

"You'll get used to it."

"I suppose, but I'm going to be looking forward to weekends even more now. It's going to be strange not talking to you every day. Having breakfast, talking while we're going through all my family's ancient crap, and just having you around. The house is going to seem so quiet again."

"It's not like I'm not going to miss you too, you know."

Lisa wanted to scream, "Then don't leave!" but managed to contain herself. He wasn't saying why he was so dead set on leaving in the morning, and she was wondering if there was something he wasn't sharing. Maybe he had a girlfriend back in Phoenix that he'd neglected to mention. How would she know?

The next morning, Lisa dropped Pete off at the Alpine Grove airport, which was comprised of one short runway surrounded by a few hangars. She and Harley watched as Pete got into a tiny plane that looked far too flimsy to get airborne.

When she saw the two-seater aircraft sitting on the tarmac, she demanded that Pete promise to call her when he arrived home to let her know he'd made it back to Arizona safely. He pointed out that she would probably be attending a party, and she replied, somewhat tartly, "so leave a message" before she gave him one last kiss goodbye.

It was too bad if he didn't appreciate her concern. That plane was scary small.

Chapter 13

Mondegreens

After Pete left, the last thing Lisa wanted to do was go to a party, but Kat's big bachelorette blowout was on the agenda and Lisa had committed herself to going. She'd called Maria earlier in the week to give her regrets, using Harley as an excuse. Without Pete at the house she had no dog sitter, and taking Harley to the kennel at the last minute seemed rude, since the party was for the kennel's owner.

Unfortunately, Maria had countered the argument, stating that dogs were invited to the event. Lisa was so surprised she couldn't think of a way out of it and agreed to attend. At least Kat had remained firm on her commitment to veto costumes and strippers.

Lisa got ready to go and loaded Harley into the truck. Maria had pointed out that the liquor was going to flow and most attendees had a ride home with a spouse, significant other, or friend. She'd said, "It's like Cinderella, where we all turn into pumpkins at midnight when our rides show up."

It had occurred to Lisa that Cinderella didn't turn into a pumpkin, but her ride did. She didn't want to get into a big fairy-tale debate, so she decided to arrive late and leave early. If she made an appearance, had some tonic water, and let Harley say hi to a few canine friends, that would be plenty.

She hadn't been to the Enchanted Moose in years. It was a motel, RV park, and convention center that stayed in business mostly because people had so few options for event venues and places to stay in Alpine Grove. It was also the only motel that allowed dogs. All of Lisa's high school reunions had been held at the Moose, but she'd been able to avoid them so far.

Lisa and Harley got out of the truck, and she wandered around the grassy areas with him to ensure his bladder was empty before they went inside. The party was being held in one of the smaller rooms in the conference building. As Lisa walked down the hallway, it wasn't difficult to determine which room it was because loud, raucous music blasted from within. When she opened the door, she entered a darkened area filled with twinkly lights that had been strategically strung in the shape of a specific part of the male anatomy.

Lisa put her hand over her mouth as she stared up at the lights. She was startled by a woman who came up next to her and said, "It's really something, isn't it?"

Lisa nodded, rendered temporarily speechless at the level of anatomical detail. Harley was wagging his tail, whapping her leg like a whip. She looked down and noticed that Harley had encountered another Labrador and the two dogs were happily sniffing one another. The woman at the other end of the dog's leash said, "I'm Jan. I think we met at the library. This is my dog, Rosa"

Lisa peered at her more closely. "Oh, yes. Hi. It's nice to see you again. That's some, uh, interesting headgear you have."

Jan took off the glittery penis tiara and held it in front of her. "Once she finds you, Maria will make you wear one too."

"I need to hide."

"Well, she's headed for the stage now, so you have a reprieve. We should probably sit down for this."

"I think so."

They settled into their seats with their dogs lying down next to them. Lisa noticed that Harley was being remarkably well behaved. Maybe all the work Pete had done training both the dog and Lisa had finally paid off. Or maybe the poor dog was in a state of shock at all the strange sights and smells.

The music died down and the two women looked up at the stage as Maria attempted to negotiate the small step up. The maneuver was challenging because the lime-green spandex dress she was wearing made it difficult for her to move her legs. She teetered a few times, then grabbed the microphone off a stand. "Welcome everyone!"

Jan leaned to Lisa. "You missed out on a number of drinking games earlier."

"That's okay. I'm not drinking, since I have to drive home."

"I'm not either. After an incident with spiked Jell-O shots, I determined that alcohol and I needed to break up. We didn't have a good relationship at all."

From the stage, Maria said, "Thank you all for being here to celebrate Kat's last few weeks as a free woman. Where are you, Kat?"

Kat waved her hand weakly from the bar, where she was standing with her gigantic hairy dog, Linus. It was a good thing the dog was so large because he seemed to be propping her up.

Lisa whispered to Jan, "Is she okay?"

"Three sheets to the wind, which is probably the only way she'll get through this. Karaoke is next."

"Wow. It's probably a good thing she won't remember it."

Maria said, "As you know, the live entertainment I had planned fell through, so the entertainment is us! My friend Fred let me use his karaoke machine from the bar. But I'm sad to say that in an unfortunate turn of events, one of the patrons of the Mystic Moon Soloan got a little too exuberant and the machine has a little problem, so the thingie that shows the lyrics is dead. But it's okay! You all know the words to these tunes, so feel free to sing along!"

She bent to turn on the music and after a belch of static, the machine burst forth with the music from "Daydream Believer" by the Monkees.

Maria belted out, "Cheer up, Lean Cuisine!"

Lisa looked at Jan, "What did she say?"

"I think she might not know the lyrics as well as she thinks she does."

"Did she say beans? I'm positive *that's* not right."

"It's not." Jan said, "The song was composed by John Stewart not too long before he left the Kingston Trio. It was recorded by The Monkees and hit the number-one spot on the Billboard Hot 100 chart in 1967. Davy Jones sang the lead vocals."

"Good heavens, you certainly know your Monkees trivia."

"I know a lot of trivia. It's a bit of an occupational hazard."

Lisa gestured toward the stage. "Is it just me, or is this version dirtier than the original?"

Maria belted out,
"I once thought of you
As a white knight on his skis.
Now there's snow and holy crap he peed
Then the glad times start and end
And the taller one will spend
But how much faith in jewelry will we really need?"

Cheer up, Lean Cuisine!
Oh, a can of beans
A daydream, I believe
I'm under the homecoming queen."

Maria completed the song and bowed deeply. "Someone else has to take a turn now."

Many of the women in the room were ducking their heads, attempting to make themselves invisible. Finally, a blonde woman held up a glass and proclaimed, "You're all a bunch of wimps!" before ascending the stage.

A woman hiding in a dark corner shouted, "Go, Tracy!" as Maria handed her the microphone.

The strains of "Blinded by the Light" came from the karaoke machine, but Lisa was only half paying attention. "White knight on skis" reminded her of Pete. Okay, he wasn't a knight and she'd never actually seen him *on* skis, but still. She gave herself a mental reprimand for going down this line of thought yet again. It was past time to stop thinking about him. Continuing to be hung up on a guy who lived in a different state was going to make her miserable.

Jan said, "I estimate that there is a less than three percent chance that Tracy will sing these lyrics correctly."

"Well, she did get the song title right."

Tracy crooned, "Wrapped up like a douche when you're rolling in the night."

"And the ninety-seven percent wins again!" Jan said. "The correct lyrics have the word deuce, not douche."

"Really? I could never understand it."

"I don't think anyone else can either. Misheard lyrics are called mondegreens. The term was coined by the author Sylvia Wright after she misheard the lyrics of a Scottish ballad as 'Lady Mondegreen,' instead of 'laid him on the green.'"

Lisa was starting to understand why Pete had said Jan might be the smartest woman he'd ever met. Trivia didn't even begin to cover it. The woman was a walking encyclopedia.

Lisa poured some water from a pitcher on the table into the glass in front of her. "I have trouble with Elton John songs, like the one with the electric boobs and the mole hair suit. I mean, that can't possibly be what he's really saying."

"In 'Bennie and the Jets' he's talking about boots, not boobs, and it's mohair."

"It sounds like boobs."

"I think so too." Jan pointed at the stage. "Poor Kat. I think Maria is trying to get her to sing."

They watched as Maria detached Kat from her grip on the large brown dog and shoved her up onto the stage. Kat was holding a glass and downed the rest of the amber liquid before trading her glass for the microphone.

Tracy stumbled off the stage and Maria deftly caught the glass and Tracy before she did an undignified face-plant on the floor.

Kat threw her tiara into the audience like a Frisbee. Maria returned to the stage and turned to the machine. She whispered something to Kat, to which Kat replied into the microphone, "But I only know four words of that song."

The microphone picked up Maria saying, "So what? Just make it up."

"Don't Bring Me Down" by Electric Light Orchestra came on and Lisa noted that Kat was right. She managed to get the words in the song title correct, which fortunately accounted for a large percentage of the lyrics. Sadly, Kat couldn't carry a tune and Lisa was pretty sure the real lyrics weren't, 'You're always talking 'bout your gravy bites. One of these days you're gonna get advice.'

When the song was over, Kat staggered off the stage and returned to her position next to her dog. He gave her a slurp for moral support and she bent down to hug him.

Lisa nudged Jan. "That's sweet. At least she has one fan."

Maria jumped up onto the stage and said, "Okay, it's time to rock some eighties now! This one is in honor of my possessed cat, Scarlett and her new kitty boyfriend, Quincy. I blame Kat for my further descent into cat-ladyhood, so this one is for you, girlfriend."

Lisa looked at Jan, who responded with an 'I don't know' shrug.

Maria clutched the microphone and wailed, "The sheep don't like it. Rock the cat box. Rock the cat box!"

Lisa said, "I always thought it was 'rock the cash bar'."

"Nope. Casbah," Jan said.

Maria announced that after karaoke, party games were next, including Twister and pin the tail on the donkey. She directed a spotlight to a huge poster of a muscular man sporting six-pack abs, a cowboy hat, and nothing else. Lisa was pretty sure that a tail was not going to be what they'd be pinning onto the guy.

By the time a woman named Robin had mangled Carly Simon's "You're So Vain" with 'You walked into the potty like you were walking onto a yacht,' Lisa had decided she'd seen and heard enough.

After saying goodbye to Jan, she went over to the bar to congratulate, or maybe console, Kat before she left.

Kat was leaning heavily on the dog, who was now wearing a tiara. She straightened slightly as Lisa walked toward her and raised a glass.

Harley and Linus sniffed each other while Lisa gave Kat a hug. "Thank you for inviting me."

"At least you can say you saw it." Kat lifted a penis-shaped straw from her drink and pointed it at her. "Because nobody would believe this unless they saw it for themselves."

Lisa laughed, "I suppose you're right. Drink lots of water before you go to bed tonight, okay?"

"Yeah, Joel will be here in...um...I don't know how many minutes." Kat turned her wrist to look at her watch, dumping the ice cubes and the dregs of her drink on the floor. "Oops. Clean up, aisle two!"

Linus slurped up the ice cubes, made a few crunching noises, and the mess was gone. Harley looked disappointed and sniffed the floor incredulously. Lisa tugged on the leash. "Come on. Let's go. You missed it."

"My consolation for all of this is that soon I'll be in Hawaii!" Kat held up her empty glass. "I put on my flip-flops. Stepped on a Pop-Tart…blah, blah, something about a heel. But there's boobs in a blender…and soon it surrenders. And something or other helps me hang on…"

Lisa gave Kat another hug and led her to a chair. "Have fun in Margaritaville."

~

Sunday morning Lisa methodically walked through the house room by room, taking notes in an effort to assess what needed to be done to finish the house. From her admittedly non-expert perspective, it seemed that most of the destruction phase was complete with the exception of the office, where Pete had stayed. The wallpaper had been removed for the most part, the carpet was gone, and some of the more atrocious moldings and built-ins had also been torn off and hauled away. Now it was time to get the house put back together.

Maybe she could manage it herself, as Pete had suggested. In addition to new drywall for the dining room wall, all of the rooms needed to be painted and have the new flooring installed. If she pulled the knobs off the kitchen cabinets and repainted them, even the kitchen was probably passable. The flooring had been ordered and was sitting at Lowell's Hardware waiting to be installed. If she could find a flooring contractor, maybe Luke and Rod could be convinced to help with painting. And she could certainly wield a paintbrush and roller herself, if it came down to it.

It was also going to be necessary to have a massive yard sale to get rid of the rest of the furniture. She'd been putting it off because of the weather, but maybe she could hold the event inside by leaving the furniture in place and putting price tags on it.

With a yard sale, people usually dragged all the stuff they wanted to sell into the yard, so valuables in the house wouldn't be visible to browsers. But in this case, if someone wanted to steal a thirty-year-old ashtray, they'd be doing Lisa a favor. From the sounds of it, Craig Maddox had already stolen the only valuable item that had been in the house. Whatever it was.

After weeks of going through things with Pete, she wanted to finally get rid of absolutely everything that was left. Selling it all would be less like a yard sale and more like an estate sale, except that no one had died.

Well, that wasn't entirely true. One thing had died. It had been only a matter of hours and she missed Pete terribly. Although she'd never say it to Bev, Lisa felt as if she had lost her best friend. At least she still had Harley to keep her company. He'd followed her on her construction assessment throughout the house like a furry shadow, making sure she was okay.

"Oh Harley, you're such a good boy." She reached down to pat his head. "I think it's time we make this official. There's no way I'm going to let anyone else adopt you."

Lisa picked up the phone and dialed Larry's office. Brigid answered in a businesslike tone and asked if she wanted to speak to Larry. Lisa cleared her throat. "Actually, do you have a second? I was hoping to talk to you about Harley."

"Is he okay? I didn't think you were leaving town yet. Larry said the house is still under construction and implied there was a delay, so I wasn't worried yet."

"I suppose he talked to my mother. Ugh. I guess I do need to talk to him about the house."

"You shouldn't have to foster Harley for too much longer, I hope. The article in the newsletter generated a few calls, and I have a family who might be interested in adopting him. They've been hemming and hawing that a Labrador is too big, but I'm hoping they'll come around."

"Tell them no. He has a home. I want to adopt Harley."

"What? Really? That's fantastic news! Foster failures make me so happy."

"I'm a failure?"

"A foster failure is someone who fosters a dog but loves him so much they decide to adopt him. Honestly, how could you not fall in love with Harley? He's such a sweetheart."

"Well, it helped that Pete trained him. Harley is so much better behaved now. He sits and lays down on command. They love him at the Alpine Grove Care Center."

"You should do therapy work with him. Dogs are so comforting for people in places like that."

Lisa looked down at Harley. "I guess I could. I'm not sure what's involved."

"Talk to the folks at the facility. I bet they'd be thrilled."

"Harley does seem to like having a job to do."

"You could consider search-and-rescue work too. He already rescued one person. How's the guy he found at Snow Grove doing?"

"Much better. Pete went back home to Arizona yesterday."

"Good for him. I'll get Harley's adoption paperwork set up for you."

"Is Larry going to be around later today? I should stop by and talk to him about the house issues. Losing my general contractor will change the money arrangements, I'm afraid."

"Yes, Larry's schedule is open. See you later. I'm so excited—I'm going to get started on Harley's paperwork right this second!"

Lisa hung up and gazed down at the dozing dog at her feet, trying to put the upcoming unpleasant conversation with her brother out of her mind. Harley seemed largely unaffected by the dramatic change in his fortunes. Seeming to sense that Lisa was staring at him, he raised his head and thumped his tail a few times. Lisa reached down to pet him. "Guess what? You're *my* dog now. That means you need to help me figure out how to fix the mess I've made of this house."

Lisa called Luke and Rod and asked them to stop by the house. Because of Craig's disappearance to the wilds of Los Angeles, both of them were out of work and eager to talk to her about earning some money again.

Bright and early Monday morning, the two men and Lisa negotiated an hourly rate that was higher than what they had earned subcontracting. By the time she left, Lisa was extremely pleased with herself. She had two people who were enthusiastic about helping her finish the job. Luke and Rod seemed relieved to be working for her directly, instead of having to deal with Craig and his cryptic rules and lists. They went over her notes and Luke suggested a couple of freelance flooring installers who generally worked with the big flooring companies, but probably weren't busy in late February.

The rest of the week Lisa spent working on the house. Most of the time she wasn't working, she was either exhausted or asleep. She successfully lined up a company to lay the new flooring and they claimed they didn't mind working around the furniture and painting projects.

The only break she took was to visit Betty at the Alpine Grove Care Center with Harley. When Lisa arrived, Betty was off getting her hair done, so Lisa ended up spending some time talking to Deanna, the nurse she'd talked to before.

When Lisa asked her about volunteering with Harley, the nurse had laughed and pointed out that because of her many regular visits, Lisa was virtually no different from any other volunteer. The residents knew Harley and constantly asked when he was returning. Deanna gave Lisa some paperwork to fill out, so her status as a volunteer could be made official. When Harley visited Pete the first time, Lisa had been asked to provide his veterinary records, so he already passed muster.

Before she left, Lisa completed the volunteer forms at the reception desk. "So I guess I'm signing my life away now."

Deanna leaned over the counter toward her. "Maybe. On that note, after your questions the other day, I was wondering if you've ever thought about working here? Like as a paid job, not as a volunteer."

"I have thought about what you said too." Lisa put down the pen. "But right now, I'm working on fixing up my parents' house. It's an all-consuming project at the moment."

"What happens when it's done? Do you already have a job? I got the impression you were looking."

"I'm not qualified to do anything, except maybe flip burgers. I have a high school diploma, but that's it. I did take a couple of classes at the community college back in Gleasonville, but I didn't know what to do with it. I mean, U.S. history is interesting, but it's not like I want to become a history teacher, so I felt like it was a waste of time."

"There are serious shortages in the health-care field. If you took one of the state-approved courses to become a certified nursing assistant, you'd get a job."

"You think so?"

"I'm sure of it. We're short-staffed and it's worse at the facility we have in Gleasonville."

"I did my rehab there years ago after a ski accident. It was before they expanded and long before this one was built."

Deanna smiled. "You're great with the residents and the CNA courses don't take years, so it might be something worth thinking about."

Lisa returned her smile. "I definitely will. Thanks."

~

By the time the weekend rolled around, Lisa had moved beyond exhausted to bone tired. She gave herself the gift of sleeping in late as a small concession to her worn-out muscles. The phone rang and Harley leaped up to bark at it.

After settling Harley down, she picked up the receiver and smiled at the sound of Pete's voice. "You're calling early."

"It's an hour later here. Are you still in bed?"

"Why would you think that? You know I get up early."

"You are in bed. I can tell."

Lisa propped her head up on her palm. "How? I thought you had to see people to tell they are lying."

"Because I know you. It's different. So how come you're still in bed?"

"I'm tired. So much has happened I don't even know where to begin."

"How about starting when I left?"

Lisa regaled Pete with everything she could think of about recent events. He laughed at her anecdotes about the bachelorette party, the construction project, Harley, and her various painting misadventures.

In her excitement to talk to him, she eventually realized that Pete hadn't said one word about what was going on with him in Phoenix. "So okay, you've heard it all now. Everything from drunken parties to questionable rumors and gossip from the geriatric community at the Alpine Grove Care Center. What's happened with you in the last week?"

"Not much, really. Went to the PTSD group that I've been going to for years. I think they were a little relieved to find out I wasn't dead."

"I suppose that's a reasonable concern."

"My level of personal risk dropped considerably when I left the force."

"Good point, but they probably don't know what a bad skier you are."

Pete laughed. "Very true."

"How's rehab going? George already asked me the other day if you were behaving yourself."

"It's all right. I kinda miss George though. He was good at making me work, but it didn't seem like it, so I didn't realize that's what he was doing. In retrospect, it was pretty sneaky and probably helped me a lot."

"Is something wrong? You sound sort of...I don't know... different, I guess."

"Not really. Maybe I'm jealous. You did all these amazing, funny, interesting things in only one week. And I sort of sat around in the air conditioning and moped. I can't believe it's over eighty degrees already. I'm not ready to deal with hundred-and-ten-degree days again."

"Moped? I thought you had all this stuff to do."

"I wanted to see my friends and the people at the group. I felt like I had abandoned my life here and things would fall apart. But really, everything is fine. It wasn't like I didn't pay my bills."

"True. You did call your neighbor and ask him to send your mail." Lisa rolled onto her back and stared at the ceiling. "As for my week, mostly, I worked my tail off. I don't know how amazing that is."

"Hey, I'm impressed. I wish I were there to help, but I'd fall off the ladder."

"I wish you were here too. Have you given any more thought to visiting?"

"We'll see."

Lisa didn't think she was getting the whole story. Something was bothering him. "I still have this huge house, you know, so there's lots of room. It does smell like paint though. Harley has paint on his tail now too."

Pete chuckled. "Given what you told me, it sounds like he's been really helpful."

"He's provided lots of moral support since you left. I thought he might stage some type of revolt after his favorite person went away, but maybe he knew I was upset and that I'm his permanent mom now, so he has to be nice to me. He actually has been really good. And when I ask him to sit, he sits."

"He was doing that before I left, but that's great to hear."

Lisa reached down to pet Harley. The word 'great' didn't match Pete's tone of voice. "Are you sure nothing is bothering you?"

"I guess I miss being there more than I thought I would. I've always been one of those people who has no problem being alone. I think spending so much time out in the world fighting crime made me desperate for quiet when I was at home. But now the silence is driving me nuts. I miss talking to you."

"Well, we could talk more than once a week. And I keep telling you, the invitation is open whenever you want to visit."

"I should finish up my rehab here. It would be nice if the next time you saw me, I could walk."

"You know I don't care about that."

"I care."

"Well, maybe you could plan to visit once I'm back in Gleasonville, then. I'm looking into doing their certified nursing assistant program. It takes less than six months and then I could get a job. Deanna thinks I can get a job at their facility down there or in Alpine Grove because they're short-staffed."

"I had no idea you were interested in that type of work, but I think you'd be an excellent nurse. Why didn't you say something?"

"When I was waiting for you to finish physical therapy, I talked to Deanna and it got me thinking. It was the day you got your cane and I was excited about that. Later, you dropped the bomb that you were leaving and I forgot about it."

"I guess that was a complicated day. Hey, I can give you a reference, since I was your patient."

"I think you might be a little biased. And in case you're wondering, I don't plan to sleep with all my patients."

He laughed. "I'm glad to hear it."

"Think about visiting, okay? I still love you. Nothing has changed."

"I don't know about that. It sounds like lots of things have changed in a good way. You're kicking butt and taking names."

Lisa laughed. "I don't think anyone has ever said anything like that about me in years."

"I know you're still the same determined woman who set her sights on the Olympics and kept unruly twins from drowning in an ocean of strained peas. Oh, and who I happen to love. I'll talk to you next Saturday, okay?"

"I'll be here, assuming I haven't fallen into a paint bucket or something."

"Don't worry. If that happens, you've got Harley there to rescue you."

After they said goodbye and she hung up the phone, Lisa looked down at the dog, who was fast asleep next to the bed. "You hear that, hero dog? You better keep an eye on me."

Chapter 14

Decisions

Spending all day every day painting gave Lisa a lot of time to reflect upon the conversations she'd had with Carol, Cheryl, and Pete over the weekend. Because her daughters were nineteen, mostly they talked about what they were doing at college and their upcoming plans for spring break.

Cheryl planned to visit a friend's home in Maryland, and Carol was trying to convince Lisa and her father that spending spring break at Mike's place in New York was a good idea. Carol claimed that her sudden desire to see her father was unrelated to the fact that her boyfriend's family happened to live in Manhattan. Lisa had vowed to stay out of the discussion. If Mike was okay with Carol staying with him, then it was his decision, not hers.

The fact that both Lisa and Mike thought Carol's boyfriend was a low-life loser was another reason Lisa wanted to avoid the fray. She was busy in Alpine Grove, so Mike could deal with that type of thing for a change.

The girls had both asked a number of questions about the roommate Lisa had staying at their grandparents' house and why the guy had left. To Lisa, there seemed to be undue curiosity on their part. Although Lisa had a good relationship with her daughters, discussing certain topics with them made her uncomfortable.

The fact was, Pete was gone and there was no way she was discussing any details of her sex life with the twins. She told them the reason Pete had returned to Arizona was because he could now walk with a cane and wanted to return home. Then she subtly changed the subject by letting them know she'd officially adopted Harley.

Cheryl and Carol both loved animals so they were thrilled that Lisa was keeping Harley permanently. As Lisa knew they would, they both chatted away about a dog named Sienna, who had lived next door when they were growing up. For years, the twins had worked together lobbying for a dog of their own, but Mike had vetoed it every time. Now that she'd spent so much time with Harley, Lisa wished she'd supported their idea of getting a dog, but she never had.

In retrospect, Lisa had caved on a lot of family decisions and she wished she hadn't. While the kids were growing up, Lisa had been the peacemaker. Much of her day-to-day life involved keeping everyone else happy. Early on, that meant keeping diapers changed and babies fed. Later it involved getting everyone to school, dealing with homework, and mediating countless sibling arguments. Then getting drivers' licenses, endless dating angst, and college exams. The entire time, Mike was busy at work, so Lisa also worked to keep him happy. She tried to be the good wife, hoping to keep her marriage from falling apart sooner than it finally did. Everyone else's needs had occupied her mind for years. It was the way her life had been.

Recently Bev, and now Pete, had pointed out that Lisa never asked for what she wanted. The reality was that she'd forgotten how. The more she thought about it, the more angry she became that she'd managed to fall in love with a person who then left town. What about what *she* wanted? Although

Pete had known she was annoyed, she didn't really do much to try to convince him to stay. Instead, as usual, she'd decided to keep the peace, augmented with some chocolate sauce for extra sweetness. How typical of her.

After Luke and Rod left for the day, Lisa found herself fretting about what had happened with Pete, while she tried to figure out what to make for dinner. Harley looked up at her hoping for a handout and she tossed him the corner of a tortilla chip. "I don't care if it's not Saturday yet and he thinks I'm clingy. I'm not clingy, I'm mad, so too bad. I'm calling him."

She reached for the phone and dialed Pete's number. After he answered and before he could say anything else, she said, "I need to talk to you."

"Actually, I was going to call you."

"Even though it's not Saturday?" Lisa sat down at the table and looked down at Harley, raising her eyebrows at the dog.

"I need to talk to you."

"That's what I just said." She twisted the phone cord around her finger, trying not to lose her nerve. "I'm not sure how to say this, but I realized something today."

"Me too."

"You said I never ask for what I really want and I don't make decisions."

There was a pause and he said, "Well, it does sound like you're getting a lot more practice lately."

"I know. Maybe I spent too much time catering to other people's needs. I spent so much time worrying about what they wanted that I didn't think much about what I wanted. I never asked for much of anything, even when I was sick."

"Why not?"

"I'm not sure exactly. For a long time, I think I was trying to keep the peace and hold my family together. Maybe I was too afraid to take a stand or disappoint people. But I don't want to do that again. What I *want* is to be with you. So I'm asking. Is there any way you can come back here sooner rather than later? Or maybe I can go see you there. I don't care."

"Actually…"

"No! Don't say no yet. We absolutely have to work something out. This is too important." Lisa stood up and began pacing across the kitchen. "I know you're unhappy too. You said so, and I can tell. This situation doesn't make any sense. We were happy living here, even in a noisy construction zone. Why should we make ourselves miserable being apart?"

"I don't think…"

"Wait! I'm not finished. Today, I was painting and I kept thinking about how life is so short and it could end at any time. I could get cancer again. Or you could have an even worse accident." Lisa stepped over Harley's prone form. "People like us—anyone who has had a life-altering illness or accident or almost died—should realize how quickly everything can change. We're being stupid not enjoying the time we have. If you love me and I love you, we should be together."

"I know. We should."

"What?"

"That's why I was going to call you. There are a couple of last little things I need to take care of here, but I talked my friend Ray into driving me and my truck back to Alpine Grove this weekend. If it's okay with you, that is."

A smile spread across Lisa's face. "Are you serious?"

"Very. Ray is going to fly back to Phoenix, so you can use my truck and give the old pink thing back to Larry. I gotta tell you, a boring, plain white 1995 Toyota pickup is a lot less conspicuous."

"I thought up a whole speech I was going to give to convince you."

"Well, that was a great start, but I didn't need convincing. I've had a lot of time to think too. I came to the conclusion that finding someone who loves me and is willing to put up with me has to be some sort of miracle. So as Shakespeare would say, 'I would not wish any companion in the world but you.'"

Lisa brushed a happy tear from her cheek. "The Bard really had a way with words, didn't he?"

"He was a whole lot more eloquent than I am."

~

The next few days seemed to pass slowly because Lisa couldn't wait for Pete to see the house. As she was painting miles of door trim, she considered how different the place looked since he'd seen it. Against all odds, the interior was starting to look nice. The flooring had been installed and most of the painting was finally done. Heck, if she were in the market for a huge family home, she'd want to buy it. But she didn't, so some lucky Alpine Grove family was going to end up with a great place for their kids to grow up.

Now that much of the largest and most bizarre furniture had been sold and the decor had been neutralized, the constant onslaught of memories had subsided as well. Lisa still needed to hold the indoor yard sale, but she no longer felt like she was living in a strange time warp. In some ways, Lisa was glad she'd been roped into the project because it had forced her to confront her past in a tangible way. There was nothing like going through thirty-year-old Barbie doll clothes to take you back to your girlhood.

Another interesting side effect of working on the house had been getting to know Luke and Rod. Before Craig had disappeared, she'd barely talked to them, but after so much painting together they'd spent a lot of time chatting about their lives and families. It turned out that during the summer Luke captained a tour boat on the lake, so he had lots of amusing stories about wildlife encounters and tourist antics. Rod had worked on many of the new condos at Snow Grove, and even though he never skied at the resort, he knew a lot about the development that had happened over the years.

Late Sunday afternoon, Lisa was upstairs painting more trim when a knock came from downstairs. Harley came roaring around the corner from the dining room, barking furiously at the front door. Lisa put down her paintbrush and ran downstairs.

She shoved the dog aside and opened the door. "Back up, Harley."

Pete was standing on the doorstep leaning on his cane with a suitcase sitting next to him. He grinned at her and pointed at Harley, who sat, but stomped his front legs in excitement at seeing his favorite person again.

Lisa wrapped her arms around Pete and gave him a hug, then dragged him inside. "I'm so glad to see you." Before closing the door, she grabbed the suitcase and peered out at the street. "Where is Ray?"

"He has some stuff to do."

"In Alpine Grove?"

"He dropped me off. I suggested he stay at the Enchanted Moose. I told him it was nice."

"Apparently, he doesn't share your gift for lie detection."

Pete laughed. "You have no idea how much I've missed you."

"I bet I do." She put her arms around his neck and kissed him.

"I guess you've been doing more painting? Tea rose and latex is an interesting combination." He pushed a stray curl behind her ear. "Your dog is sitting on my foot."

"Now that you're here, I think he's back to being your dog. Let's have something to eat and you can tell me about your trip."

"I need to tell you some other stuff too." He took her hand in his and they walked to the kitchen. "It's about Craig."

"What about him?"

"I think I mentioned that the fact he stole something bugged me."

"Yes, and I have to say not having him around has been fantastic." Lisa rummaged around in a cabinet and pulled out some plates. "I don't miss his lectures one bit."

"It turns out there was a safe in the dining room wall."

"What?" Lisa turned to face him. "He stole a *safe* out of this house? Like with money in it? Is there some Lowell family fortune I don't know about? Sheesh, nobody tells me *anything*."

"I don't know about the fortune, but I do know he can't get it open."

"How do you know that?"

Pete folded his hands in front of him on the table and smiled. "He doesn't have the combination and he's been chatting with people at pawn shops all over LA. None of them want to touch it because they think it's stolen, so he returned to Alpine Grove with it."

"How do you know all this?"

"My buddy Ray is a private detective. After he retired from the force, he took the exam and hung out his shingle. I called in a favor and he made a few calls for me. There's another PI in LA that he knows, who is great. She's the one who dug up the pawn-shop connection."

"Why are you sitting there looking so smug?"

"Because I know where the combination is. Ray is going to get the safe from Craig and then we can open it."

"Does Craig know about this?"

"Not yet, but he will. Ray should be calling here pretty soon." Pete scratched his chin. "Let's just say Ray can be persuasive when he wants to be."

Lisa raised her hands in front of her. "Wait a minute. How do *you* know where the combination is and Craig doesn't?"

"As you said, I'm the only person who has touched all those pretty leather-bound books in the Lowell family library in who knows how long. The combination is in three of the books. First, I noticed that *Treasure Island* said 'Left 34' on the flyleaf, which I thought was sort of strange, since you said no one ever read those books."

"I guess someone did."

"Betty, I'm assuming."

"She probably wrote it down so she wouldn't forget." Lisa grinned. "I guess that didn't work out too well."

"If you forget where you wrote something down, you have a problem. The other books are *Robinson Crusoe* and *The Odyssey*."

"You read the Odyssey? Really? Yuck."

"I skimmed it. That was right before you took me to the library. I told you I was getting desperate."

"No kidding. When you're down to Homer, you're desperate." Lisa went to the table and leaned over to put her arms around his neck. "I can't believe you did all this for me."

He pulled her onto his lap and kissed her. "I love you."

"I love you too. I was afraid I'd never see you again."

"And I was afraid of staying here. After all those years of being a cop you'd think I'd be more courageous."

Lisa kissed him and gazed into his blue eyes. "Maybe it's time we both stop being so scared of everything. Any day could be our last, so we should do our best to live it up."

"I like that idea." He smiled. "And given that look on your face, I'm thinking you bought more chocolate sauce, didn't you?"

She grinned. "Why, yes. Yes, I did."

Chapter 15

Epilogue

Lisa drove south on the highway toward the lake with Pete in his truck. For once, Harley wasn't sitting in between them or drooling on them from the small seats behind them in the extended cab of the Toyota. Lisa had convinced Luke to take the dog for the evening, but she wondered what the other residents of Alpine Grove were doing with their dogs since the boarding kennel was closed for the next couple of weeks.

Lisa turned onto a road that went along the lake. The North Fork Lodge was located right on the lake off Edgewater Road. "It's so strange coming back here after so many years. The North Fork Lodge had the best Halloween haunted house when I was little. There were hay rides and tons of candy. I was in chocolate heaven. I heard that over the years the place got really run down, but someone bought it and restored it not too long ago."

The sign indicating the turn for the lodge had a dinner fork on the logo, and Lisa turned down a hill toward the lake.

Pete glanced at her. "When they say fork, they literally mean a fork."

"Well, you won't forget it, which is the point of a logo, right?"

At the bottom of the hill the trees, cabins, and buildings that made up the North Fork Lodge were strewn with little white twinkly lights that reflected on the water. The main lodge building was a large log structure and its roof was rimmed with lights that sparkled in the fading late-afternoon light.

They got out of the truck and went up the creaky wooden steps to the lobby. Lisa opened the door and they walked into a large open room with huge wooden beams and a stone fireplace. Beyond the entry, people were milling around talking with one another in an open dining area that connected to the lobby. Long buffet tables were laden with food, and more people sat at round wooden tables, chatting. Everyone seemed to know one another other and for a moment Lisa felt a little awkward. Where was Kat?

She turned at the sound of stilettos marching toward her, click-clicking on the wooden floor. Maria raised her hand in greeting. "You made it!" She stopped, put her hand on her hip, and gave Pete an appraising gaze up and down. "You must be Pete. Your description precedes you."

"It's nice to meet you." He glanced downward. "The cane was probably the tip-off."

"No, I heard about those sexy baby blues." Maria gave Lisa a sly smile. "Nice."

Lisa said, "This is Maria. She threw the bachelorette party I told you about."

Pete grinned. "That sounded like quite an event."

Maria flipped her hair over her shoulder. "I'm the party planner extraordinaire."

"Did you attend the wedding?" Pete asked.

"Yes," Maria squeaked as the expression on her face crumpled. She fanned her face with her hands and swiped at her mascara with her fingertips. "I was at the courthouse and I cried my eyes out through the whole thing. Don't ask me anything else or I'll start bawling again. They wrote their own vows. If in the unlikely event I ever find a man in this godforsaken wasteland and get married, I'm getting Kat to write my vows."

"I guess she *is* a writer," Lisa said.

"You have no idea. She's wasted on that geeky garbage." Maria gulped. "I can't talk about it. What they said, it was so romantic I melted into a puddle of goo. Ask Becca; she'll tell you. She was there and was crying, just like me. I swear, it was a total weep fest. I bet even Jack shed a few tears and he's a studly outdoorsy type."

Lisa didn't know who Becca or Jack were, but she nodded politely. "Have you seen Kat?"

Maria sniffed and pointed at the buffet. "Over there with Joel. She's pigging out on some of those spinach hors d'oeuvres that Brigid makes."

Lisa excused herself and nodded at Pete to indicate they should go find Kat. At least she knew who Brigid was, so that was one person. It was odd to be at an Alpine Grove event and know so few people.

Kat waved when she saw Lisa and Pete approaching. After introducing Joel and Pete, Lisa gave Kat a hug. "Congratulations."

"I heard you found a safe in the house," Kat said.

"How did you find out?" Lisa asked.

"Larry told Maria, who told me." Kat took a sip of her champagne and continued, "So, I'm dying to know what was in it. And why was it in your parents' place?"

"My aunt Betty stashed it in the dining room wall while the house was being built. After the Cuban missile crisis in the early sixties, she was worried that the world was coming to an end, so she wanted to make sure her valuables were safe," Lisa said.

"Nobody knew?" Kat glanced at Joel. "And here I thought *my* family was good at keeping secrets."

"My grandfather was Betty's brother, and he built the house. She never told my parents and apparently Grandpa didn't either. As the years passed, it got more difficult to bring up the subject of ripping apart the wall, I suppose. Maybe Betty didn't think my parents would keep the house as long as they have. And then at some point, she completely forgot about it," Lisa said.

"How did you find it?" Joel asked.

Lisa said, "The contractor I hired, Craig Maddox, was in Betty's class in elementary school. She taught fifth grade and he remembered her saying that she had a safe in a wall."

"Now we know why he was so eager to take the job," Pete added.

"But it's all done. The real estate agent will be coming by to take pictures tomorrow." Lisa said. "And I have to say, the house looks great. My parents would appreciate it if you'd tell everyone you know to come to the open house later this spring."

Kat waved her glass at Lisa. "Wait, what was in the safe?"

"Fifty thousand dollars, some jewelry, and a bottle of bourbon." Lisa glanced at Pete. "Betty said we could have the booze. We put the money in a regular bank account for her, and now she also has a safe deposit box for the jewelry."

"That's quite a windfall," Joel said.

"She offered to give some of the money to us, but that didn't seem right." Lisa shrugged. "We're headed back to Gleasonville."

"Lisa is going to take a nursing-assistant course," Pete said.

Lisa turned to smile at him. "And Pete is going to train Harley to do search and rescue. And get him certified as a therapy dog so they can come visit me at work."

Kat raised her arms to the sky. "And at long last, I'm going to Hawaii tomorrow. Woo-hoo!"

Lisa congratulated the happy couple again, then she and Pete got some food from the buffet and sat down together at a table. "They look so happy."

"So do you."

"I am happy. For the first time in a long time, I'm healthy and I know what I want."

"I'm glad." He took her hands in his. "We know what we are, but know not what we may be."

"Hamlet!" She gave him a sly smile. "I know it's out of order, but Hawaii starts with 'h' and I've never been there. Do you want to go? I think a vacation to the tropics could be fun."

"Fun is good. I like fun."

Thanks for Reading

Thank you for dedicating some of your reading time to *Daydream Retriever*. I hope you enjoyed Lisa and Pete's adventures. I'll be writing more books that will feature Kat, Joel and various other residents of Alpine Grove who bring dogs to the boarding kennel. The eleventh book, *The Hound of Music* is available along with ten other books in the series.

If you would like to be notified by e-mail when I release a new book, you can sign up for my New Releases e-mail list at SusanDaffron.com.

I know that not everyone likes to write book reviews, but if you are willing write a sentence or two about what you thought of *Daydream Retriever*, I encourage you to post a review at your favorite book vendor site or share a message with your social networking friends.

If you would like to share your thoughts about the book with me privately, you can reach me through the contact page on the SusanDaffron.com web site.

I look forward to hearing from you!

~ Susan C. Daffron

Acknowledgements

Writing a novel is never easy and I'd like to thank my husband James Byrd for his support and encouragement throughout the publishing process.

I'd also like to thank my alpha and beta readers for their eagle-eyed reading and great feedback:

- James Byrd
- Sandra Marine
- Nancy Brashear
- Jinx Kimmer

About the Author

Susan Daffron is the author of the Jennings & O'Shea series and the Alpine Grove romantic comedies, a series of novels that feature residents of the small town of Alpine Grove and their various quirky dogs and cats. She is also an award-winning author of many nonfiction books, including several about pets and animal rescue. She lives in a small town in northern Idaho and shares her life with her husband and three really cute dogs.